CAUGHT

IN THE

CURRENT

A Novel

CAUGHT IN THE CURRENT

DANIEL HRYHORCZUK

LANGDON STREET PRESS

Langdon Street Press
322 1st Ave N, Suite 500
Minneapolis, MN 55401
612.455.2293
www.langdonstreetpress.com

ISBN-13: 978-1-62652-268-8
LCCN: 2013945006

Distributed by Itasca Books

Cover Design by Alan Pranke
Typeset by Kristeen Ott

Printed in the United States of America

To my wife, Christine, and my sons, Nicholas and Alex

CHAPTER 1

Four students killed as war protests spread. Students plan strikes.
Alec pored over the headlines. Students were strik-
ing across the nation. Nixon warned, "When dissent turns to
violence, it invites tragedy." *Who is the one inviting tragedy?* he
wondered. The editorial in the *Daily Northwestern* endorsed
the strike: *All of this misery is so useless and debilitating that we
cannot sit quietly and watch it happen around us, as Northwestern
has traditionally done in the past.*

"Hey, Alec, you going to the rally at Deering Meadow?" Tim was guarding the rock by University Hall. His Grateful Dead shirt was splattered with red paint. He was a divinity
student whom Alec had known since their high school days at
Loyola Academy. Alec had not figured him for a radical.

"I guess. I'm just not sure if it's my fight or not."

"Do you have a draft card?"

"Yeah."

"Then it is your fight," Tim said.

"I don't know. My roots are elsewhere. I'm more anti-Soviet than anti-establishment."

"Were you born here?"

"Yeah."

"Hey, man, this is America. Everyone's from elsewhere. Join the revolution."

Alec made a "V" with his fingers. "I'll see you there."

Alec's assurance was half-hearted. It wasn't his culture they were rebelling against. He had demonstrated in front of the Soviet embassy when the Soviets invaded Czechoslovakia, but he stayed off the streets during the Democratic National Convention. He was on the periphery of the counterculture. His cousin Zack, on the other hand, was a true hippie. He had fought the police in Grant Park during the convention. "The streets were ours," he'd bragged. Alec wore his hair long, though not as long as Zack's. Alec smoked grass with his friends. He played rhythm guitar in a band. He wrote songs about love, bullfights, and war.

Throngs of students and professors were heading toward Deering Meadow. Alec recognized many of the faces. It would be cowardly to walk away, so he went along with the flow. Students with white armbands were flashing "V" signs and trying to maintain order.

The rally had the buzz of a rock concert. It was difficult to hear. The bullhorn blared above the din. He could only catch phrases from the various speakers. Most spoke in favor of a strike. "Out with ROTC!" and "Disarm the police!" were greeted with cheers, while calls for calm were jeered. A petition was circulating to have the campus secede from the United States.

The speeches were interrupted by a funeral procession. A cortege of students bore four black coffins, one for each of the Kent State victims. The last carried a placard that read: "It could have been your kid at Kent." The leader of the procession seized the bullhorn and read out the names of each of the deceased.

That single act of street theater brought the war home. Alec never imagined that a peaceful college protest could have ended in such reactionary violence. He believed that truth alone could conquer power. Those who advocated struggle, like the SDS and Black Panthers, had been on the fringe. Now, after the killings, they were mainstream. It was as if all of the disparate movements—anti-war, civil rights, women's liberation—had converged into an unstoppable current that together could wash away the old world order. Calls to strike echoed through the meadow 'til thousands were chanting in unison. He too began chanting: Strike, strike, strike.

***

Alec dialed through the FM stations, searching for some Stones. He skipped through the rifts and static until he landed on "Street Fighting Man." Zack had helped him soup up his orange Karmann Ghia with some kick-ass speakers. "The time is right for a palace revolution" blared in his ears as he sped down Lake Shore Drive. *No matter what language you speak at home,* he thought, *you have to dig rock.*

Stefi was waiting for him by her high school gym, dressed in her pom-pom uniform. He hopped out to open her door. She kissed him playfully, waved to her giggling girl-friends, and eased into the bucket seat.

"Why so serious?" she asked.

"Northwestern is going on strike."

"On strike? Why?"

"To protest the war and the killings at Kent State. They want us to boycott classes."

"Will you?"

"I think so. I'll see what happens tomorrow."

"You're halfway through the semester. If you boycott, will you still get credit? Don't you need those classes for medical school?"

"I'd hate to have to repeat organic. Still, I have to stand up for what I believe in."

"Whatever you decide, it's OK with me," she said and put her hand on his knee. She was wearing his high school ring.

They had met at a dance last fall. At first, he thought she was too young to date, but when they slow-danced to "Moon River," he was attracted to her instantly. It was like the pull of opposite poles of a magnet that got stronger the closer they came together. Her sea-green eyes and flirtatious innocence were imprinted on his brain. He doubted if he could ever be so attracted to anyone again.

"I've got news that will cheer you up," she said. "My parents are going to let me go to Europe."

"Wow, that's great."

"I told them that lots of kids are going. I think they have at least three full buses. We're going to stay at a Scout camp in Munich and a convent in Rome. We fly out the last week of July and get back just before Labor Day."

"Then I'll join you in Munich after my 'Offbeat Europe' tour."

"Do you know exactly when?" she asked. "I don't know how long I can keep the boys away."

"I'm sure you can keep them away for a couple of weeks. I'll find out more tonight. Father Collins called a meeting with the parents."

He drove up to her home in Palmer Square.

"That pom-pom uniform is really sexy," he said as he ran his hand up her thigh.

"Stop it! My parents will see." As she kissed him goodbye, she opened her mouth and invited his tongue for a split second. "That's enough," she teased. "Think about that before you get yourself arrested."

***

Father Collins was a jovial Jesuit who loved to travel. He spoke multiple languages, though none of them well. The jocks on his trips joked that Father liked to play sharks in the pool, but that had not been Alec's experience. Even though Alec was in college, Father had allowed him to join his latest "Offbeat Europe" tour as an alumnus.

Father Collins traced a circle on a map of Europe that he had hung on the wall in the Loyola Academy library. Each of the countries was displayed in a different color. The Soviet Union, from the Baltics to the Black Sea, was one broad swath of red.

"We've reserved three Volkswagen minibuses in Luxembourg. In addition to me, Brother Bill and Mr. Curtis will do the driving. We will drive northeast through Germany, Denmark, and Sweden and then enter the Soviet Union through Finland."

The parents fired off questions.

"How will you get from Sweden to Finland?"

"Ferries will carry our minibuses across the Baltic Sea."

Alec's father raised his hand. "Is it safe to drive through the Soviet Union? Aren't we fighting the Cold War?"

"We're working with Intourist, their official travel agency. They're arranging our itinerary and will provide us with escorts in each city. We have confirmed stays in Leningrad, Moscow, Kiev, and Lviv. We're still waiting to hear from them about our exit route. There's a great deal of red tape. That's why we began the visa process last fall."

"Will you visit Prague?"

"No, the State Department says it's still too dangerous. We've made tentative arrangements in Constanta and Krakow, depending on where they instruct us to exit. We'll head west through Bucharest. The last leg of the trip—through Austria, Switzerland, and France—is all set. We fly back from Luxembourg."

"How many miles will you be driving?"

"We'll cover about 7,500 kilometers in seventy-five days."

Alec was less interested in hearing about the last leg of the trip. He planned to separate from the group in Lucerne and then hitchhike to Munich to rendezvous with Stefi. They had both signed up for the "Flight of Freedom" tour organized by the Ukrainian Youth Organization that overlapped with the last few days of the "Offbeat Europe" tour. He was eager to show her the Europe that he knew.

***

As Alec neared campus, he saw that police had cordoned off the main roads. He detoured through the side streets and parked by the Tech Institute. Classes had been canceled. Rumors of an impending police assault were spreading quickly. A crowd was gathering on Sheridan Road.

"You see any cops on your way in?" Tim was directing strikers to gather whatever debris they could find.

"I saw some flashing squad cars farther south on Sheridan Road," Alec replied. "They're not letting any traffic through. I had to make my way here through the side streets."

"This campus is ours," Tim declared. "We're not going to let the pigs take it over. Find something to help block the road—branches, trash, anything. Did you see the *Daily Northwestern* this morning? They called us white radicals."

"As opposed to what? Black radicals?" Alec asked.

"They're trying to divide us and label us. It's a typical establishment ploy, but no one's buying it."

The strikers who were barricading the road included whites, blacks, hippies, and even jocks in lettered sweaters. Other students were bringing in food for the strikers. Rock music blasted from one of the halls. The barricade on Sheridan Road was growing quickly. Alec picked up a sign that read "Strike the War" and stuck it into the tangled mass of tree limbs, fencing, and trash.

Plainclothesmen with cameras took up positions across the street. Students brought them food and drink with salutations of "Peace" and "Make love not war." The strikers braced for an assault. The hours ticked away without violence.

Suddenly, a striker ran into the street with welcome news. "The administration has given in to our demands!"

Euphoria spread like wildfire. Alec flashed a peace sign and hugged the kids around him. He felt the power of youth. He now belonged to the hippie generation.

CHAPTER 2

Johnny fiddled with his toothpick as he listened to Alec's story about the strike.

"Don't get too caught up in this anti-war thing," Johnny said. "Remember that you took an oath to the Brotherhood. Let's talk after practice."

The Brotherhood was an elite fraternity of the Ukrainian Youth Organization that was formed after the Soviets murdered the Ukrainian poet Vasyl Symonenko. The patriarch himself had blessed their hand-sewn flag. Their flag portrayed the key chapters in Ukrainian history: Kievan Rus, the Cossack Hetmanate, the 1918 declaration of independence, and the Ukrainian insurgency during the Second World War. After recruiting the requisite thirty members to form the new fraternity, Johnny purged all but ten. "Only the best of the best," was his motto.

Johnny had recruited Alec into the Brotherhood in 1969, shortly after the purge. He was Alec's counselor in the Ukrainian Youth Organization. Johnny was only two years older but had the bearing of a military officer. He was intense in everything he did. Alec agreed—on the condition that they also recruit his best friend, Serge. Serge was a Russian major at DePaul and had spent a semester as an exchange student in Kiev. Academic exchanges were viewed with suspicion on both sides of the Iron Curtain. Johnny was wary, but Alec vouched for Serge's integrity, and the two were initiated into the Brotherhood on a peak in the Rockies. They had drunk mead and sworn loyalty to the Brotherhood, to Ukraine, and to each other.

Alec's volleyball team practiced in the field house at Humboldt Park. In the fifties, the Ukes and Poles had the run of the park, but now it was taken over by the Puerto Ricans. After practice, Johnny put his hand on Alec's shoulder and led him down a meandering path around the lagoon. Alec had spent many carefree days of his childhood running through these nooks and dells with his cousins. Johnny stopped by the two bronze buffalos that guarded the entrance to the rose garden.

"I hear you'll be traveling to Ukraine this summer."

"I'm on a tour with my old high school," Alec replied. "We drive through Ukraine for about a week."

"You're a patriot ..." It was more of a statement than a question.

"Yes, of course."

"Then there's something I want you to do."

Alec hesitated. He had heard rumors of Ukrainian Americans parachuting into Soviet Ukraine in the 1950s to support the partisans, only to be never heard from again.

"Is it dangerous?" Alec asked.

"I'm not daring you to do something dangerous. I'm asking you to do your duty."

"What do you want me to do?"

"We just want you to gather some information. The Soviets tap the phones and open the mail. The only way we can get information in and out of Ukraine is through word of mouth."

"So you just want me to talk to people?"

"Pretty much."

"OK ... then I guess I'm willing to do my part."

"Good. CK and I were there last summer. We met some good people in Kiev. Before you go, you need to be prepared. There's someone I want you to meet."

"Who?"

"I'll tell you after I arrange the meeting."

***

Gino's East was packed. *Strange choice for a secret meeting*, Alec thought. Yet it was perfect—dark, noisy, and smoky, with as many simultaneous conversations as there were initials carved into the wooden tables. As he elbowed past the bar, he overheard a teenage boy and his girlfriend saying their farewells. The boy had been drafted and was leaving for boot camp in the morning; they would not see each other for several weeks. Chances were good that after boot camp, his unit would be deployed to Vietnam.

"What am I supposed to do without you?" she cried.

"I'll be all right. Just wait for me. I'll try to get an

assignment as a cook or something. I'll be safe."

Alec knew that the boy wouldn't be safe. Nixon was bombing Cambodia. His friends who couldn't get a student deferment had joined the National Guard. The others had to take their chances. Like so many other young men who had been drafted, the boy at Gino's was going off to fight in a strange place for reasons that he and his girlfriend did not comprehend. Alec's Ukrainian-American community had already suffered three casualties from the Vietnam War. He had known the boys but not well. They were mainly friends of friends. Their bodies had been laid out in Olenyk's Funeral Home in closed caskets. They were heroes. Now they were gone.

Boyan and Johnny were waiting in a booth. They had already ordered a deep-dish pizza. Boyan was a dark, heavyset man in his late twenties with languid eyes. From the ashtray on the table, it appeared that he was already halfway through a pack of cigarettes. Alec sat down next to Johnny and waited for an introduction. There was none. Boyan looked at Alec and raised a heavy eyebrow. "Cigarette?" he offered.

"No thanks, I don't smoke."

"Johnny says you have some Hutsul blood in you."

"My father is a Hutsul." The Hutsuls were the Carpathians mountain folk. They were dark-haired and spoke their own dialect. They had resisted occupation since the invasion of the Tatar hordes.

"And your mother?"

"She grew up on the banks of the Dniester River, fled to Germany as the Red Army advanced, and finished medicine in Munich under the American occupation." Alec was not sure why he was volunteering so much information.

"Were you born in a DP camp?"

"No, I was born in Champaign, Illinois." *In the heart of the heart of the country*, thought Alec.

Boyan lit another cigarette. "Johnny tells me you are interested in helping us."

"I am willing to do my part."

"The situation in Ukraine is evolving," said Boyan. "There is a new democratic movement that is gaining momentum in the Baltic states and is likely to spread into Ukraine. The Ukrainian dissidents are getting bolder." Boyan's gaze was magnetic. He was the keeper to a door that led to secret knowledge. Johnny had apparently already passed through that door. Alec was now the initiate.

"What would I have to do?"

"Very little. We want you to become an expert on current affairs in Ukraine. You need to know who's who ... the political issues ... even cultural issues. On your trip to Ukraine, simply keep your ears open, and tell me what you hear."

"Do you want me to meet with anyone specific?"

"No. Just talk to whomever you happen to encounter. You'll know what questions to ask."

"What if they ask me to smuggle something out?"

Boyan put out his cigarette. "You don't have to accept it. If you do, you'd better make sure it's something worth risking your life for."

After their meeting Johnny took Alec aside.

"You did well. He trusts you. I'll give you the name of a good guy in Kiev. Make sure you look him up."

***

Green Sunday is the Ukrainian feast day of the dead. When spring turns to summer, wandering souls return to the forests and streams. Flowers and trees are animated with spirits. Greenery is cut to adorn churches and homes. The dead are offered food and drink to ensure that their spirits do not turn vengeful.

As Alec's family drove to St. Nicholas Cemetery in their Lincoln Continental, his mother reminisced about her parents. She was eighteen when she fled to the West with her older sister. She had left her parents and her younger siblings behind. All she had left of Ukraine were her childhood memories. Alec and his sister and brother listened attentively; their grandparents had passed away, and this was as close to them as they would ever get.

"Even though your grandfather was a priest, we would always celebrate the Green Days. The traditions are older than anyone can remember."

"They're pagan," Alec's father added. "They date back to the ancient Greeks and perhaps even earlier. In the seminary, they instructed us to meld the old and the new, to put a Christian interpretation into the old ways."

"You studied to be a priest?" Alec asked.

"For a short while, but I never finished. When the Soviets came, I had to flee. Priests and other intellectuals were killed or sent to Siberia."

"What happened to Grandfather?"

"He was arrested and forced to renounce Catholicism," his mother replied. "They allowed him to serve, but only under the yoke of the Russian Orthodox Church. The villagers would have revolted if they'd taken their only priest away."

"When I'm in Ukraine, I'll try to visit his grave."

"No. Absolutely not. You can't let them know that you have family in Ukraine," she insisted.

"But what about your sister and brother?"

"God willing, they will find you."

The gate to the cemetery was adorned with freshly cut branches. The place was zoetic with communing spirits. Families placed branches and flowers on the graves of their dead. Priests blessed graves and accepted donations. Women in babushkas buried bread and poured libations on the ground for their loved ones. Alec's parents had no immediate relatives of their own to pray over, so the family went off in different directions, searching for departed friends.

Alec did have someone to pray for. Damian was the grandson of a second-wave immigrant. He spoke Ukrainian with an American accent. He was the pastor's favorite altar boy. When their fourth grade class went on a field trip to Humboldt Park on Green Thursday, Alec and Damian snuck away from Sister Teresa to wade in the lagoon. The lagoon was covered with water lilies and was verdant with an algal bloom. Alec dared his friend to wade across, and Damian took the dare, doffing his shorts and marching into the muck. Damian became ensnared in the vegetation and sank beneath the green slime.

At the funeral, the pastor rationalized that it was God's will. Damian's mother wailed that Rusalky had dragged her son underwater. In the Old World, these water nymphs embodied the spirits of girls who had drowned. They lured innocents into the water to join them. Sister Teresa blamed the devil. Alec blamed himself. It didn't make sense then, and it didn't make sense now. Alec broke a bough from an evergreen and wandered between the headstones, looking for his friend.

He recognized Damian's mother, kneeling over her

son's grave. She was singing a lullaby and plucking blades of grass from the patch of pansies in front of his headstone. As Alec went to lay the bough on the grave, Damian's mother grabbed his hand and refused to let go.

"Tell him I am coming soon," she entreated him.

"I don't understand."

"When you see him, tell him I am coming soon."

Alec pulled back his hand, unnerved by her implication.

"Yes, of course, of course … I will tell him you are coming soon." The image of Damian's body ensnared in the weeds surfaced in his consciousness. He turned away and ran to seek the comfort of his parents. They were chatting with some friends by the outdoor chapel.

"Mama, I think Mrs. Podelnyk is losing it. She asked me to speak to her son."

"She's not been the same since he drowned. Don't let her upset you. Think about your upcoming journey. A grand tour of Europe, essential to the education of any cultivated young man."

"It should be quite an adventure."

"Remind me to give you a letter before you go … for my cousin in Munich. I haven't seen him since we were children, but I'm sure you can stay with him while you're waiting to join the Ukrainian Youth Organization tour."

"Sure. Anything else before I go?"

"Just be careful in the Soviet Union. It's a dangerous place. Aunt Ulana will look for you. Don't call the wolves out of the woods."

***

The waves of Lake Michigan played with the shoreline. Beaches would appear and disappear over the course of the winter. Just south of the campus, the city of Evanston had bolstered a secluded section of shoreline with large rocks to combat the erosion. It was a favorite place for lovers. Alec thought it would be the perfect place for their farewell.

The moon was rising over the lake. Stefi nuzzled in his arms. Her blonde hair smelled of hyacinths.

"I wish we could sail away together," he said.

"I'm happy right here in Chicago," she replied.

"Don't you have the urge to just take off and see the world?"

"This is my world. You, the Ukrainian village … our future together is here."

"My future is up in the air after this semester. The strike might affect my application to medical school."

"Did you get credit for your classes?"

"Yes, but they switched everything to pass/fail. I'm worried how it will affect my grade point average."

"Did you have to take any exams?"

"Just take-home. I handed in my World Lit one on Friday. I had to write about heroism."

"So who did you choose?"

"Lucifer from *Paradise Lost*."

"Are you crazy?"

"It's been a crazy semester. I just wanted to do something rebellious. I was feeling some sympathy for the devil."

"I know you're rethinking a lot of things in your life. But please don't throw our future away just for the sake of rebelling."

"I'm not throwing anything away." He kissed the nape

of her neck. "You're my Cinnamon Girl. You always will be."
She hugged him tightly. "I brought you a gift," he said.

"You did?" she beamed. "I knew you loved me. Show me."

He pulled a blue Tiffany's box from his backpack and placed it in Stefi's hands.

She carefully undid the bow and wrapper as if she planned to save them. She opened the box to discover a gold charm of the Eiffel Tower.

"It's beautiful! I love it!" She kissed him on the lips and opened her mouth. Alec accepted the invitation. His hormones were racing.

"It's a reminder of our upcoming reunion," he said.

"I'll write to you at every stop on your tour," she promised. "And I'll give you a kiss in front of the Eiffel Tower that you'll never forget."

CHAPTER 3

Alec envisioned the angel of light being cast out of heaven. In his essay on *Paradise Lost* he had argued that Lucifer was a fallen hero. He had all the characteristics of a hero: leadership, vision, and youthful rebellion—he was simply on the wrong side of universal law. The Northwestern grad student reading his essay had scribbled in red: "Nice try, but morality is not relative." The fall into darkness seemed to last forever ...

Alec woke with a start. The flight careened from the turbulence as it began its descent into Reykjavik. He looked out the window to see if the plane had veered into a plume of volcanic ash. Day was just breaking in the east. Unlike the peaks of the shimmering clouds, the land beneath was still shrouded in darkness.

He pulled Stefi's photo out of his wallet and pressed it to his lips. She had written "your Cinnamon Girl" on the back and sealed it with a lipstick kiss. He put the picture back in his wallet and closed his eyes.

As the plane touched down, it seemed to slide down the runway.

"Welcome to Reykjavik," the chief stewardess announced.

Even though Iceland was only a fuel stop, Father Collins had included it on the mimeographed itinerary for this summer's "Offbeat Europe" tour. Each country, he said, had something to offer his young men.

Alec was relieved to deplane after the harrowing descent. He looked for a postcard at the airport shop. Stefi had promised that a letter would be waiting for him at every address on the itinerary. She had even mailed a letter to Luxembourg before he left. He had only cautioned her to not write while he was in the Soviet Union, because her letters might be opened.

A thermometer on the wall of the airport shop displayed the outside temperature as 12° C. The shop was filled with Icelandic handicraft. Alec ruffled through the handmade woolen sweaters, hats, and scarves until he came upon a pair of mittens. The mittens were knitted out of hand-spun wool. They were white, with a delicate pattern interwoven in darker wool. *Stefi will love these*, he thought. He knew he needed to budget his dollars, but he could not pass these up.

He recalled the day after Christmas when he had taken her sledding to the large hill in Humboldt Park. The hill had several trees, and they needed to steer the sled around them. He had sledded there many times as a child and wanted her to experience the thrill. He brought his old wooden sled with the red runners. The day had been bright but well below freezing. Stefi was bundled in a woolen sweater, cap, and scarf and black ski pants that hugged her sexy bottom. They could see their breath in the cold. A fresh snow had fallen the night before. It was perfect sledding weather.

"You first," Alec had offered. "Just be careful to avoid the trees."

"Why don't we go down together?" she suggested.

"We could, but it will be harder to steer."

She gave him a playful kiss on the lips. "I trust you."

Alec lay on the sled and grabbed the handles. Stefi lay on top of him and held on to his shoulders. Their legs were dangling, intertwined, over the back of the sled. Alec spread out his arms and dug his gloves into the snow. He pushed with his boots and gloves, the sled inched forward, and suddenly, down they went. "Stefi! Stefi, hold on tight."

The snow beneath the fresh-fallen layer was packed tight and slick. As the sled accelerated, with each bump their bodies flew up and then pressed down into each other, only to go weightless again. Alec's face was inches from the snow. He steered right, then left, and then right again to avoid the trees. With each turn their bodies swung left, then right, and then left again. Stefi screamed with delight. There was no way to brake until the sled reached the frozen lagoon at the bottom of the hill. The sled slid across the ice until they intentionally toppled off and rolled into the ice and snow.

Stefi's woolen cap and exposed blonde hair were frosted in snow. Alec took off his glove and brushed the snow off her face. Her eyes were sparkling and her cheeks were red. He kissed her lips. "You're my snow princess," he said.

"I just want to be special to someone."

"You're special to me."

"Let's do it again," she laughed, and they pulled the sled back up the hill.

The mittens in the airport shop reminded him of their romp in the snow. It wasn't just her playfulness that attracted her to him. He wanted to shelter her. His mother had read him a folktale about a boy who lost his mitten in the snow. All animals in the woods, from a cricket to a wild boar, took refuge in the mitten. Finally, when a bear crawled in, the mitten ripped. Alec wanted to nestle Stefi in that mitten and keep the other animals out.

***

Stefi's letter was waiting for him in Luxembourg. Alec decided to open it in privacy. He did not want to share his love life with a gang of horny teenagers. He rented a bike in the center of town and challenged himself to cycle to the French border and back in a single afternoon. The border was less than fifteen kilometers away, and he figured the ride would give him time to think. It was a flat, easy route, and the monotony of the pedaling would help him concentrate. He put the letter in his pocket and planned to open it in some idyllic glen far away from his fellow travelers.

As he pedaled toward the border, he focused on his mission. Boyan had sent him a large packet with typewritten notes and newspaper clippings about the Ukrainian dissidents. The "Sixtiers" were mostly writers and artists who resisted Russification. Many had spent years in the Gulag. Others were undergoing rehabilitation in psychiatric hospitals. Alec had memorized their names and their complex interrelationships. Some were connected through blood, others through marriage, and many through memberships in literary clubs. About half were currently in prison or in psychiatric institutions. Others had simply disappeared. He feared that someone would ask him to smuggle something out—a diary, a notebook, a letter. Being caught with physical evidence could result in imprisonment. He wouldn't know if the request to carry something out was legitimate or if it was a KGB setup. Boyan had warned him that it was a Cold War game and that it had its winners and losers.

Alec was proud to do his duty. His family had a history of resistance against Soviet oppression. Most of his uncles who fought against the terror had either died in battle or been executed. Not all in his bloodline were heroes. Years earlier, his father had given him a book on the history of his village in the Carpathians. At the turn of the century, his great-uncle had been elected to represent the district in the Austro-Hungarian Parliament. With pride and fanfare, the villagers had given him money and a horse for his journey. He left the village and was never heard from again. Some say he made it to Vienna, became an aristocrat, and abandoned his countrymen. Others say that he was simply eaten by wolves. The most vicious rumor was that he had absconded with the horse and the money.

Alec had no clue how far he had cycled. Rows of vineyards intersected both sides of the road. He realized that he had lost his bearings. He wasn't sure how far he still needed to go. He must have veered off the main highway because he was alone on the road. It had not occurred to him to take a map because the route looked so simple.

He turned off the road down a dirt driveway to ask for directions. A rusty sign with the words *Vorsicht bei Hund!*

was posted at the entrance. The words held no meaning but the red exclamation point seemed ominous. As he neared a farmhouse, he saw a black hound lying in the portal. Flies were buzzing around its eyes. The fur on its back and tail was eaten away by mange. The hound sprung up before Alec could retreat. It raised its hackles and bared its canines. Alec hesitated for a second to see if it was leashed; it wasn't. As he spun his bike around, the hound bolted toward him. The bike swayed from side to side as he tried to accelerate in the loose dirt. He sensed that the hound was almost upon him. He held his breath and sprinted back toward the main road. His heart was breaking out of his chest. When his front tire hit the asphalt edge, the bike abruptly stopped, and he tumbled head over heels. He blindly put his arms up to protect his face from the fangs, until he saw that the snarling hound had stopped at the sign. An old man with a long pole and keen gaze had restrained it. The hound coiled its hairless tail. The old man pointed to the road.

Alec picked up his bike, being careful to avoid their eyes. He swore at himself for not heeding the warning. He had a good hunch as to what had happened to his ancestor in the Carpathian forest those many years ago. He climbed back on his bike and retraced his route back to the city. He remembered Stefi's letter. He reached into his pocket, but the letter was gone.

✳✳✳

"Those German kids were good," said Rip, "especially that kid who megged you to score the last goal. Your defense is getting rusty."

"It's been a long time since I played soccer," Alec

replied. "We would have kicked their butts in volleyball. Let's go grab some beers."

The three friends parted from their German opponents and walked over to a *rathskeller* a few blocks from their hostel. They were careful to avoid Father Collins and his two henchmen. Mr. Curtis was a high-school science teacher who was a lifelong Eagle Scout. He wore knee socks and shorts that were too tight for his butt. Brother Bill was a Jesuit novitiate. He was a cool guy in his late twenties, serious but easy to talk to. He seemed less rigid in his thinking.

Both Rip and Luka were juniors at Loyola. They were Ukrainian Americans from the same neighborhood in Chicago where Alec had grown up over the past two decades. All three were fluent in Ukrainian and would annoy their American friends by having private conversations in a foreign language. Rip was boisterous, with a quick wit and generous smile. Luka was reserved. He was scary smart but mostly kept his thoughts to himself. Both were candidates for the Brotherhood.

"I can't wait to get to Copenhagen," said Rip. "The girls there are supposed to be gorgeous, and I heard they're willing to do *anything*! They're all into free love."

"*Drei weitere Biere bitte*," Rip called out to the waitress. He was taking German at Loyola and was eager to practice.

The beer maid was a gray-haired woman in an embroidered blouse and black skirt. She acted like the owner. She placed the liter steins on their wooden table and pinched Rip on the cheek. "*Möchten Sie etwas Apfelschnaps?*" she asked.

"She's asking if we want some apple brandy," Rip translated. "I think they're famous for it here."

"I think she likes you," Luka said. "Ask her if she has a daughter."

"*Ja*," Rip replied. "*Drei Apfelschnaps bitte*. We'll shoot the brandy and chase it with beer."

The local beer in Cologne was better than any that Alec had tasted before. Alec had developed a fondness for local brews during his travels. He, Rip, and Luka planned to drink a local brew at each new destination.

"We have to be careful not to overdo it," Alec said. As the oldest of the three, he felt some responsibility. "When Walrus and I were in Dublin on Father Collins's "Round the World" tour, we decided to have a stout at every bar between our hostel and the center of town. I remember waking up in a bar with my arm around the ugliest girl I had ever seen—that is, until I saw the girl with Walrus!"

All three broke out laughing. Walrus was well known to Rip and Luka. Other than Serge, he was Alec's closest friend. Walrus and Alec grew up a block apart in the Ukrainian hood and spent the summers together at Razz's summer home in Wisconsin until they were old enough to go to youth camps. Alec had hoped that Walrus would join him on this trip, but his parents decided against it. His father believed the Soviet Union was still too dangerous.

Despite his cautionary tale, the beer and the Apfel-schnaps kept flowing. Rip would not stop talking, and Luka was turning green. Alec did not want to wake up with his arm around another strange girl.

"I think it's time to go," he said. "We need to save ourselves for the elephant beer in Copenhagen."

CHAPTER 4

Copenhagen was even wilder than they had imagined. The hostel was packed with European youth who were chasing parties from one country to another. Father Collins was beside himself, trying to shelter his American innocents from the sin around them. Marijuana was plentiful. Alec, Rip, and Luka were sitting on Rip's bed when a black-haired Dane passed a joint around. Alec didn't refuse the hit; he didn't want to risk appearing straight.

"Creeper," the Dane said. "Creeps up on you." They all broke out laughing, though they weren't sure why.

Stefi's letter had been waiting for him when he arrived at the hostel, and Alec wanted to reply. He took another hit of the joint and went over to his bed to write her a letter.

Dear Stefi,

I got your letter this morning—it's great to hear from you! I miss you. Life here is wild and free. Right now the Swedish guys are chasing the Danish girls past my bed, and the Italians are coming in a close second—they're all high on wine and grass. Copenhagen is a magical place. The streets are full of young people. At night, everything comes alive. Rock music blasts out of the head shops. Free and easy, that's the way it's supposed to be. When we got to Luxembourg I rented a bike and got lost in the vineyards. I was almost mauled by a hellhound. Rip, Luka, and I played soccer with some kids on the street in Cologne and got our butts kicked. We ended the day drinking apple brandy at a bar owned by some old German woman. I think she was sweet on Rip.

We're only a few days away from the Soviet Union. I'm anxious to see Ukraine. I don't want to get heavy, but there's something important that I need to do. For once I feel involved. I can understand what the strike at NU was all about. It's up to us to change things. Wait for me ... but no—maybe it's better if we get to know each other all over again, like a whole new beginning. I miss you. Write.

Love, Alec

***

The Tivoli Gardens were intoxicating at night. The glow of the lights drowned out even the brightest star in the sky. *Tivoli is a cross between Disneyland and a county fair,* thought Alec. *This is where Peter Pan comes to play.* Alec needed this escape.

He was hungry. He plopped down several kroner for some French fries and a beer. The lights in the stand seemed brighter than they had to be. The fries were hot, greasy, and salty. The ketchup was not like the American standard. It was too sweet—not enough vinegar. He sat down on a bench to eat his fries and watch the world go by. The time seemed to go on forever.

Unlike Stefi, Alec was keenly aware of his existence. There's a big difference between feeling alive and knowing that you are alive. He envied her ability to not dwell on the meaning of life. Tonight was going to be different. It would be more fun to dream walk through this whimsical place than to watch it from a bench. He stood up and joined the crowds that were wandering through this Neverland of Oriental palaces, roller coasters, and fun houses. The music changed with each new venue. The din of laughter and cries of fright and delight were constant.

Just behind the carousel, Alec saw the entrance to a fun house called the Magical Mystery Tour. At first, he thought it might be a showing of the Beatles movie, but the hawker at the door kept shouting the equivalent of "cheap thrills" in multiple languages. He reminded Alec of Serge. As a child, Alec had loved fun houses and scary rides. His cousin Zack would take him and his younger cousin Tatiana to Riverview Park and chase them through the fun houses. They would pass on the roller coasters and find the creepy rides instead that plunged them into darkness filled with fake Spanish moss, opening caskets, and screaming banshees. Alec was a sucker for cheap thrills. He bought a ticket and went in.

The swinging door into the Magical Mystery Tour opened into an inlaid wooden room. *Beautiful, but not scary*, he thought. He noticed, however, that the room appeared to be getting progressively smaller. The lights were getting dimmer. The walls seemed to be closing in. The door where he had entered disappeared into the intricate inlay. He felt disoriented. He hated confinement. Panic began to creep up his spine. He started to push on the panels, looking for a mechanical release. *There has to be a way out*, he thought. *I'm paying for this!*

He had to think his way out of the box. Rather than push, he tried sliding the wall sideways. It gave way. This was much too complicated for a fun house. The opening revealed a long tunnel, bathed in blue. The floor of the tunnel was squishy, making him lose his balance. It undulated with the weight of each step. He realized it was like a long waterbed and that he had to carefully calculate each step. He lurched right, left, and right again. The sides were frustratingly just a few inches wider than his outstretched arms. He learned that if he slammed right and then recoiled left that he could maintain his forward momentum. It was as if he were in the hold of a ship being tossed in a storm.

At the end of the tunnel, he stumbled into a room filled with brambles. A fog machine pumped in an algae-colored ether. He thought of Brer Rabbit hiding from Brer Fox. This was more an obstacle course than a magical mystery tour. How could they let children in here? He remembered when he and his cousin Tatiana had played in the thick brambles at his parents' lake house. He was five, and she was just five days younger. He would lead her by the hand through the thicket. *Someday I'll marry you*, he'd promised her. That was a long time ago. The brambles were tearing at his clothes. He kneeled to the ground and touched the floor. *I can crawl below them*, he thought.

He was satisfied with himself for outsmarting the fun-house tricks. It felt like cheating to crawl through the place, so he stood up to face the next challenge. He entered a black room with a flashing ultraviolet strobe light. *What's so creepy about a disco?* The walls were covered with angled mirrors. The mirrors gave the impression that his torso had been torn into a hundred pieces. With each step and each flash of the strobe, a different part of his body would reflect back and back and back again. His white shirt, iridescent in the strobe light, was the only unifying feature.

He burst out the exit into the cool of the evening. He had gotten what he paid for. A dog was barking in the distance. He really had to pee.

The closest WC was in a dimly lit part of the Gardens, only a few hundred meters from the fun house. As he walked into the unlit section marked "Herretoilet," he saw a blonde girl with her skirt up, sitting spread-eagle on a urinal. A dark-haired boy, not all of eighteen, was thrusting into her, oblivious to the world. Her blouse was open, and her moonlit breasts bounced with each thrust. Neither seemed to care that Alec had just walked in.

She was beautiful, wild, and abandoned in her passion. Alec felt himself getting hard. Still, he really needed to pee. He walked over into the urinal next to them, opened his zipper, and unleashed a golden stream that hit the top of urinal. The blonde turned her head. One hand was on her lover's shoulder. With the other she flipped Alec a bird. It was not a disdainful gesture. It was slow and deliberate. More like ... wait, you can be next.

Alec turned red, zipped up his zipper, and hurried out the bathroom door.

"Silly boy," she said.

CHAPTER 5

Alec unfolded his map of Stockholm. It had been a week since he had last seen Stefi, and he was lonely. He asked the young female clerk at the desk if there was any mail for him. She checked the name on his passport and then handed him a postmarked lavender envelope. He wanted a private place to read it. The Haga Park was just north of the city. It would be a pleasant place to stroll on a sunny June afternoon. The pastry shops along the way to the bus stop were too tempting to pass up. He dropped ten kronor for a Napoleon pastry and ate it while he walked. The custard and currant jam squished out the sides as he bit in. The powdered sugar stuck to his lips. He put his hand into his pocket to make sure that Stefi's letter was still there. It was, but his sticky fingers stained her lavender letter with jam.

Stefi's letters had been waiting for him at every new destination, as promised. Between the "*I miss you*" and "*I love you*," she would describe the wonderfully ordinary goings-on of a high school girl on a boring summer vacation. "*Marta and I went to North Avenue Beach and saw Chou and Razz. We're planning to go to Round Lake on Sunday, but it won't be the same there without you.*" There were three more letters in addition to the latest: the first in Luxembourg, a second in Cologne, and a third in Copenhagen.

He wondered if he really loved her or if he loved the idea of loving her. Was she simply reflecting his affection like the light off the moon? Was there a dark side to her that he hadn't yet seen? *She's just a schoolgirl.* They had dated for less than a year. How much about love could they possibly understand? *I guess,* he told himself, *that whatever age you are, you're as wise as you've ever been.* He remembered what his mother had told him: "It's better to love than to be loved." He hoped their love would last. Stefi was spontaneous and overflowing with life. She was also damn sexy. He hoped their lust would last forever too.

He was getting nervous. Every stop on the itinerary was a step closer to the Soviet border. He needed to relax. A stroll along the meandering paths of Haga Park was the way to do it.

There were surprisingly few people in the park—some tourists, mothers with strollers, and lovers holding hands. The trees were casting long shadows in the late afternoon. He walked past the butterfly houses toward the Temple of Echo. The temple was a lovely, round, open edifice seated on the top of a small hill. According to the inscription, King Gustav III had it built in 1790 as an outdoor dining room. The design allowed sound to echo, and he could hear all of the conversations in the room, even if his guests were seated far away.

Alec climbed the stone steps and entered the temple. The high, open arches provided views in every direction. He thought of the children's game King of the Hill, in which boys try to knock each other off the top of a hill until only one victor is left standing. You always had to watch your back, because if you were king, someone was always trying to knock you off. *Here*, he thought, *the king made it clear who was king and designed a structure in which neither friends nor enemies could conspire against him. It was ingenious.* Now the king was gone, and only his temple remained.

"Alec!" he yelled out to test for the echoes. "Alec ... Alec ... Alec ..." The echoes reverberated more like a whispering crowd than echoes off the mountains. *Ghosts*, he thought. He was alone in the temple, and he felt like King of the Mountain. He put his hand in his pocket and pulled out Stefi's jam-stained letter. He could still smell the faint fragrance of hyacinths. He put his forefinger under the flap and gently pried the envelope open. The flap looked like it had been glued, opened, and re-glued.

Dear Alec, I miss you. Yesterday Marta and I went for a party at Razz's. I had a little too much to drink, and Serge drove me home. He was asking about you.

Serge had been Alec's best friend since Damian died. Serge had the hairdo and magnetism of Elvis Presley. He was everything that Alec was not. Their initiation into the Brotherhood was the culmination of their friendship. Alec's other friends warned him that Serge was all about Serge, but Alec wouldn't listen. Their companionship was mutually beneficial. They played well together. Serge would usually attract the girls and pass the ones he didn't want to Alec. Stefi was the exception. She had always seemed more interested in Alec than in Serge. It was one of the reasons he loved her.

The weekends are especially lonely, her letter continued. *I go to North Avenue Beach with my friends, but it's not the same without you. Next week I leave for camp in Wisconsin. Those three weeks should pass quickly. I can't wait to see you in Europe. I'm sewing some new outfits just for you.* Another thing that Alec loved about her was that she sewed her own clothes. She had three other sisters, and he had likened her to Cinderella. "I have money to buy clothes," she retorted. "I just like to make my own."

He folded the letter and put it back in the envelope.

He went over the itinerary in his head. Take the ferry to Helsinki and then enter the Soviet Union at the Finnish border. There were only four days to go. He began to compose a cryptic reply to Stefi.

I need to do something that I can't tell you about just yet. Don't worry. I won't be able to write while I'm in the Soviet Union. They go through all the letters …

***

Father Collins encouraged the boys to take advantage of the sauna next to the hostel—he had gone there the day before and found it invigorating. Alec convinced Rip and Luka to go check it out with him. The sauna was housed in a three-story stone building on the corner of a busy intersection. Last winter Alec and his friends from the Brotherhood had taken an excursion to the Turkish baths on North Avenue in Chicago. It had been an interesting male-bonding experience, complete with hot and cold baths, dank green walls, and masseurs who spoke to them in German. The boys had taken a group picture while wrapped in their towels.

The men's locker room in the Swedish sauna was on the second floor. The three friends put away their clothes, tied towels around their waists, and stepped into the hallway that led to the saunas. The door at the end of the hallway opened into a spacious two-story hall with a swimming pool. Sunlight streamed into the room from the skylights. The swimming pool had a high dive that was also accessible from the third floor.

"Let's go see what's up there," Alec suggested. They climbed up the stairs to discover three sauna rooms with escalating temperatures. They entered the mildest and sat down on the aspen benches. Two Swedes were sitting in the corner, but the room was large enough that they didn't feel cramped. The temperature was hot but tolerable. Alec could feel the heat engulfing his body. Beads of sweat began to form on his skin. After a few minutes, the sweat began to trickle off in little streams. He poured a ladle of water on the hot stones.

"Let's try the next room," Alec said. "I can't believe it could be much hotter than this."

It was. The heat was no longer relaxing; it was oppressive. The bench was so hot it was difficult to sit on. Rip and Luka lasted only a few minutes.

"It's crazy hot in here," Rip said. "Luka and I are going to jump into the pool."

"I'll join you in a minute," Alec replied. "I want to see how long I can last in the third room."

The door leading to the third room had a sign in Swedish that he could not decipher. The metal handle to the door was too hot to touch with bare hands. Alec used his towel to grab the handle. A blast of superheated air rushed out of the room. He stepped into the room and sat down. The room was empty. He was determined to last at least a minute. He closed his eyes and began to count backwards from sixty. When he inhaled his first breath, the air burned his throat. He put his towel to his mouth to cool the air, but it was still too hot to breathe. Sweat was streaming down his body and pouring into his eyes. Fifty, forty-nine, forty-eight …

He felt himself getting dizzy. He lost count of the time. He and Walrus were back on the bank of the Wisconsin River, checking their lines. They threw sand balls at a wasp nest that was dug into the bank. Sister Teresa dragged him to the front of the class by his ear. He and Serge were tuning their guitars by the campfire. The band was playing "Moon River." Boyan asked him if he wanted a cigarette … Stefi laughed as she brushed the snow from her hair …

"Wake up! Alec, wake up!"

Alec felt a bruising grip under his triceps. Someone had lifted him and was dragging him to the door. A blast of cold air brought him back to his senses. The temperature in the hallway felt alpine by comparison. He was drenched in sweat. His towel was soaked. Brother Bill kept dragging him down the hallway.

"No, no, I can walk. I'm OK."

"You need to jump into the pool."

"I can make it on my own."

Bill did not let go of his arm. A swinging door opened into the blue two-story natatorium. Alec and Bill staggered onto the high dive and dove naked into the pool.

The steep drop in temperature was exhilarating. It was like fire and ice. Father Collins was right. He felt alive. *Escaping death sharpens your senses.* He slowly swam up from the bottom of the pool and opened his eyes to see Rip and Luka laughing at him from the shallow end.

"Pretty cold, huh?" Rip yelled out. "Pulls your nuts right up!"

The cold blue water was a soothing escape from the intolerable heat.

"Want to do it again?" asked Luka.

"No, once is enough."

Bill was watching from the deep end of the pool.

Alec swam over. "Thanks, I owe you one. I just sort of drifted away."

"You shouldn't have gone in there alone."

"I just wanted to show my friends I could do it."

"You don't have to prove anything to anyone. You just need to be at peace with yourself. I know. I've been there."

CHAPTER 6

The drive from Helsinki to the Soviet border crossing seemed interminable. While their previous immigration checks had been perfunctory, here the Finnish immigration officers insisted on checking every passport to make sure it had a valid Soviet visa. Their three Volkswagen minibuses were the only vehicles on the road. Alec stared out the passenger-side window at the desolate fields that even nature seemed to have abandoned. The fields were like ancient battlefields—sacred to some and profane to others. A place can be many things through the course of time. He imagined that the ghosts of underage soldiers still wandered these fields, bewildered as to their fate.

A metal signpost marked the distance to the border, ten kilometers away. Alec began to sweat. He steeled himself as they drew nearer. He had nothing to hide. He was a tourist in a minibus caravan with thirty other students. He, like the others, had applied for his Soviet visa six months ago. What could possibly take six months to process? If they had investigated him, what could they find? The son of political immigrants ... graduate of Ukrainian Saturday school ... Northwestern University student. And who would carry out such an investigation? A trusted schoolteacher? A counselor? A friend? *Don't get paranoid*, he scolded himself. Then he remembered what his cousin Zack had told him: "Just because you're not paranoid doesn't mean that they're not out to get you."

Alec was riding with Father Collins in the lead van. He saw the Soviet border station in the distance. A series of parallel barbed-wire fences stretched perpendicular to the road as far as the eye could see. A solitary crow breached the perimeter. Guard towers broke the skyline every five hundred meters. A heavy red-and-white gate blocked the road. Border guards with oversize hats and automatic weapons manned the gate. Beyond the gate, the road veered into a complex of gray cinder-block buildings with metal roofs.

As the vans approached, a border guard stepped into the road and waved them to a stop. Father Collins rolled down the window to ask instructions. The guard barked out commands in Russian.

"He's telling us to step out of the van," said Alec. Knowing Ukrainian, he could understand enough Russian to get by.

The Loyolans filed out of the van, joking and laughing nervously.

"Don't they know we're Americans?"

"Just shut up," said Alec. "Do what they say."

The guard checked out the van to make sure that no one else was hiding inside. Two other guards simultaneously checked the other two vans. Satisfied with the head count, the guards ordered everyone back into the vans. They directed the vans to park by a windowless building in the center of the complex. The boys watched as their luggage was emptied out of the vans.

Two more border guards walked out of the windowless intake building. One of them was clearly a commanding officer. He was older and ruder than the others. He spoke some broken English.

"Everyone alone take luggage," he said. By now the nervous laughter was replaced with an uneasy seriousness. Father Collins handed the officer the stack of thirty-three US passports. The entire group filed into the intake building to await processing. The commanding officer flipped through each of the passports and then handed the stack to his subordinates.

Rip nudged Alec in the ribs. "We're in big trouble," he said. "Some of the guys bought porn in Copenhagen—magazines, Super 8 film."

"Idiots," said Alec.

As the guards checked the visas, they would call out the names. The person called was then led into a customs line.

Alec heard his name called. He picked up his green knapsack and tried to nonchalantly pick a customs line. When he tried to cross the red immigration line, the officer grabbed him by the arm.

"Come with me," he said in Russian. "I know you can understand me."

The officer led Alec into a brightly lit room and ordered him to sit down. The room had the sickly, sweet smell of

Soviet tobacco. He had Alec place his knapsack on the stainless steel table that separated them. He spoke to Alec in Russian, and Alec replied in Ukrainian. The questions were clear. There was no need for an interpreter. *Why did they single me out?* he wondered. He was not the only Ukrainian American in the group.

The officer fingered Alec's passport with his yellow fingers. "Alec Dmytrovich Korol."

"How do you know my father's name?" The patronymic wasn't written in his passport.

"Where were your parents born?" the officer continued.

"My parents were born in western Ukraine."

"What did they do during the war?"

"They were in displaced persons camps in Germany." Alec had wanted to say that they fled the advancing Red Army, but he knew better. When the war broke out, his father had been studying to be a priest, and his mother was studying to be a doctor. They were intellectuals. They would have been shot or sent to Siberia, had they not fled. Alec's uncles had died fighting in the Ukrainian Insurgent Army, but there was no way his interrogator could have known that.

The officer opened Alec's knapsack and began to remove the items one by one. He had the bloated face of a morning drinker and stank of sweat and acetaldehyde. Alec's knapsack had a transparent plastic pocket on the inside flap where he kept Stefi's letters and other valuables. The officer flipped through the letters until he came upon one from Alec's mother. The letter was in Ukrainian. He looked at Alec as though he had just uncovered a hidden stash of heroin. He took the letter, walked out of the room, and locked the door.

Alec waited. An hour went by. He stared at the cin-der-block walls. Another hour went by. *What could they possibly want with my mother's letter?* The letter was addressed to a distant uncle in Munich. She had simply written, *"My son will be arriving in Munich a few days before the tour. We would greatly appreciate if you would take care of him for those few days. Please give our best wishes to the rest of the family."*

Alec heard the door unlock. He was hoping that Father Collins was coming to get him out of this place. Instead, the officer came back with two armed guards.

"Stand up," he ordered. Alec quickly stood up. "Take off your clothes."

Alec's heart was pounding. He had no choice but to comply. As he took off each article of clothing, the officer would tell him to wait while he examined it for hidden pockets or other contraband. It was like a perverted game of strip poker.

Alec stripped down to his underwear. The officer examined him closely.

Alec had the lithe physique of a volleyball player. He was in the best shape of his life. He trained with his team twice a week and worked out between classes at Patten Gym. Under the leering eyes of his alcoholic interrogator, however, he felt helpless and humiliated. He was like a fly whose wings had been ripped off by a sadistic child.

The officer began to open Stefi's letters while Alec stood in his underwear. Alec couldn't tell if his interrogator could read English. From the colored paper and the handwriting, it was clear that the letters were from Alec's girlfriend. He smelled the letters. As he opened each envelope, it was as if Stefi was being violated in front of his eyes. He felt powerless. He wanted to protect her, but he couldn't.

The officer opened Alec's wallet and began to pull out the few photos that were tucked into the plastic holders. He leered at Stefi's photo and read the inscription on the back. Before he could question Alec further, there was a rapid knock on the door. A female guard brought back Alec's mother's letter and whispered something to the officer. The officer seemed disappointed. He looked at Alec. "Get dressed," he said.

Alec was led back into the large customs room where Father Collins and Bill were waiting. The rest of the group had cleared customs hours ago and were waiting in the vans.

"Are you OK?" Father Collins asked him. "Apparently there was some mix up with your visa. It took a while to figure out. I had to call the Intourist agency in Moscow, and they eventually straightened it out. It's next to impossible to make a phone call from here."

"No one else was held up?" asked Alec.

"No, no, it was a slow process, but there were no other problems."

Alec wondered how the pornography had gotten through untouched.

CHAPTER 7

The white nights of Leningrad made it difficult to sleep. The Intourist hotel room had two narrow single beds with over-starched white linens and rough woolen blankets. Pigeons cooed on the sill just outside the window overlooking Nevsky Prospect. A painting of a black locomotive with a red banner adorned the wall. The room stank faintly of sewer gas. Father Collins made Alec share the room with Bill, the Jesuit novitiate chaperone, probably to keep Alec out of any further trouble.

"Uneasy dreams?" asked Bill.

"It's hard to fall asleep. I can't tell if it's day or night." Alec didn't want to talk about himself. He thought the room might be bugged. "Thanks for getting me out of that sauna in Stockholm."

"No problem. It's my job to make sure you guys don't get into trouble."

"What made you decide to become a Jesuit?"

"The Jesuits are different from other orders—they think for themselves. I respect that."

"No, what I meant was, what made you decide to devote your life to God?"

"I had a calling when I was in high school. I wasn't sure though, and I'm still not 100 percent sure. I led a wild life. I needed some sense of order."

Bill can't be more than thirty, thought Alec. *What kind of wild life could he have led?*

"Those pigeons are eavesdropping," Alec said jokingly. Bill got up out of bed to shoo them away. He tried to open the window, but it wouldn't budge. He rapped on the glass until they finally flapped away.

Bill began to open up. "During college I spent a semester abroad in France. I met a girl, Emilie, at the library in the Sorbonne."

"She was Parisian?"

"She was from Languedoc. They're more down-to-earth than Parisians. She loved the coast and the sea. When the semester was over, we took off for the south. I bought a red Honda motorcycle, and we tried to do every beach from Cannes to Collioure."

"She spoke English?"

"A little, but we mostly spoke French. I majored in French literature in college."

"It sounds like you really cared for her."

"She was a beautiful person. I loved her."

"Then why did you leave her?"

"I didn't. One night I got drunk in Collioure and crashed the motorcycle. I survived—she didn't."

The conversation had veered into an uncomfortable direction. Alec pulled the stiff sheet up to his chin. Bill lay back in bed. The pigeons fluttered back to the sill and resumed their cooing.

"Do you think that everything that happens is preordained?" Alec asked.

"No, I think that we get to choose our actions. I chose to drink and drive. I have to live with the consequences of that decision."

"I guess that's better than the alternative," said Alec, but he wasn't sure. He pretended to go to sleep.

***

The Hermitage Museum was housed in the complex of buildings that comprised the Palace Embankment along the Neva. The beautiful architecture was eclipsed only by the art within. The opulent rooms in the Winter Palace hoarded the riches of a vast empire. *It was enough to foment a revolution,* thought Alec.

Alec imagined what St. Petersburg was like in the 1840s, when the Ukrainian poet Taras Shevchenko was a student of the Academy of Arts and an apprentice in Bryullov's studio. Alec had read Shevchenko's works in Ukrainian Saturday school. The young Shevchenko was a promising painter, but his true genius was poetry. His words celebrated the soul of Ukraine: the steppe, the Black Sea, the Cossack burial mounds. His characters were fictional and historical: shepherd boys and lovelorn maidens, blind kobzars, and Cossacks who defended their land against the Turks and Poles and foolishly signed a peace treaty with Russia. The tsar exiled him to Orenburg and then Orsk, "under the strictest surveillance, with a ban on writing and painting." Respecting his last will and testament, Shevchenko was buried on a hill in Kaniv overlooking the Dnipro River. Even the Soviets considered his burial place a shrine. He had fought against the type of Russian chauvinism that was embodied in the tsarist Ems Ukaz: "Ukraine does not exist, it never existed, and it will never exist."

Alec had the same burning nationalism, and until now he had not questioned why. He spoke Ukrainian at home. He learned English from Howdy Doody, the Lone Ranger, and the Blue Fairy on black-and-white television. It was strange that he felt so tied to a place he had never seen. He had sung the words to the Ukrainian national anthem—"We will lay down our body and soul for our freedom"—at Scout camp, Ukrainian school, and political commemorations a thousand times. *Is nationalism in my blood,* he wondered, *or was it imprinted in me by my upbringing?*

As the crowd pushed them from room to room, Alec made sure to stay close to Luka. Both were looking for the same painting. Masterpieces flashed by them like scenes from the window of a moving train.

"There it is!" said Luka. Luka was referring to Ilya Repin's painting *Reply of the Zaporozhian Cossacks to Sultan Mehmed IV of the Ottoman Empire*. It portrayed the hetman and his staff writing what is officially recognized as the most obscene letter ever written to a head of state.

"Look how they're laughing!" Luka said. "I can imagine them composing the next insult. It makes me proud to be Ukrainian. What do you see in the painting?"

"It depicts freedom," Alec replied.

"Still … it's odd that it was painted by a Russian."

"Yes, but a Russian who was born in Ukraine. The Cossack blood is mixed into the land."

"Do you hate Russians?" Luka asked.

"No, I'm not anti-Russian. I like Russian music and literature. I enjoy reading Dostoevsky and Lermontov. I love the Red Army band. I even think I understand the Russian soul. What I hate is Russian chauvinism and imperialism."

As the masses pushed through the Hermitage, they chanced upon Leonardo da Vinci's *Madonna and Child*. Luka stared at her naked breast; Alec was captivated by its innocence. Even though the Madonna had exposed her breast, the composition with her suckling Infant was the epitome of purity. Whenever Alec needed solace, he prayed to the Blessed Virgin. *Hail Mary, full of grace … It's how the world was meant to be*, he thought, *and not how it was*.

His mother had told him how her cousins, who were idealistic young teachers, had been lured by Stalin to eastern Ukraine to promote "Ukrainianization," only to be executed on arrival—three bright lights methodically extinguished in some unknown railroad station by bullets to the back of the head. She had told him how his namesake, her brother Alec, had died at Brody, the quiet killing field where the poppies grow, fighting the advancing Red Army. Ukraine was now the outland rather than the ancient seat of the empire. The Russians had even expropriated the name of Kievan Rus. Ukrainians were little brothers to their Russian oppressors. He had experienced none of it personally, yet he felt like he had suffered through it all.

***

The drive through Russia was bleak and boring. In the late afternoon, the Loyola caravan pulled into a Soviet open-air sanatorium. Sanatoriums were widespread throughout the Soviet Union. The Pine Tree Sanatorium just south of Moscow was famous for its spring-fed lake that the workers had artificially excavated to three times its original size. The waters were rumored to have healing properties. The sanatorium had originally served as a Pioneer youth camp.

Intourist had arranged this rest stop to impress the young Americans with the quality of Soviet life. The housing was Spartan—little more than army tents wired with electricity that sat upon plywood floors. That was part of the open-air charm of the place. The communal toilets were separated into men's and women's sections, each of which had a hot shower. There was a small, tin-roof cafeteria with long tables and plastic chairs. Most families brought their own food and grilled pork *shasliks* on the numerous metal-grate grills that were scattered throughout the camp. Securing a grill for one's family was crucial to the success of the holiday. The campers would mingle with friends, drink vodka, and share their secrets for marinating pork. The ultimate in status was to have one's own stainless steel skewers with the heat-resistant plastic handles that were a by-product of the Soviet space program.

Each tent held four metal spring beds. The boys had an hour to unpack and rest before convening for supper at six in the camp cafeteria. Alec threw his knapsack on the bed and wandered out of the tent to explore the camp. He chanced upon a pair of couples who were firing up a grill by the lake:

two perky brunettes who looked like sisters, a shirtless man with a tattoo of a swallow on his chest, and a short, wiry man with curly blond hair. They had claimed an idyllic spot nestled between the pines on the grassy shore of the lake. Alec could see from the swirls in the water that the fish were beginning to feed on the white moths that flittered above the surface. Their muddy Zaporozhets was parked just a few feet from the water.

"*Zdrasvite*," the man with the tattoo called out to Alec. "*Priluchish do nas.*"

Alec replied in a mix of Ukrainian and Russian. "*Zdrasvite*. My name is Alec. I am a student from America."

"American?" the man replied in Russian. "Then absolutely you must join us. I am Igor, this is my friend Anna, and this is Boris and his wife, Maria. We are on holiday. Boris and I are steel workers. He was once a champion wrestler, and now he is a specialist of impenetrable alloys. The girls are students at Moscow State University. Boris prepared the *shaslik* with the help of his mother, and I prepared the *samohonka* using a recipe I learned in the navy." The other three laughed when he mentioned the moonshine.

"Nice to meet you. I can only stay for a little while." Unlike his previous few days in the Soviet Union, this encounter seemed genuine and unrehearsed. Alec was eager to connect with real people.

Boris pulled a large glass jar out of plastic GUM bag. The jar was filled with chunks of pork shoulder marinated in apple-cider vinegar, onions, and bay leaves. Igor proudly produced two unlabeled bottles of moonshine and some water glasses. He unscrewed one of the bottles and poured a little on the fire to demonstrate its potency. The moonshine flared in an instant. "Pure enough?" he asked with a broad smile.

"How is it that you speak our language if you are an American?" Anna asked him.

"I was born in America, but my parents are from Ukraine."

"Then you are a Slav like us," Igor replied. He poured everyone a shot and raised a toast. "To the sons and daughters of Mother Rus, wherever fate has taken them."

"Alec, I have an anecdote for you," said Boris. "Comrade Brezhnev decides to visit a village so that the people can meet the man responsible for their quality of life. He first encounters a seven-year-old boy on a bicycle and says, 'I am the one who gave you your clothes, your bicycle, and the food that you eat. Go tell the others.' The boy pedals home and calls out to his mother, 'Mommy, Mommy, come quickly. Our uncle from America has come to visit!'" All five broke out laughing.

Igor poured a second round while Boris skewered the shasliks and expertly arranged them on the grates over the wood fire. "Quickly, Boris, or we shall die of thirst. The next toast is yours." Igor winked at Alec and said, "What shortens life the most is a long pause between the first and second toast."

When Boris was satisfied that the skewers were the correct distance from the fire, he raised his glass and said, "To Alec, our brother from America." With that familial toast, even the girls had to finish their glasses.

Boris turned the skewers while Igor laid a plastic tablecloth and five mismatched plates on the hood of the car. Anna sliced a loaf of wheat bread, while Maria fished pickled tomatoes, cucumbers, and yellow mushrooms out of assorted jars. Boris pulled the skewers off the fire and served each of them a generous portion of roasted pork.

As the Igor refilled the glasses, Alec felt compelled to

respond. "I would like to raise a toast to my brothers—"

"No, no," Igor interrupted. "The third toast must always be to women."

Alec laughed. "Well, in that case, I would like to raise a toast to Anna and Maria, the two most beautiful women I have met in the Soviet Union!"

"Well done!" Boris said. "To our beautiful wives and girlfriends! May they never meet!"

Alec wasn't sure if it was the moonshine or the hospitality, but for the first time in days, he felt genuinely happy. His new comrades did not probe or interrogate him. They simply welcomed him. They joked and laughed and enjoyed each other's company. When Igor pulled a balalaika out of the trunk of his car, Alec realized it was time to go.

"I'm afraid I have to rejoin my group. They are expecting me in the cafeteria. I don't want them to come looking for me."

"Ah yes, we understand," Ivan replied. "The watchful eye of Father Brezhnev. Before you go, you must have some honeycomb for dessert." Maria sliced a square of honeycomb, wax and all, and gave it to Alec. As he bit into the wax, the sweet pockets of honey burst open in his mouth.

"It's delicious, and thank you," he said. "I hope that one day we can meet again." His Ukrainian schoolteachers had warned him that all Communists were evil, but he realized the folly of such generalizations. When he returned to his tent, he saw that everyone but Bill had already left for the cafeteria.

"I'm glad you're back," Bill said. "I was getting worried. I told them you were having some stomach trouble."

"It was my stomach all right," Alec replied, "but it was anything but trouble."

Alec forced down a second dinner in the cafeteria. He wasn't at all hungry, but he did not want to stand out. The dinner was unusual, but tasty enough: green borscht, pickled herring, and a mystery meat with fried potatoes. Father Collins was pleased with the arrangements. Before allowing the boys to eat, he stood up and said grace. After the amen, he said, "Our hosts have arranged a meeting this evening with the Komsomol youth. It will give you a chance to meet Russian teenagers. They have studied English in school and are eager to converse with you. We'll be meeting with them back here in the cafeteria at eight o'clock sharp."

When they returned to their tents, Ronnie, one of Alec's tent mates, let out a cry. "My camera's gone! Somebody stole my camera!"

"You probably just left it in the van," said Alec.

"No, no, it was right here on the bed. Just before we left for dinner!"

Father Collins and an English-speaking camp manager came in to quell the disturbance. Ronnie explained what had happened.

"It is not possible," said the manager. He gave Ronnie a cold stare to determine if this was some sort of American provocation. He quickly determined that the boy was not capable of such subterfuge. "Do not be alarmed. We will locate your camera by the time you return."

The Komsomol youth that filed into the cafeteria at eight looked well past their teenage years. They looked self-assured—no nervousness, no awkwardness, no hesitation. They had the sorts of fixed smiles and skyward gazes that Alec had seen on Soviet propaganda posters. Each Komsomolets chose an American boy to sit across from. The pairings were seemingly random until Alec found himself staring at Stefi's face—he knew it wasn't Stefi, but the resemblance was re-markable. She had the same green eyes, wheat blonde hair, and high cheekbones. She was just a little older and a little taller than Stefi. Her hair was pulled back, like a schoolteacher's; it seemed ready to be unleashed with the pull of a pin.

"Hello, my name is Myra."

"Alec."

"I am Komsomolets … as you say in English, Communist socialist youth," said Myra. "Are you American Scout?"

"Well, yes and no," said Alec. "I belong to a Ukrainian American youth organization."

"My father is Ukrainian," said Myra, "and my mother is Belarusian."

"Do you speak Ukrainian?" asked Alec.

Her gaze was unnerving. It never left his eyes. "Only a little. We speak Russian at home. I learned some words from my grandparents."

"It's funny, but even living in America, I didn't learn to speak English until I was in the first grade."

Myra smiled. "We are instructed to talk about Lenin and workers' rights and the glory of my country. Perhaps we should talk about ourselves instead."

"I'd prefer that."

Myra undid the clasp in her hair. "Do you know the meaning of my name?" she asked.

"Yes, in Ukrainian, Myra means peace."

Myra seemed pleased. "Would you like to go for walk by lake? I enjoy the evening air."

Her offer startled him. It seemed too good to be true. It might be the call of a siren.

"A walk?"

"Yes, by lake," she replied. "It is beautiful by sunset." Her foot touched his ankle under the table and ran up the back of his calf. "Do you know the meaning of your name? It means defender of the people," she continued. "Who is it that you defend?" She moved her foot from the outside of his leg to the inside.

Alec was moved by the provocation. He weighed the risks. "I'm sure it's beautiful, but I'm very tired," he lied. "It's been a long drive." A look of concern flashed across her face, as if she had in some way failed her country. She quickly regained her composure and withdrew her leg. Her whimsy evaporated.

"Here are my coordinates. Write to me."

It's strange, thought Alec, *that she did not request my address in return.* Alec felt like a coward. He wasn't sure why he was so uncomfortable with her proposition. If this was a game, then surely he could play it. What harm could there be in a walk by the lake with a beautiful girl who would talk about internationalism and socialism and how religion was the opiate of the people? It would have been a pleasant diversion. He would have been strong enough to resist any further temptations. *I should have played it differently*, he thought.

Alec walked back to the tent ahead of the others. He saw the camp manager at the entrance to the tent, speaking in Russian to a young man dressed in a black sweat suit. The young man was barely perceptible in the dark. He moved quickly and quietly, like a cat.

"Have you located the camera?" the camp manager asked.

"No, it is not anywhere."

"Are you sure that one of the Americans did not take it and hide it in his luggage?"

"I am absolutely sure. I have already gone through all of their things."

CHAPTER 8

A plain signpost that read "Ukrainian SSR" marked the crossing of the border. There were no guards or barricades—the political border had been torn down long ago. The covered bus stops along the road were stenciled with the red-and-black motifs typical of embroidery from the Chernihiv region. Alec looked out the window, hoping to see a change from the bleak Russian landscape. Sunflowers grew along the fences of the country cottages, known as *dachas*. The earth seemed blacker. Communist graffiti stilled defaced the whitewashed walls of the public buildings. "Glory to work!" was a ubiquitous slogan.

The road to Kiev led through the town of Kruty. The battle at Kruty had been one of Alec's questions on his Ukrainian Saturday school *matura* exam. He strained to see any evidence—a monument, a historical marker, a graveyard—of the massacre that occurred here on January 29, 1918. The Central Rada had declared independence on January 22 but did not have a standing army. A Ukrainian People's Republic Unit of four hundred students was sent to the front to resist the advancing Bolshevik force of about four thousand men. Half the students lost their lives in the futile battle at the Kruty railroad station.

A policeman with a baton motioned the cars and trucks to slow down, as there was an accident ahead. The minibuses came to a stop behind a truck that was idling and spewing black diesel fumes. As the policeman let the truck go on, Alec saw what had happened. A lone motorcyclist had collided with a horse-drawn plow. The horse was lying on its side, panting. The motorcycle rider was not moving. Father Collins signaled to Mark and Bill to pull over to the side of the road. The Loyolans peered out the windows in morbid curiosity. They pushed each other aside, trying to get a better view. Father Collins pulled a small leather bag from the back of the minibus and put his white stole around his neck. The policeman crossed himself in the Orthodox style and let him pass. Even in the land of the godless, the seeming disbelievers were willing to hedge their bets. Father Collins said a few words over the body and made the sign of the cross. He then got back in the van and drove on without saying another word.

Dusk was creeping in as they reached the Kiev Left Bank. The caravan drove through rows and rows of *Khrushchyovkas*—the drab apartment buildings where most of the populace lived. There were lines of people waiting everywhere—at bus stops, grocery stores, and even by the street vendors who sold *kvass*—a drink fermented from black bread—from trucks that looked like small oil tankers. All drank from a common glass. As the caravan neared the bridge that would take them over the Dnipro, Alec saw the majestic expanse of this mighty river. It was as wide as the Mississippi and dotted with sandy islands. The right bank swept up sharply, revealing the green hills where fortifications once stood. The setting sun reflected off the golden domes of the Pecherska Lavra. *It feels right,* he thought. *I belong here.*

***

Their hotel was on Kreschatyk Street in the heart of the city. It was built in the same neoclassical Stalinist style as the rest of Kreschatyk. A uniformed doorman guarded the entrance. At breakfast, their Intourist guide—a short woman with a staccato voice and black, cropped hair—explained the day's excursion. They would begin their tour at the Pecherska Lavra. They would visit the historic monastery and enter its catacombs. From the Lavra, they would drive along the river to Podol. They would walk up Andriyivsky Uzviz to the Andriyivsky church. They would finish in the Sofiyska Ploscha and see the museum of St. Sophia's Cathedral and the ruins of Myhaylivsky Sobor.

As the group crammed into their minibuses, Alec was careful to avoid the lead bus with the Intourist guide. He sat shotgun in the one that Bill was driving.

Alec leaned over to Bill and whispered in his ear. "I need to ditch the tour. I need to meet some family, and they're afraid to come to the hotel."

Bill nodded. "When we make a right turn at a light, I'll stop for a moment until they pull out of view, and then you can jump out. I'll tell the other boys to not say anything. Just meet us back at the hotel by dinnertime."

The lead van flashed a right-turn signal as it came up to a stoplight. Tall stone buildings and flowering chestnut trees hid the view from around the corner. Beyond the intersection a policeman with a baton was randomly flagging down cars.

"This is the spot," said Alec.

As the lead minibus turned, Bill waited for several seconds until it was out of view. "OK, now!"

Alec jumped out. "Thanks!" he said. "See you tonight."

As Alec darted down the street, he heard the policeman blow his whistle. *Damn*, he thought, *of course he was watching. No locals would be driving Volkswagens!*

Alec ducked out of the main street into an alleyway. It smelled of urine. A woman who was hanging laundry off her porch pointed to a gated wooden fence. Alec tried the gate but it was locked. He jumped, grabbed the top of the fence, and pulled himself over just as the policeman ran into the courtyard.

The woman continued hanging her laundry.

"*Babushko, chu tut prebih khlopets?*" the policeman called up to her.

The woman shrugged. "*Nicho ne bachyla.*"

Alec wondered why the woman would lie for him. *Maybe she's had had her own run-ins with the authorities*, he thought. The policeman tried the locked gate, swore, and then went back to his traffic patrol.

Alec cut through some backyards and alleyways until he emerged on Muzeyna Street. His escape had not gone as smoothly as planned. He had memorized the address of Taras, the "good guy" that Johnny had referred to at their meeting several months ago at Gino's. After his close call with the policeman, he decided to take a circuitous route to make sure he wasn't being followed. He backtracked and descended into the fluorescent underground beneath Kreschatyk Street. Scores of workers plodded toward their government bureaus. It was easy to avoid eye contact because no one wanted to be noticed. He emerged at Bessarabsky Market and walked up the street to Shevchenko Park.

Taras' apartment building was close to Kiev State University. The university buildings were painted in revolutionary red. Alec saw students from all continents in the park in front of the university—African, Asian, South American. It was strange to hear them speaking Ukrainian. The first floor of Taras' building housed the university bookstore. Through the bookstore windows, Alec could see the monotonous tomes— *Man of Steel, Traitors on Trial, Soviet Nuclear Power.* The propaganda was mind-numbing. He wondered how Ukrainian youths could stand it. In the States, students were protesting the war and challenging the very culture of America. *Here,* he thought, *they're being fed a steady diet of bullshit.*

The vestibule of the apartment building looked like a rundown tenement. It was dark and windowless, with a single naked light bulb. There was trash in the stairwells, and paint was peeling off the walls. This space belonged to everyone and to no one. Alec walked up to Apartment 4A and knocked on the door. He heard a shuffling inside. He knocked again. After several minutes, he heard the locks open. He counted at least three, including the sliding of a tight bolt.

When the door opened, he spoke quickly in Ukrainian. "Hello, my name is Alec. I'm a friend of Johnny's from Chicago. I'm looking for Taras."

The man, dressed only in a bathrobe, studied Alec. It

was clear from the look of the apartment—at least as much as Alec could see through the opened door—that he lived alone. Newspapers and books were scattered on the floor. A sewing machine was tucked in the corner, surrounded by piles of plastic aprons.

"Johnny who?" the man asked, trying to read Alec.

"Johnny with the Ukrainian Brotherhood. He was here last year with his friend CK."

"Yes ... Johnny from America. Please come in. I am Taras."

"I hope I am not intruding."

"You are visiting Kiev as a tourist?" Taras asked as he looked past Alec into the dark hallway. After closing the door behind Alec, he bolted all of the locks. "You must excuse me, but my neighbors are inquisitive." He pulled out a chair by the lone table. "Please, sit down. You said something about the Brotherhood. I forget—who is your patron?"

Johnny had warned Alec that he might have to answer questions that only a few, select people could answer. Taras would have to be sure that Alec was a real American and not a KGB agent, trying to entrap him.

"Vasyl Symonenko," replied Alec. Vasyl Symonenko was a dissident poet who had helped ignite the national democratic movement in the 1960s. He had died at the age of twenty-eight after a brutal beating by operatives from the Ministry of Interior.

"Yes, of course. 'You can choose everything in life except your homeland.' I was just preparing breakfast. Would you like some tea? I'll be right back." Taras went into the adjacent room of the three-room apartment and returned wearing a white shirt, black pants, and sandals. He then busied himself with being a good host. He brewed some tea in a samovar, sliced some wheat bread, and opened a can of smoked mackerel. He took the pile of plastic aprons off a second chair and placed them on the floor. "I'm sorry, but I have not had a chance to buy fresh vegetables. Do have some pickled tomatoes." He nodded toward the emptied chair, indicating Alec should sit, and then asked, "Do you go to church, Alec?"

"Yes, to St. Nicholas Cathedral."

"You are Orthodox?"

"No, Ukrainian Catholic."

"Your roots are in western Ukraine?"

"My parents were born there, but I'm not sure exactly where." Alec did not want to put his relatives in danger.

"The Great Patriotic War was difficult for all."

"The war was before my time. I'm more interested in current affairs."

"In Ukraine?"

"Very much so."

"How much do you know about our life in Ukraine?"

"Johnny has told me a great deal. I've also followed the news, as little as gets out."

"I am being a rude host. Let's eat and drink, and then we can talk about the present." Taras placed some smoked fish, a pickled tomato, and a slice of wheat bread on Alec's plate. He then put equal portions on his own.

"I'm curious," Alec said. "Why do you have so many plastic aprons?"

"Oh, these," Taras said, seeming apologetic. "I make them. I work at a plastics factory, and they occasionally let us 'liberate' the remnants of the rolls. I cut them out, stitch them, and sell them. They are quite popular. It's a way to make a living. I also write when I am not working."

"What do you write about?"

"Loneliness, escape, freedom …" Taras opened a bottle of vodka the size of a Coke bottle. The screw cap was such that once it was opened, it could not be resealed. He placed two water glasses on the table and poured two fingers of vodka into each. "Let me raise a toast to you, Alec, for having the courage to come here."

They clinked glasses and downed the vodka in one gulp. Taras refilled each of their glasses. After a few mouthfuls of bread and fish, Alec raised the second toast.

"To Ukraine—may we free her from her chains."

Taras nodded in agreement and both emptied their glasses. "Words can be more powerful than bullets," Taras said. "I'd like to present you with a memento of your visit." He went into his bedroom and brought back a small book of poetry titled *Sunflower* by the Ukrainian dissident poet Ivan Drach. Taras wrote an inscription on the inside cover:

To Alec,
In remembrance of your meeting with a brother from gold-domed Kiev.
Taras, July 2, 1970

"Thank you," Alec said when he read the inscription.

Before he could say more, Taras interjected, "Have you swum in the Dnipro?"

"No, I just arrived yesterday."

"Then we must go." Taras put away the half-finished tin of fish, and after opening and re-locking the door, he led Alec down the stairs of the tenement to embark on their adventure. They entered a nearby metro and descended down an escalator for well over a hundred meters. The metro station looked like an underground palace. It was lined in white tiles and graced with crystal chandeliers. *Very different from the dark, graffiti-plastered stations in the Chicago subway*, thought Alec. *Perhaps there is some merit in socialism.*

The Hydropark metro stop opened on an island in the middle of the Dnipro River. There were already hundreds of bathers on the sandy beach. This was a place where the communist ideal of "to each according to his need" seemed to work. The bathers looked genuinely happy.

"I don't have a bathing suit," said Alec.

"No need," laughed Taras. He took off his shirt and pants and jumped into the river in his underwear. Alec stripped down to his white Fruit of the Looms and dove into the Dnipro River. The warm, dark water enveloped him as in a womb. He came up for air, feeling reborn. *This is why I was born*, he thought. The same river flowed through the same banks in the same way it had one thousand years before. St. Vladimir had christened the population of Kiev in this same river, delivering them from a culture of pagan gods and rituals, to the enlightenment of Christianity. Shevchenko overlooked this river from his grave in Kaniv. The Cossacks had used the rapids to protect their freedom on the island fortress of Khortytsia. He was now here to continue the flow.

"Every Ukrainian should swim in the Dnipro at least once," said Taras. "It is our sacred river."

"I agree. I wish my parents had the chance. They have never been east of the Zbruch River. They fled west during the war. I hope that someday, they'll have a chance to return and swim in the Dnipro, as I did."

"God willing. A small group of us believe that we will see freedom in our lifetimes." As they dried off on the banks in the heat of noon, Taras said simply, "There's someone I want you meet."

***

The *sobors*, or Orthodox cathedrals, were more than just solitary churches. They were religious complexes with buildings, orchards, and workshops that belonged to the clergy. Taras led Alec to a small workshop located in the shadow of a great sobor. He knocked twice and then three times and twice again. The door was not locked. He waited a moment and then went in as though he was no stranger. A woman was pulling a ceramic plate out of a kiln.

"Greetings!" Taras said.

"Greetings," she replied. She looked through Alec, as if he wasn't there.

"Alec is my friend," Taras explained. "We've been enjoying the afternoon, talking and swimming in the Dnipro. We were discussing Vasyl Symonenko. Alec, Mariana is a Distinguished Artist of the Soviet Union. Her ceramics are displayed in the Mariinsky Palace."

Mariana eyed him more carefully. "You are not from here," she said.

"I am a Ukrainian from America."

"You seek knowledge," she stated. Taras' peculiar knock on her door must have been some kind of code.

"I'm trying to learn as much as I can about the current situation in Ukraine," replied Alec. He knew that Taras had taken a risk. He had brought him into the inner sanctum of the Kiev cell of the Sixtiers.

Mariana led Alec to a table that was scattered with ceramic talismans in various shapes and colors. "Pick a piece," she said.

He wasn't sure if she was presenting him with a gift or testing him. Alec picked up a black talisman. It was a non-human face with a tortured smile.

Mariana sighed. "Show it to Maksym when you see him."

"We should visit Maksym?" asked Taras.

"Yes," she replied and then turned her back and went to tend her kiln.

CHAPTER 9

Alec could not believe his good fortune. He had successfully ditched his Intourist guide, had found Taras at home, and had been accepted as a confidant into the Kiev cell. Now he was going to meet Maksym, one of the heroes of the dissident movement. Boyan had told him to simply keep his ears open; Johnny had given him the connection he needed. They would both be so proud of him.

The dispensary where Maksym was recovering from an unknown ailment was located on the outskirts of the city. It was reachable by bus after about an hour's ride. A high, stucco wall surrounded the dispensary, so one could not see in from the outside. Taras and Alec hopped off the bus and walked across the street to the guard gate.

"We'll have to sign in," said Taras.

"What shall I write?"

"What is your father's name?"

"Dmytro."

"Then write Alec Dmytrovich."

The guard was an old, fat woman in a colored ba-
bushka. "Who are you here to visit?" she asked.

"Maksym Ivanovich," Taras replied.

"And the young man with you?"

"He is my cousin from Kolomiya." Taras chose Kolomiya as Alec's fictitious address because it was a part of Galicia and because Alec's Ukrainian, while fluent, had traces of a
Hutsul dialect that was only spoken in the Carpathians. The
language that Alec spoke with his parents in the diaspora was
an anachronism, frozen in a place and time before the Great
Patriotic War.

The guard seemed to know Taras. She nodded, made
them sign the register, and then let them pass.

The gates opened into an expansive park with tall oak
trees. Walking paths wove through the landscape like a ragged
web and converged at a statue of Lenin. Workers quietly tended to the landscape with shears and hack-scythes, rather than
with the loud lawnmowers and power hedgers more common
in the West. It was tranquil by design. It was a place where the
infirm could recuperate through fresh air and sunlight.

Taras led Alec to a secluded bench beneath a clump of
birches and said, "Wait for us here."

Alec ran through the list of questions in his head, but
they were all becoming blurred. Should he say who sent him?
Should he mention Boyan? Should he listen or ask questions?
He was becoming unnerved. He knew that Maksym was an im-

portant figure. He knew of his books, though he had not read them. He knew of the years that he had spent in the Gulag. He was a man who had sacrificed everything for Ukraine. Would he view Alec as a frightened schoolboy, or would he see in him the inner strength embodied in the oath of the Brotherhood?

From the bench, Alec spied Taras coming up the path, pushing a man in a wheelchair. As they came closer, he could better discern Maksym's features. He was a thin man in his forties or fifties—most likely forties, because one had to account for the effects of the Gulag. He had a full head of hair and a mustache that could be twirled. He was wearing a Ukrainian embroidered shirt. His most striking feature was his eyes. They were blue-gray in color and twinkled with the idealism of youth.

As they approached, Maksym gave Alec a broad smile, as if he'd just seen a long-lost relative. "Welcome. I apologize for these humble surroundings. I can walk, but my doctors prefer that I view the world from a wheelchair."

"I am Alec Dmytrovich. It is an honor to meet you."

"Would that Ukraine had more young patriots such as yourself," said Maksym. "I thank your parents that they have taught you about our homeland. Taras tells me that you are a member of the Ukrainian Brotherhood. Please tell me more."

"The brotherhood is a fraternity. While most of the fraternities date back to the time of Petlura, ours was founded only three years ago. We felt that we needed a band of brothers who could relate to Ukraine as she is now, rather than as she was."

"Both are necessary," replied Maksym. "The past illuminates the present. Tell me about your parents. I am very interested in their life in America."

"My father was studying to be a priest when World War II began. He fled to Germany when the Soviets invaded western Ukraine. He would have been killed if he'd stayed."

"And his family?"

"He was an orphan. He was raised by an aunt in the village of Lower Berkut."

"And your mother?"

"She was studying medicine in Lviv. Before the Communists came, she and her sister fled to Germany. She was able to finish her medical studies at Munich University."

"How old were they when they fled?"

"My father was twenty, and my mother was eighteen."

"Did your mother leave anyone behind?"

"Yes. She left her parents, her brother, and her younger sister," Alec said sadly.

"And what is their life like now, I think Taras said in ... Chicago?"

"They are doing well. We live in a neighborhood in the city where almost everyone is either Ukrainian or Polish. My mother is in the private practice of medicine. My father is a businessman and is active in the cooperative movement. We even have our own Ukrainian credit union."

Maksym looked pleased. He studied Alec with the intensity of one who knows that he will never see that person again. "Alec, let us go toward the statue of Lenin. We can continue talking on the way."

Alec took the handles of the wheelchair from Taras. He released the brake and slowly wheeled Maksym down the winding path.

"Do you hear any news in America of what is happening in Ukraine?" Maksym asked.

"Only bits and pieces. We have Ukrainian American newspapers and radio programs, but they mostly deal with events in the diaspora. We have heard, however, about your struggles and those of the other Sixties. Some of your works have been smuggled out of the country."

"It's a peculiar thing," said Maksym. "We are allowed to write but not to circulate our works. They give us only the appearance of freedom. It is like my medical condition. They tell me I can't leave without a diagnosis, and they refuse to give me a diagnosis."

This dispensary, thought Alec, *epitomizes the Soviet appearance of freedom—open yet closed; guarded but easily entered. Beautiful walking paths but the patients are in wheelchairs.*

"Still," Maksym continued, "I am an optimist. These repressive times come and go—they always do. Ukraine will be free, though it may not be in my lifetime. Democracy is already taking root in the Baltics. They will be the first of the imprisoned nations to break free. Then it will be our turn."

"I have heard that the KGB apparatus is ruthless. Children turn in their parents. People are afraid to pray," said Alec.

"That is exactly why they will fail," Maksym insisted. "My wife is a physicist. She says our captors are putting more energy into maintaining the system than the system is producing. It is not sustainable." Maksym pointed at some workers in the distance. "Tell me, what do you see?"

Alec stopped the wheelchair. He noticed that Maksym was missing three fingers on his right hand.

"Ah, you are looking at my hand. Frostbite. It's an occupational hazard in the camps. It is nothing. I can still write with my left hand."

Alec nodded, feeling guilty for focusing on something so mundane when he should be concentrating on the exchange of ideas. He surveyed the grounds. "I see many workers—probably more than this park needs—raking, pruning, and looking busier than they really are."

"What of the path beneath our feet?"

"Grass and weeds are breaking through the cracks in the pavement."

"Why don't they cut those down?"

Alec thought for a moment before answering. "Their hack-scythes would scrape the pavement and would soon be dull. The scythes are only good for the tall grass. The workers would need to pull the weeds out by hand."

"And why don't they?"

Alec shrugged. "It's probably too much work, and they don't seem to care."

"Exactly. They don't care, because it doesn't belong to them. They would rather be planting and harvesting on their own land than landscaping a workers' paradise."

Alec thought of the public hallway in Taras' apartment building, with its naked light bulb and heavily bolted doors. *He's right*, he thought. *No one cares about what they don't own.*

"That is what fascinates me about this place," continued Maksym. "It is a struggle between man and nature, between order and disorder. Freedom is a force of nature. It is like a river. You can dam it, but you cannot stop it. It will not stay dammed forever. It is a mistake to believe that you are greater than God. Even this dispensary, a place where the infirm should have respite from their miseries, is a perversion. They say I am ill but refuse to tell me why. They say I can leave this place when I am healthy but won't tell me when. I fear I may not see the day. Yet today, nature has found a way to bring you to me."

Maksym's wife is right about the waste of energy, thought Alec. The party was indeed putting huge effort into maintaining the status quo. Their system needed constant pruning—or more accurately, suppression, imprisonment, and execution. The highest blades of grass were cut first, yet new ones sprouted to replace them, growing in the unlikeliest of places. The labor to maintain the suppression of freedom would one day exhaust them.

The late afternoon sun dipped behind the statue of Lenin. Alec needed to get back to the hotel before supper. Maksym saw the anxiety in his face and said, "I'm afraid we don't have much time. Did Mariana give you something to show me?" Alec showed him the black talisman. Maksym's face became more serious. His bright eyes saddened. "Someday, Alec, I hope to travel to America and meet your Ukrainian Brotherhood. But for now, we most focus on the present. Stop here, by the statue of Lenin."

"Why here?" Alec asked.

Maksym grinned. "I want Lenin to judge the deeds of his comrades." He turned his wheelchair to face Alec. "Listen carefully." For the next fifteen minutes, Maksym relayed state secrets as if by telegraph—quickly, efficiently, and to the point. He listed the titles and authors of samizdat literature that was being smuggled to the West. He talked about the latest repressions—who was arrested, who was imprisoned, who was institutionalized, and who simply disappeared. The charges against the dissidents were always the same. The names and events came at Alec faster than he could assimilate them. Alec recognized the names, but he did not know the people. They were as anonymous to him as the students who'd died at the railroad station at Kruty. Still, he felt he was shouldered with a grave responsibility. They were counting on him to tell the world their stories.

"They chose to sacrifice their lives for their country," said Alec.

"Many did," replied Maksym. "For others, their country chose them." Maksym reached into his pocket and pulled out a pen and a photograph of himself as a young man. On the back of the photo, he wrote, *I hope that one day I will have the chance to meet the members of your Brotherhood.* He handed the photograph to Alec and placed his hand with the missing fingers on Alec's shoulder. *"Heroyam slava,"* Maksym said. "Glory to heroes."

***

When Alec returned to the hotel, the Intourist guide was waiting in the lobby. She did not question him about the events of the day, but she looked at him with the arrogance of a judge who has decided on the punishment before hearing the verdict. She insisted that he ride with her in the lead minibus for the duration of their stay in Kiev. "It is easy for tourists to get lost in our country," she said, "especially if they do not obey the rules."

Their itinerary the next morning included an obligatory visit to the Museum of Atheism. Father Collins warned his boys that rather than succumb to the sacrilege, they should use the opportunity to reinforce their faith. The rooms were organized chronologically, beginning with depictions of cavemen and the worship of animal spirits. The mass christening of Kievans in the Dnipro in 889 by Volodymyr the Great was rationalized as an expedient political act. Sacred relics were displayed under harsh lights to demonstrate that they were simply old bones, devoid of any spirituality.

Alec came across a seventeenth-century Bible that had been confiscated from an Orthodox church near Kharkiv. It was printed in Church Slavonic and was open to the book of Ecclesiastes. He had learned to decipher the cryptic language by reading the inscriptions in St. Nicholas Cathedral in Chicago. He might miss words and even entire passages, but he could get the gist of the meaning. Now, Alec tried to see how much he could decipher.

Vanity of vanities. All is vanity … All the rivers flow into the sea, yet the sea is not full … unto the place from where the rivers flow, there they return again …

He had difficulty deciphering several of the lines until he came to the last:

He who increases knowledge increases sorrow …

CHAPTER 10

The highway from Kiev to Lviv was lined with an unending row of poplars that obscured the fields beyond. *Why go to these lengths to hide what surely are just collective farms?* thought Alec. *Some apparatchik, years before, probably was given the task of beautifying the road, and this was his straightforward solution.* Still, Alec felt elated. He had found his reason for being in the meeting with Maksym, although there was too much to remember. He'd jotted down a few notes in acronyms that only he would understand, tore the paper into tiny pieces, and hid them in the bottom of his knapsack. Anyone ruffling through his knapsack would mistake it for rubbish.

Alec knew that his mother had passed a message to her sister to meet him in Lviv. "Don't look for her," she had said.

"She will find you." He had only seen pictures of her when she was a child, so he wasn't sure if he would recognize her. *A group like ours will be hard to miss*, he thought. *If she is anything like my mother, she will be clever enough to find me without raising suspicion.*

As they drove down the poplar-lined highway, the vegetation seemed to get greener. It was not the pale green of spring, but a verdant, almost overripe green of summer. The whirring poplars added to the illusion. Every now and then, Alec would catch a glimpse of the fields behind the trees, though never enough to form a complete picture. He closed his eyes and thought of Stefi. *I'll write her as soon as I cross the border into Romania*, he thought. *I will tell her what I did, and she will love me all the more.* He had not written to her since Stockholm. He wondered what she was doing to pass the days.

The minibuses arrived at the campsite near Lviv in the late afternoon. The camp was similar to one where he had met Myra, but it had wooden cottages with tin roofs instead of tents. The cottages were scattered throughout a thick forest. There was no lake to get one's bearings. The camp was dark from the shade of the trees, even in the late afternoon sun. Alec asked to room with Rip and Luka. While Kiev was the heart of ancient Ukraine, Alec's roots, like Rip's and Luka's, were in Galicia. Their parents had never ventured east of the Zbruch River. Galicia had been under Poland until the Second World War. In Lviv, the common language was Ukrainian, rather than Russian. The three friends would have much to experience and share.

After dinner Alec walked over to the communal bathroom to shower. The path was muddy from a recent rain and mined with puddles. He stepped on patches of grass, knowing they would provide better traction than the mud. A woman and her daughter were leaving the bathroom as he approached.

The daughter was dressed in a tight white blouse with a black skirt. She was barefoot and carried her shoes in her hand. Her breasts stuck straight out in a pointed bra. *Strange way to dress at a campsite*, thought Alec. She looked precocious; her figure was between plump and voluptuous. As they navigated past each other and sidestepped the puddles, the girl intentionally slipped so Alec could catch her. Her pointed breasts pressed against his chest. "Excuse me," she said in Ukrainian and then giggled with her mother. Alec turned his eyes away, being careful to avoid her gaze.

When he got back to the cottage, Luka stopped him at the door. "Look what I found," he said. He made Alec kneel to look under the bed. A single black wire led from the mattress into the wall. Alec realized that his brush with the girl by the bathroom was no chance encounter.

***

Alec awoke to the sound of rain pattering on the tin roof of the cottage. His shoes were still muddy from the night before. The idea of his mattress being bugged had spooked him. It was not subtle; it was utilitarian. He couldn't even joke with his friends without being recorded. He got up out of bed and gently woke up Luka, handing him his glasses that were on top of the Samsonite suitcase under the bed. Luka was blind without his glasses.

Alec motioned to Luka to step outside, and he didn't speak until they were away from the cabin. Then he said, "Last night, Father Collins said that we'll be taking the minibuses to Halych after breakfast to see the ruins. I need to hang around here in case someone shows up."

"Rip and I are also going to ditch the Halych tour. We want to see Lviv on our own. We'll just tell Father that we're sick."

"There's a bus that runs into the center of the city every hour," Alec replied. "I'll meet you and Rip at Lychakiv Cemetery at one. Wait for me at the entrance. If I'm not there by 1:30, just go on without me."

Luka nodded his assent. He knew that Alec had been up to something in Kiev, but he didn't question him. He wanted to be a good friend.

The minibuses left after breakfast, as planned. Alec moped around the camp, hoping his aunt might find him. The plump girl and her mother had tried to get his attention at breakfast, but he knew to avoid her. She was still dressed in the same tight outfit. Her hair was damp from the rain, and her pointed nipples stared at him through her wet blouse. The mother was fussing over her as if she was a prize horse.

He quickly realized that it was too dangerous for his aunt to meet him here. The camp was under surveillance, and she would have to sign in. What could she say? That she was here to meet the Americans? He decided to forgo the rendezvous and head into the city to meet his friends.

The bus stop was located at the entrance to the camp along the main road. He sat down on the solitary bench to wait, next to two ladies who seemed oblivious to his presence.

"And what do you think Raya would have done under such circumstances?" the younger woman said to her elder.

"She would have told Bohdan to pack up his things and leave," the older woman replied.

"Olya always had a temper, but she's a saint compared to Irina."

Alec brightened immediately as he recognized the code. Olya was his mother's name. Bohdan was her brother. Irina was her older sister. He slid closer to the women, saying, "Aunt Ulana? I'm Alec from America, Olya's son."

"I knew it!" replied Ulana. "See, Vera? I told you it was him!"

Alec pulled a new hundred-dollar bill from his wallet. "My mother asked me to give you this."

Ulana quickly took the bill and tucked it in her sock, making sure no one would see. "I've seen photos of your father," said Aunt Ulana. "You clearly resemble him." Alec took that to mean that he didn't resemble his mother. "Tell your mother that we are very grateful for her packages," continued Aunt Ulana. "We sell the babushkas to buy things that we need."

Alec nodded. He'd always wondered why his mother sent babushkas to a distant cousin in Lviv, as the head scarves seemed ubiquitous here. Now, he guessed they were innocuous, easily bartered, and passed the controls at the border without exacting high tariffs. They were a form of gray-market currency.

"Tell your mother we are all well. Uncle Bohdan has written a book on medicinal plants that is being used in agronomy schools. He has a large dacha and several beehives. My own husband has not been as fortunate. He developed hepatitis from a blood transfusion when they were replacing his heart valve. We expect him home from the hospital soon."

Alec relayed the details of his family's life in Chicago. He recalled birthdays, graduations, and family gatherings. Ulana and Vera listened with delight until the bus pulled up to the stop. Ulana's esprit was as refreshing as an artesian spring.

"Will you go with me into the city?" asked Alec.

"No, we need to go," Ulana replied. "We'll take the

next bus." They had come 130 kilometers from their home in hopes of finding Alec, but they did not dare spend more than an hour talking to him or ride with him into the city.

Alec kissed his aunts and wished them health and good fortune, wondering if he would ever see them again.

***

Lychakiv Cemetery was nestled on a forested hill overlooking the city. It was the one place where both Ukrainian and Polish patriots peacefully coexisted. The Polish nobility were interred in the most elaborate crypts. The graves went back centuries—most gravestones were worn and neglected and had little relevance to the present. Others, like Ivan Franko's, were adorned with daily bouquets of flowers.

When Alec got off the bus at the entrance to the cemetery, he saw that Rip and Luka were not alone. They were talking to three young men, of university age, who wore jeans and American T-shirts.

Rip saw Alec get off the bus. "Alec, over here!" he called out. "We want you to meet someone." As Alec joined the group, Rip explained, "Luka and I ran into these really cool guys by the opera."

The alpha Ukrainian student was handsome enough to be a movie star. He wore his hair slicked back, and his Ukrainian was perfect. "Hello, my name is Kolya," he said, speaking in the same dialect as Alec did, "and these are my friends, Yuri and Ivan."

All solid Ukrainian names, thought Alec.

Yuri and Ivan just seemed to hang around, letting Kolya do most of the talking. "Rip and Luka have been telling

us about your tour," said Kolya. He pronounced "Rip" without rolling the R. "It is very exciting for us to meet Ukrainians
from America who understand what we are going through.
The fucking Russians have taken over the whole country. Only
a few of us have the balls to stand up to them."

Alec stayed polite but cool. He learned that he could
trust no one. Rip and Luka, on the other hand, were enamored
with their new friends. They were seeking to make a difference
in their ancestral homeland. Meeting and helping real Ukrainians like Kolya was the way to do it.

Rip and Luka stepped away for a few minutes to converse with Yuri and Ivan. They seemed to be negotiating. Rip
motioned to Alec to come over.

"Kolya, Yuri, and Ivan are trying to get into Lviv
Polytechnical University. They don't have the cash to pay off
the admissions officer. When we were talking to them about
our trip, I told them that several of our American friends had
bought porn movies in Copenhagen. They said that if they get
their hands on even one such movie, it would be enough to get
them into the university."

"So what are you saying?" asked Alec.

"Luka and I are just going to introduce them to the
guys who have the movies. They said they would take it from
there."

"Are you out of your mind?" Alec demanded.

"No, no. We're not handling anything," replied Rip.
"We're just going to make some introductions."

Kolya saw that Alec was not buying into the plan and
quickly changed tactics. He pulled him aside as said, "Alec, I
really came here to meet you."

"Me? Why?"

"I have something for Johnny."

"Johnny? What Johnny?" Alec asked incredulously.

"Your friend Johnny from Chicago. The founder of the Brotherhood."

"Why do you think that I might know him?"

"Your friends Rip and Luka said that you know him."

"Johnny didn't mention you to me."

"It's understandable. It's not safe to speak about such acquaintances," Kolya replied.

"Let us walk over to Ivan Franko's grave where we can talk privately."

Alec was dumbstruck by Kolya's revelation. He felt ensnared by spirits who were crying out for justice. Kolya led him through the necropolis of crypts and moss-covered tombstones until they came upon the one marked "Ivan Franko." The monument depicted a stonecutter with a pickaxe battering a cliff, with the poet's name chiseled into the granite. Fresh-cut flowers were strewn across the base.

Kolya picked a flower from a nearby grave and laid it on the monument. "*Vichnaya pamyat*," Kolya said. "Eternal memory."

Alec struggled to recall the words ... "Break down this cliff! I read his poem, 'The Stonecutters,' in Ukrainian Saturday school. Franko was a nationalist and a socialist."

"The two are not incompatible," Kolya replied. "His grave is worshiped by nationalists and communists alike."

"He was definitely controversial. Writers are agents for change."

"But only if others can read their work. Our authorities do their best to suppress them."

"Terrorize them is more like it," Alec countered.

"They are heroes. We must support them."

"How?"

"By having others read their work."

Alec felt as if the dead had turned in their graves.

"When Johnny was here last summer," Kolya continued, "I introduced him to a dissident—a poetess. She is hoping that someone from the West might help her."

"You're asking me to smuggle her poems across the border? Why should I trust you?"

Kolya pointed to the sculpture of the stonecutter. "You are heroes. Johnny said that members of your Brotherhood pledge their lives to Ukraine."

"We pledge allegiance, not martyrdom. I am not a hero," Alec said.

Kolya picked up another flower from a nearby grave and handed it to Alec. "Can you at least talk to her?"

"What's her name?"

"Her name is Nadia—I must confess ... Nadia is my wife. I want to give her a ray of hope from the West." Alec had little interest in meeting Kolya's wife, but Kolya persisted. "She works nearby, just a few minutes away by trolley. She's a seamstress."

"I'll ask Rip and Luka to join us."

"No, no," Kolya insisted. "They'll be fine with Yuri and Ivan. They are discussing some business. I'll tell them we'll be back in an hour."

What if he is telling the truth? Alec thought. *These writers are heroes. How can I tell Johnny that I refused to meet her?* Alec relented. He placed the flower on Franko's grave. They descended the hill and boarded a trolley at the entrance to the cemetery. After a few stops, they were in the heart of the old city.

Lviv resonated with Alec. It was his ancestral home. His parents had gone to school here. It was much more European than Kiev. It had been a jewel in the Austro-Hungarian crown. The cobbled streets were lined with elaborate stone buildings adorned with decorative metal grates and intricately carved wooden doors with brass knockers that dated back centuries. Kolya pointed out the places of interest. "Masoch lived in this building," Kolya said. "You may have read his *Venus in Furs*. The book is banned in the Soviet Union, but I found an old translation on my father's bookshelf. She's right down here," said Kolya as he scampered down the stairs into the basement of an old stone building.

Alec stopped at the top of the stairs. *Don't go down the rabbit hole,* he warned himself. He looked behind him. The street was empty. No one would see him descend. *Am I being paranoid? Rip and Luka saw me leave with Kolya. How could Kolya return alone?*

A pretty girl, not all of sixteen, appeared in the bottom of the stairwell with a box of buttons. She bumped into Kolya, apologized, and hurried up the stairs.

"Good day," she said to Alec in Ukrainian. When he smiled, she blushed and brushed back her bangs.

"She's much too young for you," Kolya joked from the bottom of the stairs. "Please come down. Nadia is just inside."

Alec descended the stairs. *It seems safe enough,* he thought. The staccato of sewing machines sang from the open door. To his relief, the basement did indeed house a small-scale workshop. There were rows of women cutting cloth, stitching, and sorting buttons of all shapes and colors.

Kolya walked up behind one of the button-sorters and turned her face toward Alec. "Nadia, there is someone I want you to meet. This is Alec from America."

Nadia was the most beautiful woman Alec had ever seen. She looked to be in her late twenties and seemed too mature to be Kolya's wife. She had long, raven hair, dark eyebrows, and the face that one would imagine in a Ukrainian heroine. She appeared startled and flustered when she saw Alec, as if not knowing how to behave. She blushed and offered the back of her hand to Alec, as if she intended him to kiss it. The other women at the table kept their eyes on their work.

"Beautiful, isn't she?" said Kolya. "And quite a poetess. Nadia, do you have a photograph?"

Nadia fumbled in her purse and pulled out a six-by-eight-inch black-and-white photograph of herself, dressed in a seductive silk blouse that was unbuttoned on top. It was voluptuous, the type of picture that one might submit to a modeling agency. She looked nervous. Kolya looked at her sternly. Nadia brushed back her hair and handed the photo to Alec.

"Write down your address," Kolya admonished her.

Nadia took back the photo and wrote her address and phone number on the back. "Write to me," she said, handing the photo back to Alec.

"Open the button on your blouse, just as in the photo," Kolya demanded.

What the hell? Alec thought. *Is this guy pimping his own wife?*

CHAPTER 11

Alec admired Nadia's picture in the morning light. *How could someone so devastatingly beautiful work as a seamstress? In the States, she could be a movie star.* He put the photo back into the plastic flap in his knapsack. He had agreed to take her photo but nothing more. The skies were gray, and a light drizzle had begun to fall. He did not want to risk any more unexpected encounters. He had seen enough of the Soviet Union. *Three more days 'til we cross into Romania,* he thought. Rip and Luka had left after breakfast to join up with their new friends. Father Collins had scheduled an excursion to St. Yuri Cathedral for the afternoon. The girl in the tight blouse and her mother were nowhere to be seen.

The camp now seemed confining. Alec had the feeling that the guests were watching him. The chance encounters had been too contrived. He did not want to risk falling into a trap. Better to stay put and play dead. He fell asleep on his bugged bed, dreaming of Stefi. He desperately wanted to reunite with her in Munich, far away from this dreadful place. There was a chill creeping into his bones that he hadn't felt before. He took the woolen blanket, covered his head, and curled up his knees.

"Get up!"

Alec had the sensation that his heart had stopped in his sleep.

"Get up now!" A uniformed militiaman was standing over his bed. "Take your knapsack with you and follow me."

Alec rose, hoping he would wake from this nightmare. The militiaman watched as Alec picked up his knapsack. Alec remembered the torn notes inside, and his blood froze. The knapsack looked undisturbed, it was as he had left it.

The militiaman escorted him into a larger cottage that belonged to the camp administration. Father Collins was seated in a room across from two men in dark suits. One seemed affable. The other looked like he could strangle a child with his bare hands.

"You are here only to answer some questions," the more affable man said. "Place your knapsack on the table." Both men looked identical, with thick necks that were too large for their shirts. *Good twin, bad twin*, Alec thought nervously.

"Just answer their questions," Father Collins instructed Alec.

Alec pulled his shoulders back and sat erect, studying the two men. He then retorted in a strong, clear voice, "What are your names?"

"My name is Vladimir," the good twin replied.

"My name is Vladimir II," the other replied. "Please unpack your knapsack."

Alec opened the knapsack and began with the plastic fold that held his letters. They did not seem interested in those. Clearly, they had already photographed and read them. He pulled out the picture that Maksym had given him. Vladimir II took it from him and laid it on the table. He motioned to the militiaman, who was holding a flash-bulb camera. The flash lit up the room. He turned the photo over and flashed again. They confiscated the modeling photo of Kolya's wife.

"Continue," Vladimir II said.

Alec pulled out the black talisman that Mariana had given him.

"Where did you get this?" asked Vladimir.

"I bought it from a souvenir vendor on Andriyivsky Uzviz," replied Alec. He knew they were checking to see if he still had the notes. He desperately tried to think how he could avoid their taking the scraps of paper. Could he grab them and eat them? Not enough time. He couldn't get them all, and that would just demonstrate his guilt. Could he claim the papers were planted? All eyes in the room watched his every move.

The pieces of the notes were still at the bottom of the knapsack, but Alec knew they'd seen them already—he was sure they'd removed every piece and then laid it back exactly as it was before, to play this charade of discovery in front of Father Collins.

Alec steeled himself. He pulled out the first piece of torn paper. "D-47" was scribbled in black pen. Vladimir II took it from Alec, showed it to Father Collins, and then laid it on the table to be photographed. The next piece read "70-8-ms."

The ritual continued until all fourteen pieces had been photographed.

"What is the meaning of these?" asked Vladimir in a gentle voice.

"I had torn up some notes. They're meaningless."

"Why would you tear up your notes? Why did you not throw them away?"

"An oversight."

"These inscriptions—what do they mean?"

"It's my own shorthand. '70' is the year, '8' is the month, and 'ms' is for ... medical school. It's a deadline for my applications."

"And the photograph?" asked Vladimir II, pointing to the photo of Maksym.

"It was given to me by some students I met in Lviv," replied Alec smoothly.

Both Vladimirs were irritated by his answer. Vladimir II stood up and slapped Alec across the face. "You cur," he snarled.

Father Collins rose up to defend Alec but was immediately restrained by the militiaman. "You can't do this! We're Americans!" he protested.

Vladimir slowly stood up and told the militiaman to release Father Collins. "Reverend Father," he said. "Calm yourself. Everything will be illuminated."

"Pack your knapsack," ordered Vladimir II. "All except for these pieces of paper."

As Alec placed his things back in his knapsack, Vladimir carefully picked up each piece of paper and placed it in a metal box. Alec was surprised that they let him keep the photo of Maksym but not Nadia. *There must still be room for maneuvering*, he thought.

The militiaman grabbed Alec by his upper arm with such force that it might have dislocated his shoulder. Before Alec could recoil, the man pulled him outside and along the forest path into another one of the administration buildings. Father Collins followed with Alec's knapsack. The room was filled with reporters. Rip and Luka were sitting on a bench, flanked by Donny and Leslie, two of the American boys from their group, who had mindless grins plastered across their faces. Rip sat motionless. Luka looked terrified. Bill and Carl were standing by the wall, blocked by another militiaman.

The militiaman with the bruising grip opened a seat on the bench for Alec by roughly pushing the other boys aside. Donny almost fell off the bench but was quickly propped up by one of the militia. It was as if they had been lined up for a firing squad, and the executing commander did not want any of them to faint before they were shot.

Vladimir II walked into the room and saw that everything had been arranged according to plan. He opened an attaché case and walked around the room so all could leer at the contraband within. He took out several pornographic magazines and carefully pulled out the centerfolds so that the staples would not tear the naked women in their lurid poses. He gave a centerfold to each of the sitting boys and told them to open it wide.

"This is how the West corrupts our Soviet youth," Vladimir announced to the reporters.

As he handed a centerfold to Alec, Alec looked him in the eyes and said, "You know this is total bullshit." Vladimir II just smiled, knowing that Alec was cornered. "The truth is what we say it is," he said.

He stepped back and told the waiting reporters,

"Shoot away." The room lit up with the flash of a dozen bulbs.

* * *

Alec, Rip, Luca, and the two other Americans were placed under house arrest. They were confined to the camp and forbidden from having contact with anyone outside their group. Father Collins had tried to phone the American embassy in Moscow, but the circuits were busy. He would try again tomorrow. A tribunal of judges would hear the charges against them on Friday.

Fear gripped Alec in the black of the night. He could hear Luka softly sobbing into his pillow. Alec's thoughts were beginning to spin away in dangerous directions. Rip was awake but afraid to speak. They knew with certainty that whatever they said would be used against them. *Let them use the truth against us,* thought Alec.

"Rip?" Alec whispered.

"Yeah?"

"Tell me how you and Luka got arrested."

"They're listening to us."

"Don't tell them anything they don't already know," replied Alec.

"We're innocent!" said Rip. "Kolya and his friends came to the camp yesterday morning. We told them that all we would to is introduce them to Donnie and Leslie. They asked that we join them in the room to translate. When Kolya was handing over the money, these guys in uniforms burst into the room and took us into the building where they took the photographs."

"What happened to Kolya and his friends?"

"I have no idea," replied Rip. "Why the hell did they drag you into it?"

"I don't know," Alec said. But he did. He had hurt Rip and Luka enough. He did not want to drag them down with him. Alec closed his eyes, wanting to block everything out. The questions kept intruding and his thoughts spiraled downward. What would be the consequences of his political activism? What would happen to Maksym and Taras and Mariana? Arrest? Siberia? Or worse? He feared for the safety of his relatives. And what would happen to him? Just a few weeks ago he was holding Stefi in his arms. Now he might never see her again. He would break her heart as well. He would lose his youth in some barren prison camp in the Gulag. Stefi would need to go on with her life. He couldn't ask her to wait for him. He was falling into the darkness …

Alec felt someone shaking him. "Wake up," said Rip. "You're having a nightmare. You're screaming in your sleep."

Alec woke from the terrifying sensation of falling and never reaching bottom. "What was I saying?" he asked.

"You kept screaming 'I am the angel of death.'"

***

The tribunal hearing was set up outdoors in the square in front of the opera. The judges sat behind a long table covered in red cloth. There were three judges—two men and one woman. Rows of metal chairs, enough to seat a hundred people, were lined up facing the tribunal. Militia patrolled the perimeter. Only those with a pass could enter. Alec and his co-defendants were seated in the front row next to Father Collins. Father had the look of a man who realized that prayer would not be enough. The row across was reserved for the prosecutors and defense attorneys. It was difficult to tell them apart.

Alec glanced at the people who were filing into the seats behind him. Half were military or police or KGB. They were dressed in uniform, in their finest regalia, as if they were going to a parade. They wore medals upon medals, all undoubtedly heroes of the Soviet Union. Alec imagined how in the Middle Ages, crowds would gather to witness public beheadings. Now the people ruled, but the beheadings continued. Several television cameras encircled the makeshift stage. One was always focused on the Americans to record their reactions. Alec wondered whether his relatives were watching or if they too had been arrested.

The trial was conducted in Ukrainian. There were no translators, so Father Collins, Donnie, and Leslie had no idea as to what was going on.

The lead judge looked into the cameras. "The people of the Ukrainian Soviet Socialist Republic bring the following charges against Alec Korol, Justin Ripenko, Luka Dorchuk, Donald Abrams, and Leslie Schneider: smuggling contraband, selling pornography, and corruption of Soviet youth. In addition, Alec Korol is charged with bourgeois political activism."

Alec was surprised that the charges against him were so general. There was no mention of clandestine meetings or cryptic notes.

Kolya was the first witness called by the prosecution.

"Comrade Nikola Ivanovich, please tell us how the Americans approached you."

"My friends and I were at Lychakiv Cemetary paying our respects to our departed comrades. The Americans approached us and asked if we wanted to buy some Western films."

"What kind of films?"

"They said they were bootleg American films, like *Goldfinger.*"

"You agreed to purchase these films?"

"Yes."

"You did not know that they were selling pornographic films?"

"No, no. They probably wanted to lure us with the promise of American films before demanding more money for pornography."

"That's a lie!" Rip yelled out.

The lead judge banged his fist on the table. "Silence, or you will watch the proceedings from a cell."

Kolya did not look at Alec during his testimony. Instead, he played his part to perfection, seeming nervous and contrite. Kolya's two friends corroborated his story. Alec noticed that they were not detained.

Vladimir was the next to testify. "We apprehended the defendants as the money and films were being exchanged."

Alec wanted to protest that he was not at the exchange but decided to keep his mouth shut. The defense attorney did not raise an objection.

"Can you point to the individuals engaged in the exchange?"

Vladimir pointed to all five defendants. The cameras captured their facial expressions.

The prosecutor passed out an enlarged photograph of the defendants holding centerfolds in their outstretched arms. The judges gasped in front of the cameras. Father Collins looked frustrated.

The mother of the girl in the tight blouse was the next

to testify.

"You said in your statement that one of the Americans groped your daughter?"

"Yes. That one," she said, pointing at Alec.

"Please tell us what happened."

"We were returning from the showers. The path was muddy, and there was no place to pass. As we were stepping over a puddle, he pretended to slip and groped my daughter's breasts."

"How old is your daughter?"

"She is fourteen." She glared at Alec as if she had prevented a rape.

The prosecutor proceeded to present and catalog each of the pornographic films and magazines as evidence.

Alec was surprised that Nadia was not called to testify against him. They had found her picture and address in his knapsack. Perhaps she was scripted for some future role.

The tribunal dragged on for hours. Alec was becoming numb. It was like being trapped in the cold. At first there was stinging pain, then numbness, and then the calmness of death. Each judge delivered his or her hegemony to the cameras on the evils of capitalism, the corruptive influence of the West, and the purity of the Communist ideal.

The lead judge announced that they had reached a verdict. Alec forced a grim smile—they had not even deliberated between themselves. The defense had not presented an argument. The entire proceeding was scripted, from the opening charges to the final verdict. This would not be apparent to the television viewers, as hours of proceedings would be edited down to a few key sound bites.

"We find the defendants guilty," the judge said. The

guilty verdict was a foregone conclusion. All that interested Alec was the sentence. "We sentence them to immediate deportation."

Alec felt a huge wave of relief.

"What did they say?" asked Father Collins.

"They said we have to pack up and leave the Soviet Union immediately," Alec translated. "We can never return."

CHAPTER 12

The drive from Lviv to the Romanian border at Chernivtsi went straight through the heartland of Ukrainian insurgency. The small villages in the foothills of the Carpathians had given birth to countless patriots who fought against the Soviets, the Germans, the Poles, or whoever was trying to occupy their land at the time. The minibuses were ordered to follow an escort vehicle directly to the border. They were not allowed to stop, except for a single bathroom break, and the villages and towns rolled by in a blur. Alec, Rip, and Luka were sequestered in the backseat of Father Collins' minibus.

"For how long were we deported?" asked Luka.

"For life," Rip replied.

"What am I going to tell my parents?" Luka asked.

"Tell them they can't go back either, at least until the Soviet Union breaks apart," Alec replied. "Tell them you share their exile. They'll think you're a hero."

"For selling pornography?"

"No, for being important enough to bother with," Alec replied.

Their original itinerary was to have taken them through the most scenic points in the Carpathians. They were supposed to drive through Yaremche, where the Prut River rushed out of the mountains, and view the old wooden churches that were the centers of communal life in these ancient mountains. Alec was hoping to see the places where his father had grown up as a young Hutsul. The Ukrainian American community had built a resort in the Catskills in New York called Soyuzivka, to try and recapture the magic of life in the Carpathians. The kids simply called it Suzy-Q. Alec had been to Suzy-Q many times. It now seemed like heaven. The Loyola caravan was expelled through the shortest route to the border that cut through the foothills and bypassed the mountain passes. Alec wondered if he would ever have a chance to breathe that Carpathian air in his lifetime. Still, he was relieved. Each passing village brought him closer to the other side of the Iron Curtain.

Their exit point was in Bukovyna, the land of the beech trees, just a few kilometers past the city of Chernivtsi. Chernivtsi was the crossroads of several cultures: Ukrainian, Russian, Romanian, Moldovan, Armenian, and Jewish. Goods from Turkey would cross customs at Chernivtsi and find their way into the black markets and bazaars. It was warmer and sunnier in Bukovyna than in the heartland. Alec even spotted some vineyards as they neared the border. As they approached the checkpoint, his heart was racing. He recalled his rough treatment at the Russian-Finnish border. Now he was a *persona non grata*. He was a "bourgeois political activist," who had no right to remain in their Communist paradise a minute longer than the time it took to throw him out.

The border station looked similar to the one in the north. It was a solitary complex of buildings surrounded by watchtowers, barbed wire, and open fields. The minibuses were again waved down for the usual ritual of search, head count, and processing of passports. Father Collins' vehicle was in the lead, and as it came to a stop, two border patrol guards approached with guns drawn. They immediately ordered Alec to step out. He felt paralyzed in his seat. A guard grabbed him by the arm and forcibly pulled him out of the minibus.

"Come with us," the guard said. "You can walk, or we will drag you."

Alec stumbled onto the concrete. Father Collins tried to get out too but the other guard would not allow it. Alec felt like he was drowning. It was as if he had woken up out of a nightmare, only to awaken in the very same nightmare.

"Where are you taking me?" he asked. The guards did not respond. They led him into a building, through a series of doors, and up the stairs into an interrogation room. The room was different from the one in the north in that it had windows overlooking the wide-open fields.

"Hands against the wall!" the guard ordered. He searched Alec for weapons, sparing no hiding place. Then he barked, "Sit and wait." He walked over to the single door and stood at attention, as if waiting for a superior officer.

Alec looked at the mirror in the room and saw a ghost staring back. He averted his head, looking out the windows at the open fields. The glass seemed several inches thick, but he could see that the wind was gently waving the tall grasses. *Just beyond that point*, he thought, *is the Romanian border.* He wondered how many desperate souls had tried to escape through those mine fields. In the distance, he could see dogs patrolling the zone between the perimeter fences.

When the door opened, Alec's first impression was that he was saved. A man in a light brown suit calmly entered and smiled. *He's probably a representative from the embassy*, Alec thought with relief. But when the guard saluted the man and exited the room, Alec's hopes sank.

"Can I offer you some tea, Alec Dmytrovich?" the man asked.

"No," Alec replied. "And who are you?"

"You can call me Damian," he replied.

So this is the game, thought Alec. How could his inquisitor possibly know about Damian? Demons were pulling him beneath the weeds. He needed to suppress his panic. The trial in Lviv had been a show trial for the cameras. This would be his real trial, except that there would be no jury.

"Do you prefer to speak in English or Ukrainian?" Damian asked in perfect English.

"We are in Ukraine. Let's speak Ukrainian," Alec replied. His motive was not nationalistic. If they spoke in Ukrainian, he could at least claim that he did not understand certain words and that his true meaning had been lost in translation.

"Yes, of course," Damian replied in Ukrainian, as if appreciating the wisdom of his opponent's move.

Alec examined his interrogator more closely. He was in his early forties with thin, sandy hair. He was wearing a tailored suit with matching shirt and tie and what looked like Italian shoes. He had a gold wristwatch. His face was boyish,

and he had a mild-mannered demeanor—totally unlike the
Vladimirs that had interrogated him in the camp near Lviv. His
wire-framed glasses made him look intellectual, except that
his eyes were lusterless, almost dead. *He has …* Alec searched
for the word. *Refinement. And he likes to play mind games.* Alec
thought of the executioner in Nabokov's *Invitation to a Behead-
ing.* There was no way to beat him. The most he could hope for
was a draw.

"I see, Alec, that you are admiring my watch. It's a gift
from an adversary." Alec wondered whether the giver was alive
or dead. "Alec, you remain a mystery to me."

"Why?"

"I can understand your misguided motivation. But I
need to know who sent you."

"What will become of me?" Alec asked, as if he was
asking for directions to the bathroom.

"That all depends on the outcome of our conversation," Damian replied.

"I am only twenty," pleaded Alec.

"Twenty is old enough to take responsibility for your
actions."

Alec tried to dispel fear through reason. He did not
know exactly what Damian knew, though clearly, he knew a
great deal. Alec had signed the register at the dispensary. He
had seen Maksym's photograph with the inscription to the
Brotherhood. But did he know about Johnny and CK and Boyan? If Damian caught him in a lie, the game was over. Alec decided upon a desperate strategy, like a child playing chess, he
would mimic his opponent's moves. He would try to divulge
only what his interrogator already knew.

"Who sent you?" Damian repeated politely.

Alec took a chance. "I am a member of a brotherhood."

"Very good, Alec. We are well aware of your Brotherhood." He opened an attaché case and pulled out a photo. "These boys, Alec ... can you name them?"

Alec looked at the photo. Johnny, CK, and he were planting a Ukrainian flag on a snowy peak in the Rockies. *They already know everyone in the picture*, Alec deduced. *But where did they get the photo?* He tried to recollect who else was on the trip, but his mind went blank. He blocked the panic. "This is Johnny, me, and CK." *Strange*, he thought, *that Damian did not ask for our family names ... unless he already knows them.*

"You are Ukrainian nationalists," Damian said matter-of-factly. "I too am a patriot of Ukraine."

Alec knew they were being recorded. "I can't breathe in here," Alec said. "Can we continue our conversation in a different place?"

"Excellent idea," Damian agreed easily. "Perhaps we should go for a walk. You must stay very close to me, or our guards may shoot you. Do you understand?"

"Where is my group?"

"They have been detained indefinitely," he replied, as if annoyed that Alec was asking something so inconsequential.

Damian made a gesture at the mirror and within a few seconds, the door opened. Damian led Alec down a flight of stairs and then through a long corridor, decorated with photos of Lenin, Khrushchev, and Brezhnev. At the end of the corridor was a double-door that opened into a field beyond. Alec suspected that few detainees ever made it back from that field. Outside, a walkway led to a guard tower several hundred meters away. The sun was low in the west. It would be dark in another hour. His senses heightened, Alec could hear the crickets

chirping as if they had crawled into his ear. He could smell his
sweat and see each shimmer of sunlight reflect off the wavy sea
of grass. He wondered if all condemned prisoners felt the same
sharpening of senses before taking their final breath.

Damian walked with his hands behind him, as if he
was trying to solve a perplexing puzzle. "Tell me, Alec, who
were you supposed to meet in Munich?" The *supposed to* sent a
chill down Alec's spine.

"A relative of my mother's. She told me to stay with
him until the rest of the group arrives."

"Have you ever met this man before?"

"No."

"Would you recognize him if you saw him?"

"No, and he wouldn't recognize me. That's why my
mother gave me the letter."

"And Johnny sent you to see Taras?"

Alec was trying to solve the same puzzle, only backwards. *They know about us in Chicago.* Johnny and CK were am-
ateurs. But did they know about Boyan? He decided he could
not mention Boyan under any circumstances. They might er-
roneously conclude that Alec, too, was a professional. "Yes,"
replied Alec. "I received Taras' address from Johnny."

"Did you contact Taras beforehand?"

"No."

"So how were you sure that you would find him at
home?"

"I wasn't sure. I took a chance."

"And Taras took you to meet Mariana?"

Surely they know, thought Alec. They'd either been
under surveillance from the beginning or someone had already confessed. "Yes."

"It was she who gave you the black talisman?"

He wondered if Mariana had a premonition when he picked out the black talisman. "Yes," he replied.

"We know that you met Maksym at the dispensary. Tell me what you talked about."

"He asked about life in America. I asked about life in Ukraine."

"We have deciphered your notes," said Damian calmly. Alec wondered whether their whole conversation by Lenin's statue had been recorded. "The people you discussed are enemies of the state. That makes you, Alec, an enemy of the state."

Alec let the verdict sink in. He scanned the long rows of barbed-wire fences that led to the guard tower in the distance. The blue sky had turned red, casting a reddish hue over the golden fields. The joker's line in Dylan's "All Along the Watchtower" popped into his head: "Let us not talk falsely now, the hour is getting late."

"What … what about Father Collins?" The severity of the situation was becoming clear, and Alec knew that Father Collins would be his last chance to communicate with the outside world.

"He knows you have been detained for questioning."

"What will happen to me now?" he asked quietly, hoping his voice didn't betray his fear. He imagined that they would send him back to Lviv or Kiev to face charges of espionage. The outcome of the trial would be decided in advance. He would be imprisoned for months, awaiting trial, and then most likely would be sentenced to years of hard labor in the Gulag. He pictured himself emerging a broken man. His parents would be dead. Stefi would have found a new lover. *My life is over*, he thought.

"There is still a way out of your predicament," offered Damian. "You have been honest with me. You asked to walk to avoid being recorded. I must now ask you to put down our discussion in writing."

Is this another trap? Alec wondered. Still, he had already been declared an enemy of the state. He had nothing left to lose. "What would I have to write?"

"A simple transcript of our conversation."

"Shall I write in Ukrainian?"

"Yes." They retraced their steps to the interrogation room.

"My written Ukrainian is not as good as my spoken Ukrainian," Alec lied. "I will need your help with the grammar." *Maybe I can find out how much he knows*, Alec thought, *if he dictates to me.* "How shall I begin?"

"Begin with 'My name is Alec Dmytrovich. I arrived in the Soviet Union from Finland with a school tour on June 11 ...'" Damian relayed the events in plain, simple Ukrainian, but he omitted the swim in the Dnipro. *They must not have interrogated Taras*, Alec thought, *or it isn't important.* When Damian dictated Maksym's full name, Alec only wrote "Maksym," omitting the patronymic and surname. When Damian got to the details of Alec's shredded notes, it was clear that most had not been deciphered. They seemed more interested in the general fact that Alec had met with Maksym than in the details of their conversation. Or perhaps the details were already recorded and did not need to be reiterated. Alec wrote the confession on white lined paper with a blue ballpoint pen. At the end of the narrative, Damian simply said, "Sign here." Then he scrutinized Alec's signature to make sure it was not intentionally distorted. He pulled a rubber stamp out of his case and authorized the confession with the stamp, date, and his initials.

He put the document in his attaché case and turned to look at Alec. "I know that you think you are a patriot. But consider the fact that you are a pawn. You risk your life for ideas that died long ago. I am the true patriot. I am sworn to serve and protect our Ukrainian Soviet Socialist Republic. We both love this land, but you view her from the past, and I view her from the present." He opened his briefcase and returned Nadia's modeling photo to Alec. "At some point in the future, Alec, I may need to call on you again."

Damian opened the door and led Alec down the stairs to the first floor. When he opened the door at the bottom of the stairs, Father Collins was there, pacing. He was wearing his cassock and collar and looked like he had aged ten years.

"You may proceed," Damian said. "Alec's papers are in order."

Father Collins took Alec by the hand and led him back to the van. "You look like hell. What did they do to you?"

Alec felt like a dissected cadaver. "They wanted information," he tried to say, but his lungs were dry.

"Never mind about it now," Father Collins reassured him. "We're getting the hell out of here."

CHAPTER 13

It was pitch black when the minibuses crossed the Romanian border. Romanian immigration and customs was quick and perfunctory. The boys were mostly silent and gave Alec his space. Father Collins had not said a word since they'd left the Soviet border patrol station. After they had driven past the buffer zone beyond the Romanian border, Alec asked Father Collins to stop the minibuses.

"I need to pee," Alec said.

"Just don't wander off," Father Collins replied. "Rip, go with him."

The only visible light came from their headlights. Alec stepped out of the light, knelt down, and kissed the ground. He wanted to cry, but he bit his lip to suppress the tears. He felt the relief of a hanged man who has the incredible fortune of having the rope break before it snaps his neck. He needed to escape all that happened. He needed redemption, but he did not know for what or from whom.

"Hurry up," Rip said. "They're going to come looking for us."

Alec and Rip peed into the darkness. Before heading back to the minibus, Rip turned to Alec and hugged him. "I'm sorry for getting you into this."

"I'm the one who's sorry," Alec replied. "Someday, I'll have to tell you the truth about what happened back there."

Alec could hear the boys murmuring as he climbed back into the minibus. He tried to tune out what they were saying. What could he tell them? He couldn't even confide in Rip or Luka. Damian's ominous words about contacting him in the future put them all in danger. He had become a threat to the people around him.

The unexpected events of the past several days had thrown the Loyola tour off schedule. They had missed several scheduled stops and now needed to head for a place where they could rest and get back on track. They set out for Constanta on the coast of the Black Sea. Their route would take them south through the foothills of the Oriental Carpathians and down the Siret River valley before turning east to the sea.

It proved impossible to navigate the winding roads in the dark. After a few dozen kilometers, they pulled off the road into a secluded field on the bank of the river. It was an unscheduled stop, and Father Collins instructed the boys to stay in their vehicles except when they needed to relieve themselves. They left the windows closed to keep out the mosquitoes.

Alec wasn't sure if he had slept or not. When the black

sky turned gray, he quietly opened the door and escaped the stale air and tangled mass of bodies. The outside air was fresh, and the grass was wet beneath his feet. The landscape was still untouched by the dawn. He saw the black outline of the river and looming hills in the distance. Even the mosquitoes were silent.

This is what limbo must be like, he thought. *A place caught between twilight and dawn.* His stomach burned. The river flowed out of the darkness, back into the darkness. He gazed into the Stygian River and saw faces staring back: Johnny, Stefi, Damian ... they were daring him to cross. So what if the current carried him away? He had bargained for his own life with the lives of others. He had failed them all.

He wondered what it would be like to be lost in the flow. Would death free him, or would it be the last cowardly act of his life? Would he find peace or torment or nothing? The image of Damian being pulled underwater by Rusalky haunted him. He was entangled in his roots and needed to break free. He knew that Stefi would never abandon their heritage. She meant so much to him, but now she too was pulling him into the deep.

Alec felt a hand on his shoulder. "Damian?"

"No, it's me—Bill. What are you doing out here?"

"I must have been sleepwalking."

The break of dawn illuminated the mist rising from the river.

"Anyone else out here with you?" Bill asked.

"Only ghosts."

***

Alec was surprised to see that the Black Sea in Constanta was really blue. In Shevchenko's poetry, the sea always seemed to be turbulent and forbidding. Here, it was calm and inviting. Alec wondered if the poet had ever seen the Black Sea. Waves from the east gently lapped the western shore. Sea gulls guarded the water's edge like sentries. They would chase each receding wave in hopes of snatching a fresh shell and then quickly retreat to avoid the next wave. They were oblivious to Alec and the only two other humans on the beach at this early hour, a mother and a child in a baby carriage.

Alec had awoken at daybreak to be the first in line at the Constanta post office. The youth hostel was only three blocks from the sea. The young woman at the desk had drawn him a map: go three blocks east until you hit the beach, one block south along Unirii Street, and then look for the post office next to the shop with the leather bags. Alec had crossed Unirii Street and gone onto the beach to wait until the post office opened. He needed to contact Johnny urgently. He was afraid to telephone, because they might be listening. He was afraid to send a letter, because it would never get there. *Buffalo Springfield are right*, he thought. *"Paranoia strikes deep."* He decided his best choice was a telegram. He composed it on a napkin at breakfast. It read: "Arrested. Deported. Will call when safe. A."

The post office door opened exactly at nine. Alec followed the clerk back to the counter.

"Telegram," he said. "Western Union?" He tried Russian. *"Telegrama?"*

"Da, da," the clerk replied. *"Telegrama. Mesaj? La care?"*

Alec handed the napkin to the clerk and pointed to Johnny's address.

The clerk counted the letters, and Alec handed him the money. The clerk placed the note behind the counter. Alec pointed to the note. "Please send it now," he said in broken Russian. "It's very important."

"*In aceasta dimineata,*" the clerk replied. "*Oamenii sunt in aseptare.*"

Alec had no idea what the clerk was saying. He turned around and saw the woman with the baby carriage. "*Da, da,*" Alec said and turned to walk out. As he passed the woman with the carriage, he saw that the carriage was empty.

"Where's your baby?" he blurted out in English. The woman bent over the carriage, as if to protect a baby that wasn't there. Alec looked around the post office. The baby was nowhere to be seen. *Don't panic,* he thought. *Try to act ordinary. If you run, they'll chase you.* "Sorry," he said in English. "My mistake. I thought you were someone else."

He hurried out of the post office into the sunlight. The door to a luggage shop next door was open, and he ducked into the shadows. Most of the leather in the store appeared to have come from Turkey. The store also sold flags and national emblems. Alec saw a gray cloth shoulder bag; he needed something that he could carry with him at all times.

"Can I see that?" he asked the shopkeeper in English.

"Canadian?" the shopkeeper replied, also in English. She was about Alec's age, with dark eyes, and wore a sheer, black cover-up over a bathing suit. Constanta was a resort town, and the merchants needed to know a few phrases in multiple languages.

"Yes," he replied.

The shopkeeper handed him the bag. She then looked through her assortment of emblems and proudly handed him a cloth maple leaf to sew on the bag.

"Do you have anything more international?" Alec asked.

"I have United Nations." She showed him a small blue-and-white United Nations emblem.

"I'll take the shoulder bag and the United Nations emblem." He paid her and stepped out into the street. The lady with the baby carriage was nowhere to be seen.

***

Alec quickly walked back to the hostel. He sewed the United Nations emblem on the outside flap of his shoulder bag. He took his letters from the inside flap of his knapsack and put them into his new shoulder bag, along with his Zeiss camera. There was no film in the camera—his exposed rolls had been confiscated—but he had been careful to not take any pictures of anyone except the boys in his tour group. He pulled Nadia's photo out of his pack and tore it into a hundred pieces.

Luka walked in as Alec was tearing the photo. "Alec, what are you doing?"

"I'm leaving."

"For where?"

"I'm going to join the Ukrainian Youth group in Munich."

"But that's not for another four weeks."

"I know, but I can't stay here."

Luka did not inquire why, saying only, "You're going to miss Bucharest, Vienna, Lucerne, and Paris."

"I need to head west," Alec replied. It was not so much heading west as getting off the grid. His interrogators had gone through all of his papers, including the Loyola itinerary that detailed the date, address, and telephone number of every place they would be staying. He was out of the Soviet Union, but he was not out of their reach. He needed to disappear. Last October, an earthquake had struck the city of Banja Luka in Yugoslavia. He had heard that many young people from all over Europe were headed there during the summer to help re-build the city. It seemed as good a place as any to hide. Still, he dare not tell anyone where he was headed.

Alec found Father Collins and Mr. Curtis in the laun-dry room. Father Collins saw that Alec was packed and ready to go.

"Father, I need to leave. I am being followed."

Mr. Curtis glowered at Alec as if he was an escaped convict. *He might be a teacher and a Scout,* thought Alec, *but he is not an enlightened man. He can't see the world as it really is.* Father Collins was different; he had listened to enough confes-sions to know not to judge.

"Your parents said you will be joining another tour?" Father asked.

"Yes, I'm meeting them in Munich."

"It's not for another four weeks."

"I have an uncle in Munich. I don't feel safe here. I'll wait for them there."

"Did you let your parents know?"

"Yes," he lied. "I sent them a telegram this morning."

"You'll need your passport and some money," Father replied. "I can't refund most of your expenses, but I can spare about two hundred dollars."

"That's fine," said Alec. "Just give me what you can."

Alec followed Father Collins to the hostel safe. He

handed Alec his passport and money.

"I'll send Brother Bill to see you off, at least part of the way."

"That would be great," Alec replied. He'd feel safer with Bill.

"Let your parents know when you are safe."

"I'll let them know soon." He wasn't sure, though, when he would be safe. "I appreciate everything you've done for me. I mean that. I followed you all around the world. I hope we can do another trip sometime soon."

"Business or pleasure?" Father Collins asked. He then blessed Alec and hugged him good-bye.

CHAPTER 14

Bill proved to be an experienced traveler. "They'll be monitoring the buses and trains," he told Alec. "We'll need to hitchhike out of Constanta." Hitchhiking in Eastern Europe was not difficult; it was a common mode of travel. The drivers expected to be paid fairly for their kindness.

The road west out of Constanta was replete with outgoing traffic. Bill and Alec had to compete with a flotsam of fellow hitchhikers. There were young adventurers, mothers with babies, and men with chickens. Bill pushed his way to the head of the crowd and put a US ten-dollar-bill in his outstretched hand. Their fellow hitchhikers knew they could not compete at those prices and were eager to expedite their departure. When a police car would drive by, all, including Bill and Alec, pretended to be waiting for one of the many buses that stopped fifty meters down the road.

When the first trucker stopped, Alec pretended to negotiate a price and then refused the ride. He did not want to take any chances. The next trucker who stopped a few minutes later was hauling crates of tomatoes to Bucharest. For twenty dollars he would take them both, but they would have to ride in back with the crates. Alec and Bill hopped in the back.

"You can drop me off in Bucharest," Alec told Bill, "and I'll go on from there. I'll take a train out of the country."

"I'm sure you'll be fine," said Bill.

"How can you be so sure?"

"You have the soul of a sailor."

"How do you know?"

"You love the thrill of the voyage," Bill said. "I know; I was like you once."

"Why ..." Alec stopped his question in midstream because he already knew the answer.

"Life has a way of wearing you down. You can give in, or you can get up and start over. That's why I joined the Jesuits. And now that's why I want to join the Peace Corps. I'm too young to follow just one path."

"Yeah, you never know where these journeys will take you," Alec agreed. "Hmm ... the soul of a sailor. You might be right about that."

The distance to Bucharest was only about 170 kilometers, but the drive lasted well over five hours. There were traffic jams while waiting for trains and goats and overheated cars. The road was bumpy and noisy. The stench of diesel fumes was constant. Still, Alec was relieved. He was finally off the grid.

***

Alec bought a ticket for Belgrade at the Gara de Nord station. The train was scheduled to leave from platform three at 2030. He still had two hours to kill.

"Let's get some dinner," suggested Bill. "I'm starving." They stored their bags in a locker and walked toward the city center. "This place reminds me a little bit of Paris," Bill said.

"Maybe Vichy Paris," Alec replied. The nineteenth-century architecture was defaced with propaganda posters.

"It's my treat," Bill offered. "I don't know if we'll ever be here again. Let's splurge and find something really special."

They chanced upon a grand hotel that looked like it had survived the Communist takeover with its civility intact. The concierge assured them that their dining room was renowned among foreigners. He called upstairs to make sure they would get a table by the window. Bill gave him a dollar bill for his effort.

The dining room recalled the grandeur of a bygone era. Crystal chandeliers illuminated idyllic hunting scenes on the gilded ceiling. The velvet drapes on the large windows were neatly pulled back and tied with gold cord to display the lights of the city. Heirloom china and silverware were perfectly arranged on the white linen tablecloths. The waiters were dressed in white tuxedos. A string quartet was playing Strauss.

"We can't afford this place," said Alec.

"Don't worry," Bill replied. "We might not have a meal like this again for a while."

The maître d' met the Americans at the door and seated them at a table for two near a large window. There were only five other diners in the spacious room: an elderly American lady who appeared to be dining alone, two men who were raising toasts and smoking, and a young couple who could have been celebrating their first anniversary. It was still early for dinner. The American lady introduced herself as Ms. Agnes when they were seated at the adjoining table. She was wearing a white evening gown and a beaded white hat. Apparently, the maître d' had let her know that two Americans would be dining with them this evening. She was too polite to ask them to join her but was seated close enough to overhear their conversation.

The waiter brought them two leather-bound menus and an expansive wine list. Fortunately, the menu was written in both Romanian and English. Alec's menu did not have any prices.

"We'll have the same white wine as Ms. Agnes," Bill ordered, "and please offer her a glass from our bottle.

"It's called the White Maiden," Ms. Agnes chimed in. "Very fragrant but a little sweet."

"We'll have the prix fixe menu with the veal goulash," Bill said, pointing at the Today's Special card that had been inserted into the menu. "Alec, is that OK with you?"

Alec nodded his agreement.

The waiter brought out the appetizer: Russian caviar served with blini and crème fraiche. The caviar was served in a glass cup atop a silver bowl filled with crushed ice. The waiter gave each of them a spoon that looked like it was made of mother-of-pearl. The waiter poured them each 50 grams of Russian vodka, even though they had not ordered it. Apparently, it came with the caviar. He poured Ms. Agnes a glass of the White Maiden and put the bottle on ice between them.

Bill raised his shot glass and proposed a toast. "To America, the land of the free," he said, loud enough so that the others in the room would hear. The two men who were smoking raised their glasses in solidarity. Bill clinked glasses with Alec and reached across to clink glasses with Ms. Agnes. She was delighted with the attention.

"I am waiting for my niece," Ms. Agnes volunteered. "She is teaching English here in Bucharest. She married a man from here. I'm afraid she's running a bit late."

Alec wasn't sure if there really was a niece, but he felt sorry for Ms. Agnes. *Old age is a terrible time to be alone,* he thought. *At least when you're young, you can still make a family and gain new friends. What do you do when your family and friends are gone?*

"Will you take the train back to Constanta?" asked Alec.

"No, I'll wait for them here," Bill replied.

"I guess I'll see you back in Chicago."

"Perhaps," Bill replied. "I may take some time off before I complete my vows."

"Where will you go?"

"I have some friends in Panama. I might go work there for a while."

"Will you sell your motorcycle?"

"My bike is still in the south of France. If you want it, it's yours," offered Bill. The waiter brought them two steaming bowls of wild mushroom soup.

"I might consider it. Thanks."

Bill pulled a small rumpled notepad out of his pocket. He wrote a note, tore out the sheet, and gave it to Alec. "My bike is still in Emilie's parents' garage in St. Cyprien. They're holding it for me. I won't be going back for it. Just show them this note and tell them I said you could have it."

The note was in French, but Alec could make out the address.

The veal goulash and buttered noodles were delicious. Alec could see that Bill was recalling something painful, and he didn't want to intrude with small talk. Ms. Agnes's niece had still not arrived, and she had taken the liberty of ordering her main course.

Alec looked at his watch. "Jesus, my train is leaving in twenty-five minutes!"

Bill snapped out of his funk. He seemed embarrassed that he had let the time slip away. "Don't worry; we'll make it!" He pulled a roll of leu out of his wallet and looked for the waiter. He was nowhere to be seen. He handed the bills to Ms. Agnes.

"We can't wait for our check, or we'll miss the train. This should cover it. Please give these to the waiter when he returns."

Ms. Agnes nodded in agreement. "God bless you boys," she said.

Alec and Bill bolted out of the dining room and down the circular stairs. As they were heading for the front door, they saw the waiter chasing down the stairs after them.

"We don't have time to explain," Bill said. "Just run as fast as you can."

The waiter was young and fast, but he gave up the chase after a block. They ran into the train station with seven minutes to spare. They grabbed their things from the locker. The conductor was waving the last few passengers onto the train.

"Let me know what you decide to do," Alec said. "Maybe I'll visit you in Panama next summer. You've been my guardian angel."

Alec hopped on the train as it started to pull away. He ducked into the nearest compartment and looked out the window. Bill was still standing on the platform. Alec knocked on the window and waved, but the train kept pulling farther away. *Bill was a good friend*, he thought. *He didn't judge me.* Bill had simply found a way to connect with Alec and guide him. *Someday, when someone needs a friend*, Alec thought, *I'll remember to repay the kindness.*

***

Alec shared the compartment with a young Canadian architect who was touring Eastern Europe for the summer before starting a new job in Montreal. He had heard great things about the Dalmatian coast and invited Alec to tag along. It sounded like great fun, but Alec knew that he could not afford to trust anyone.

Alec slept most of the way except for the brief stop at the border. Romania didn't seem to mind his leaving, and Yugoslavia was welcoming to foreigners. The train rolled into the Belgrade station in the early morning. Alec hopped off the train and rushed out of the station into the morning crowd. The bus station was just down Zeleznicka Street, but he wanted to make sure he wasn't being followed. He zigzagged through several side streets before backtracking to the bus station.

Alec checked the board and saw that a bus was scheduled to depart for Banja Luka at noon. He bought a ticket and waited. He slung on his shoulder bag, put on his knapsack, and sat down on the floor with his back to the wall. If he were to doze off, they couldn't steal his things without waking him.

The bus to Banja Luka departed on schedule. The only empty seat was in the back of the bus next to a young man wearing a black-and-white kaffiyeh. He was staring out the window and did not look at Alec when he sat down. The bus drove out of Belgrade into an approaching weather front—a thunderstorm from the south. Black clouds billowed over the hilltops and rolled into the valleys. Lighting illuminated the silhouettes of distant tree lines, seconds ahead of the thunder. The patter of rain accelerated into a downpour making it impossible to see the road. The driver pulled off the road to wait out the storm.

The man with the kaffiyeh pulled a leather-bound journal out of his briefcase and began to write from right to left. After he had written his entry, he replaced the journal and looked at Alec. "Why do you wear the UN insignia?" he asked.

Alec was taken aback. "You speak English?"

"I studied economics in London."

Alec raised his guard. Could they have followed him here? He had crossed two borders in the past three days. This was most likely a chance encounter, he reasoned. It would not be the first. On his trip with Walrus, he'd met a Muslim prince on a beach in Malaysia. The youth spoke English and claimed to be a son of the king. Alec had no reason to doubt him. They had discussed America's ignorance of the Muslim world.

Alec now replied. "It seemed most appropriate."

"But you are an American?"

"Yes, but my parents are from Ukraine. I did not learn to speak English until the first grade."

"Where is your allegiance?"

Where is my allegiance? Alec thought. At his Ukrainian Youth summer camps there were always two flag posts: one for the American flag and the other for the blue-and-yellow flag of independent Ukraine. He pledged allegiance to the United States on weekdays and to Ukraine on weekends. If the United States competed with the Soviets in team sports, he would root for the States. If an individual Ukrainian athlete competed, he would root for the Ukrainian.

"I am American, but I seek freedom for Ukraine."

"The United Nations recognizes the Ukrainian SSR as a nation."

"There are no independent nations in the Soviet Union. There are only captive nations. And what about your country?" asked Alec.

"I am Palestinian."

Alec had visited Palestine two years ago, on Father Collins's world tour. He had even stayed in a kibbutz in occupied Bethlehem. He was vaguely familiar with the Arab-Israeli conflict but felt ashamed that his understanding was so superficial. In his study of all things Ukrainian, he had lost sight of the rest of world.

"I have been to Palestine," Alec replied, "two years ago, when I took a trip around the world with my school."

"You are a Jew?"

"No, I am Ukrainian Catholic. We visited the Holy Land and stopped in Jerusalem, Bethlehem, and Nazareth." *Ironic*, he thought, *to be mistaken for a Jew.* It was not the first time. In Jerusalem, a rabbi had taken him by the arm and led him up to the Wailing Wall. That same day, the Israeli police had mistaken him for a Palestinian and asked him to produce papers. Several of Alec's Ukrainian friends were anti-Semitic without realizing that some of their close friends were Jews. Alec was not among them. His father's business partner, Ami, was an American Jew. His wife was born in Israel to an Irgun hero who had a street named after him in Tel Aviv. Alec's father and Ami were good friends. When Ami would come over the house, he would always bring Alec a toy. Once, he gave him a red electric car with a wireless remote that made him the envy of the neighborhood. Ami was a kind man. There was enough hatred in the world; Alec did not want to contribute more.

"My country, like yours, is captive," the Palestinian said, looking for a common chord. "You are CIA?"

Christ! thought Alec. *He is as suspicious of me as I am of him.* But some shadowy arm of US intelligence had sent him to Ukraine on an intelligence-gathering mission, so in a way, he was CIA, after a fashion. Was he a patriot or a pawn? And of which country? The UN insignia did indeed seem most appropriate. "I am a student. I work for no one."

"What is your destination?" the Palestinian asked.

"I am going to Banja Luka. There was an earthquake there several months ago. I hear they're asking for volunteers to help with the reconstruction."

The Palestinian seemed satisfied with the answer. "I am going to Sarajevo," he offered, "to recruit for our cause. How do you feel about what your government is doing?"

"We are against the war in Vietnam. We march in the streets."

"How do you feel about what America is doing in Palestine?"

"I'm afraid I don't follow events in the Middle East very much," Alec replied. He felt ashamed of his ignorance. The Muslim prince in Georgetown had been right. Americans knew little about the Muslim world.

The Palestinian went back to writing in his journal. There was no more to discuss. The rain abated enough to drive on, though the sky was still menacing.

***

The bus from Belgrade had arrived late at night, so Alec slept on a bench at the bus station. It was quiet enough, and no one tried to rob him or chase him away. At dawn, the station began to bustle with people, and he went to the bathroom to clean up. He hadn't washed or shaved for the past several hundred kilometers. He stuck his head under the faucet and washed his hair with the counter soap. The cold water woke him up.

Outside, the sky was blue, and the morning sun warmed the white buildings. A café across the street was serving breakfast. He had changed some dollars to dinars in Belgrade, and so he ordered a Turkish coffee and roll with butter and jam. He had difficulty communicating with the waiter. While Ukrainian and Serbian shared the same Slavic base, the languages were more different than similar. The waiter acted busier than he really was, and Alec was getting frustrated.

A woman at an adjoining table overheard his questions to the waiter.

"You are looking for a Ukrainian church?" she asked in a mix of Ukrainian and Serbian. "There are several in the area. Which one are you looking for?"

Alec had heard that there were villages around Banja Luka that were completely inhabited by Ukrainians. During the time of the Austro-Hungarian Empire, thousands of Ukrainians had emigrated from Galicia to Bosnia. "Any church," he replied. "I am a Ukrainian American from Chicago. I'm looking to help with the reconstruction. I thought a church might be the best place to start."

She thought for a moment. "The nearest church would be St. Sava's on top of the hill. You can take a bus, or it is about a five-kilometer walk." She pulled a piece of paper out of her purse and drew him a map. Alec thanked her and paid his bill without tipping the waiter. He decided to walk.

The destruction from the earthquake was apparent but random. Some buildings were completely intact, while those adjacent were reduced to rubble. The work of reconstruction was proceeding mainly by hand and donkey. There were few bulldozers or cranes. The road from the station to the church soon led from the old urban center to more residential areas, with fenced-in homes, vegetable gardens, and plum orchards. The asphalt road devolved to a dirt road that was muddy from the rain the night before. The puddles were quickly evaporating in the sun.

The map the Ukrainian lady had drawn pointed to a church on top of a steep hill. Alec could see the hill but the roads were not marked. A narrow path, large enough for a donkey, veered off the main road and up the hill. The climb was tiring. The woman had said that the church was on top of a hill. *More like a small mountain*, he thought. As he climbed the path, the plum trees and willows that were common below gave way to birch trees that gave way to Serbian pines. He welcomed the alpine scent of pine. St. Sava's was on top of the hill overlooking the Vrbas River and valley below. It looked more like a chapel than a church, except for its tin, gold-painted dome and white walls. The Orthodox cross on the dome cast a shadow over the yard in the midmorning sun.

The morning services were over. A young priest with a full black beard was tending to repairs behind the carved wooden iconostas.

"Glory to Jesus Christ," Alec said in Ukrainian to get his attention.

"Glory to Jesus Christ," the priest replied. "Mass is over. Have you come for confession?"

Why not? thought Alec. He believed in God but was not a dutiful Christian. Every day of his grammar school had started with morning mass. He had listened to well over a thousand masses in Church Slavonic and knew most of the mass by heart. He had even considered being an altar boy, but the Basilian brother who tended to the altar boys had made Alec feel uncomfortable—he would slap boys for missing a line of the antiphons.

Alec entered the confessional and knelt down. "Forgive me, Father, for I have sinned. My last confession was several years ago."

"Tell me your sins, my son."

"I have betrayed my family and my country. I am losing faith in the things I believed in."

The young priest sensed that this was no ordinary confession. This young man had not made some girl pregnant or stolen money or beaten up a friend. His troubles ran deeper.

"Why are you here in Banja Luka?" the priest asked.

Alec looked through the grille separating their faces. "I am trying to find myself. I am looking for a way to serve God."

CHAPTER 15

The Orthodox priest introduced Alec to the commandant of a Yugoslav work camp. The camp was organized for Yugoslav youth—Serbs, Croats, Slovenians, Montenegrins, and Kosovars who came to help their fellow Bosnians rebuild Banja Luka. The priest and commandant conversed in Serbian, and Alec could not understand what they were saying. He heard the word "America" mentioned several times. Most of the youth slept in tents. The commandant led Alec to a brick building that served as the camp dispensary. He pointed to an empty cot and said something in Serbian, which Alec assumed meant, "You sleep here."

The camp nurse, a young, buxom Bosnian named Sonja, had dark, flowing hair that she tucked into a Lenin cap made of straw. She was delighted with her new "patient." The few words she knew in English were "pretty boy" and "take me to America." She brought him dinner and *slivovitz*, a type of brandy. Alec could not understand what she was saying but smiled and toasted to her health. She called over several of her female friends to look at the American. Alec felt like the latest acquisition at a zoo. His inability to communicate with them, other than through body language, was frustrating. Still, he was amused how they doted on him.

In the morning, the youths were divided into brigades and sent to assist construction workers in various part of the city. They had no technical skills and so were relegated to manual labor: digging ditches, carrying bricks, removing stones. Alec was assigned to a group of five, whose task for the day was to help install electric utility poles. The work was hard, and Alec's hands blistered. The utility workers barked orders in Serbian and had little patience for Alec. When he did not understand a command, they would simply say it louder and look at him as if he were a dunce. He would take his cue from whatever the other youths were doing and try to do the same.

Two Serbian woman prepared lunch for the work crew in a vacant single-story home. Half the roof was missing and sparrows were flying back and forth, searching for crumbs. The women prepared a spicy bean soup in a large pot that they placed in the middle of a long wooden table, along with some freshly baked country bread. There was a pecking order to the lunch line. The workers were the first to eat. They were talking and laughing and filling their soup bowls to the brim. Next came the Yugoslav youth. Alec went last. There was just enough soup left to fill half his bowl. A worker sitting across from him was noisily slurping his soup. The man reached across the table for the pepper, keeping his eyes on Alec's bowl the entire time, as if resentful that some foreigner would be getting the last drop of the soup and denying him a second portion.

Alec returned to the camp in the late afternoon, exhausted. The youths in the camp had already formed cliques. They would say a few words to him in passing, but mostly they talked about him, rather than to him. Alec sighed and went to the dispensary, pulled out a paper and pen, lay down on the bed, and began to write.

>*Dear Stefi,*
>
>*I'm sorry I haven't written for so long but I could not. I left the group in Constanta and hitchhiked to Banja Luka to help rebuild after the earthquake. I needed to get away to find myself.*
>
>*Last summer, Serge and I wrote a song called "To My Own." The first stanza goes:*
>
>>*I leave to find tomorrow*
>>*On roads with one-way signs*
>>*I long to find a place*
>>*Where I can ease my mind*
>
>*I'm now living what I wrote. I tried to be a hero, but it didn't work out as I planned. I was arrested in the Soviet Union for political activism. I can never return to Ukraine. I feel as if I've failed everyone who believed in me. A few days ago, I felt so low I was thinking what it would be like to end it all. Reading your letters is the only joy I have.*
>
>*I'm the only American in a Yugoslav youth brigade. I arrived here two days ago and was directed to their camp by a Ukrainian Orthodox priest. They gave me a bed in the dispensary and have been giving me meals in exchange for my work. The kids in the camp point at "the American." They speak to me in broken*

Russian, French, and even Spanish. If I stay here much longer, I'll speak an international language. Some of the younger girls look at my American clothes and say, "You are pretty, yes?" I think that if they leave me to myself, I'll manage well enough. New brigades arrive daily, and I'm waiting for anyone who can speak English. If no one comes, I'll most likely spend a week here working in the brigade and then maybe go to Prague or Venice. Brother Bill even offered to give me his motorcycle, which is somewhere in the south of France.

A student here offered to help me ham radio an "I love you" message to you, but then I remembered you're away at camp. The past seems almost too far away to recapture. Except for you, I'm not sure I even want to go back home. It's all so confusing. I think of so much now.

I hope we can meet in Munich the way we parted at the beach by Northwestern.

Love, Alec

PS. I'm waiting for your kiss by the Eiffel Tower.

The spicy bean soup from lunch was beginning to work its way through his system. There was no WC in the dispensary. He went outside to look for an outhouse but could find none. He went to find his only friend, Sonja, to get directions.

"Toilet? WC?" he asked.

She shook her head as if she didn't understand. Alec resorted to body language. He rubbed his hand over his stomach and pointed outside. Sonja laughed, and Alec blushed. She pulled out a flashlight and led him by the hand to a newly constructed building on the edge of the camp. It looked like a school. She pointed at the door, and then moved her fingers as if walking downstairs. Alec nodded, thinking, *Toilets in the basement. Got it.* The building was dark, so she handed Alec the flashlight.

He found the stairs and walked down to the concrete basement, wondering why the electricity wasn't hooked up when the plumbing was working. As he reached the bottom of the stairs, he covered his nose—the area reeked of shit. He shone the flashlight at the floor and saw countless individual piles of shit. The campers had turned the basement of the unfinished building into a public toilet. He found a bare corner, squatted, and made his contribution. *This is disgusting*, he thought. *Why not just dig outhouses? Why build a schoolhouse and simultaneously defile it?* Had Communism destroyed even their most basic values of decency?

When he exited the basement, Sonja saw the disgusted look on his face. She said something like "stupid Croats" and led him back to his bed in the dispensary.

***

The next morning Alec was assigned to help replace a sewer pipe on the road that led from the camp to the center of the city. Local farmers were hurrying to the market to set up their stalls. As he was walking with his pickax, he passed a second work camp on the left side of the road. A broad field adjacent to an elementary school was being excavated to lay a foundation for an addition. The youths digging the foundation looked different than the Yugoslavs. The girls were almost as pretty, but they were a mix of blondes, brunettes, and even some redheads. The boys were wearing T-shirts and cutoffs. Some were excavating the ditches with pickaxes and shovels; others were resting and talking. They seemed to enjoy what they were doing. A tent camp was set up adjacent to the excavated field.

Alec cocked his head. He could hear that they were definitely not speaking Serbian. It sounded more like German. Their supervisor, a blond man who looked to be in his late twenties, was wearing a Rolling Stones T-shirt. His assistant, about the same age, was wearing a shirt with lettering that Alec could not read. They seemed to be studying architectural plans and laying out the contours of the foundation with ropes and stakes.

Alec approached them. "Cool T-shirt," he said.

The supervisor looked up from his plans with a welcoming smile. "Ja, Rolling Stones. Altamont. You must be the American. We have heard rumors about you. Our Yugoslav coworkers tell us an American had joined their work camp. Quiet, they say, but a good worker."

"I guess that's me. And who are you? Where are you from?"

"Ah, I'm sorry. My name is Nico. I am an architect and the leader of this group. This is my friend Hans. We are Swiss. Our sponsor is Swisscare. We are building a school."

Alec looked over the Swisscare corps. Most seemed to be between the ages of eighteen and twenty-five, equally boys and girls. A few, like Nico and Hans, were a bit older. They were all Swiss and much more hip than the Yugoslav youth.

"Do others here speak English as well?"

"Yes, not all but many. Some better, some worse."

"I joined the Yugoslav camp because I didn't know that there were any international groups here," said Alec. "I'm having a difficult time communicating with them. Is there any chance that I could join your group instead?"

Nico turned to Hans and had a brief discussion in German. They seemed to be in general agreement. "We can use a good worker. The digging is going slower than we expected. Yes, you can join us if you wish. The Swisscare official will be returning to Banja Luka next weekend. She will have to make the final decision. You can work with us until she returns. Then we will see."

Alec was elated. He could escape the seclusion, drudgery, and dismal conditions at the Yugoslav camp to join a group of Western Europeans who had volunteered their summer to help build a school. His luck was changing. "I will get my things and return in the afternoon."

"Hans will find you a place in one of the tents. Welcome to Swisscare."

Alec rushed back to the dispensary to pack his things. Sonja frowned.

"I am going to join the Swisscare group down the road," he explained. "They speak English. It will be easier for me. Thank you for your kindness." He hugged her and kissed her on the cheek. "You will be the only person I will miss here, but I'll be just two kilometers down the road. Perhaps I'll see you again. Please tell the commandant that I have joined the Swiss. I think he will understand."

Alec did not know how much of his farewell speech Sonja understood, but she understood enough to know that he was leaving. She touched her cheek where he had kissed her, and she smiled. She then pulled back her shoulders and huffed out of the dispensary without saying a word.

CHAPTER 16

Life in the Swisscare camp was hard work but good. Alec slept on a straw mattress in a tent with four other boys. The girls slept in the adjacent tents. Life in the camp was communal—everyone took turns cooking and cleaning. The elementary school for which they were building the addition had running water and a shower. Each morning, the girls would shower in the cold water and run back to their tents in their towels. The towels got looser as the days went on.

As the only outsider at camp, other than the Yugoslavs they had come to help, Alec was a celebrity. He quickly learned everyone's names and that about half spoke English. When they tried speaking to him, it was usually a mix of English and German.

The morning routine was always the same—wash, breakfast, and dig—except for the days when he was assigned to kitchen duty. Swiss efficiency even trickled down to the bathrooms. The men's bathroom had three sinks and three stalls, so everyone had their place in the queue. Alec usually washed next to Alan, a wiry boy with a wispy beard. They tried to make small talk while brushing their teeth, but their conversations were usually incomprehensible.

Alec had run out of deodorant and asked Alan if he could borrow his. Alan fumbled through his wash bag, not quite sure what he was looking for. Alec pointed to his armpit and Alan's face lit up. "Ya, das ist ein anti-shtink spray!" Communication, however banal, helped strengthen the friendships. Alec's ear was becoming attuned to the cadence of their language. He could almost tell what they were saying from the flow of the words without understanding the words themselves.

Work on the foundation proceeded slowly, shovel by shovel, meter by meter. The ground was hard and would not yield easily. Each trench was about waist deep and as wide as their outstretched arms. Boys and girls alike would chip at the face with the pickax. The rubble was shoveled into wheelbarrows and discarded in a large pile near the road. Every few days, a dump truck would come by, and the dirt would be shoveled into the truck and hauled away. The entire project could have been done in several days with a backhoe and front-end loader. It would take a month and forty workers to complete by hand.

Alec could feel himself getting stronger through the hard labor. He had never worked so hard in his life. They would dig from nine until noon and again from two until six. They dug in shifts, because only three people could work a single face at the same time. There were about ten trenches, so half would dig while the other half carted away the soil. There was a well on the school property that provided clean, fresh water. They were constantly sharing canteens because the sun evaporated sweat from their bodies faster than it could be replaced. The boys worked without shirts, and the girls wore T-shirts and shorts or bikinis.

Alec couldn't help but notice when the sweat on a girl's T-shirt would accent her nipples or when her shorts would run up her cheeks. Except for a few couples, it was hard to tell who was with whom. Many of the girls in the camp were pretty, and they became prettier as the days went on—the girls went out of their way to make Alec feel comfortable. They would try to start conversations and laugh when he misunderstood their meaning. Alec hadn't been to Woodstock, but he thought this was what it must have been like to live on Yasgur's farm and set your soul free.

He found one of the Swiss girls especially attractive. Her name was Maya. She had long, kinky hair, like the girl on the cover of the Blind Faith album, except that her hair was dark brown. She had full lips, round breasts, and ample hips, and she exuded sexuality. If Stefi was the moon, then Maya was the earth. Alec was drawn to her. If he was questioning everything he believed in, then maybe Maya was the answer.

As Alec and Maya were walking into town, she took his hand and asked him in her broken English, "My hair ... do you like it?" Her hair flowed down to her waist. She stroked it from her crown to the small of her back.

"You have beautiful hair."

"It is what word in English?" she asked. "A girl who dances for men?"

Alec's first thought was an exotic dancer. "You mean a stripper?"

"What is a stripper?"

"A girl who takes off her clothes."

"No!" She hit him playfully. "A gypsy!"

***

On Friday the camp was abuzz, anticipating the arrival of the Swisscare inspector. After breakfast, Nico assigned the campers into work details to prepare for her visit. The sleeping bags needed to be shaken out and placed neatly over the mattresses. Any wet clothes were to be dried out. The bathrooms needed cleaning. All garbage was to be picked up and hauled out. In appreciation for their volunteer work, Swisscare would treat them to a Yugoslav banquet at the Palas Hotel in the evening.

Ms. Klein arrived at the camp at noon, as scheduled. She was a short, Teutonic woman in her late forties. She wore a white dress and elevated shoes, which made it difficult to navigate the work zone. At lunch she sat with Nico and Hans and did not seem to stop talking. She pointed at several of the girls in their bikini tops to indicate her disapproval. After lunch, she walked through each of the tents, shaking her head. Several of the boys and girls had already paired up in the tents, and she seemed to indicate that it was strictly forbidden. When they arrived at the trenches, she made Hans hold the plans while Nico outlined the excavations. In one section, Nico explained, they had to deviate from the plans to bypass a gas line.

From his vantage point in the trench, Alec could see that Nico was getting angry. Ms. Klein was pointing at Alec as if she had discovered a rodent in the trenches. Their hitherto polite discussion was turning heated. Nico had apparently had enough. He positioned himself so she would have to look up at him into the afternoon sun. He pulled back his shoulders, accentuating his height. Hans moved over to his side. Nico took the plans from Hans, rolled them up, and put them back into their cylindrical case. Ms. Klein would obviously have no more need to look at the plans.

Nico walked over to where Alec was working. "We have a problem," he said. "Ms. Klein is insisting that you leave. She says that their insurance does not cover you."

"I'll be responsible for myself," Alec replied. "I have my own health insurance from school."

"She is also insisting that the boys and girls sleep in separate tents and that we all wear shirts when we are working. I explained that some of the campers were living together long before coming here and that we are forced to work shirtless because of the heat."

"You can pretend to agree and go back to our usual ways once she leaves," Alec suggested.

"Yes, but she wants us to also excavate the foundation along the original plans. That would mean relocating the gas line. We don't have the time or expertise to do it. I told her it's a simple matter of making one of the classrooms a half meter smaller, but she won't listen."

"What are you going to do?"

"I told her we are a camp of volunteers. I am the assigned leader of the camp. This evening at the banquet, we will put things up for a vote. She decided to make you the main issue. If she convinces the camp that you need to leave, then we will both leave."

"I don't want to be the reason for your leaving," Alec protested. "I can leave the camp today."

"No, you must stay. It is a matter of principle." Nico then proceeded to walk about the camp, talking to his friends and garnering support for his position.

Alec jumped back into the trench and swung his pickax with renewed purpose. From his vantage point in the trench, he could see that Ms. Klein was now working on Hans.

* * *

The tables in the banquet room in the Palas Hotel were set with white linen, china, silverware, and crystal. Chandeliers reflected in the mirrored walls like starlight. The house band donned folk costumes and played a medley of songs from the various regions of Yugoslavia. The waiters were dressed in their white tuxedos. The only incongruous elements were the guests, who were dressed in casual work clothes. The Bosnian banquet was served family style in porcelain serving dishes. The food was an exotic mix of Balkan, Turkish, and Austro-Hungarian cuisines. The antipasto platters were piled with cold meats and cheeses, pickled tomatoes, peppers, mushrooms, and eggplant. Waiters ladled hot tarhana soup with pasta from large serving bowls. The main courses included a variety of local delicacies—rolled burek, bosanski lonak, sataras, and sarma. The guests had their choice of bottled water (still or carbonated), fruit juices, and wine from Mostar. For dessert, the waiters brought out tufahije and baklava, served Bosnian coffee, and poured glasses of slivovitz. Ms. Klein had spared no expense to impress her volunteers.

The tension between Nico and Ms. Klein was palpable. They sat on opposite ends of the hall. Alec sat at the table with Nico, Hans, Maya, Bridgette, and Dominique. Ms. Klein had asked Hans to sit at her table, but he refused. Alec had not wanted to attend, but Nico insisted, even though he knew Alec wouldn't understand a word of the proceedings. He was the evidence in the case that was best presented live to the jury.

Rumors of the confrontation had spread quickly through camp, and his fate had become a cause célèbre. Alec rationalized that if Nico and Ms. Klein weren't arguing about him, they would have found something else to disagree on. It reminded him of the confrontations at Northwestern between the students and college administration. It was not so much about the actual issues as it was about confronting authority. It was about demonstrating the power of youth.

The others at the table were having a conversation in German that Alec could not follow. He could tell from their body language that they were reinforcing each other's positions.

"Why is Hans so riled," Alec asked Nico. "I don't often see him like that."

"Ms. Klein offered him my position if he defected to her side—and he refused."

Alec gave Hans a thumbs-up to show his appreciation. Hans smiled and returned the gesture. "He's a true friend," Alec said.

"Yes, he is," Nico replied. "It is a rare thing to have true friends. Never take it for granted."

During coffee, Ms. Klein abruptly stood up and demanded everyone's attention. She proceeded to make her case. Bridgette would translate a few phrases for Alec, but not fast enough for him to keep up. The key points seemed to be that Ms. Klein was the designated Swisscare official, that their liability insurance did not cover outsiders, and that Alec's presence posed a threat to their mission to help build a school for the children of Banja Luka. Nico countered that they were all volunteers, that Alec had worked side by side with all of them as an equal for the past week, and that the Yugoslav camp had accepted him without any reservations. Swiss laws did not apply here.

As the debate intensified, Ms. Klein sensed that reason and largesse would not be enough to sway the group to her side. Nico's points were greeted with *Ya*, while her points were rejected with jeers. Her expressionless face belied her frustration. Her final play was to threaten to disband the camp and send them all home. Nico responded that they would stay in Banja Luka, with or without the backing of Swisscare. There was only one way to resolve the issue, proposed Nico. They would put the question to a vote. Alec would stay at the risk of the camp's being disbanded, or he would be ordered to leave. Ms. Klein insisted on an anonymous written vote. Hans handed out pieces of paper and asked for a simple yes (he could stay), or no (he must leave). Hans would tally the votes.

For Alec, this was democracy in action. It was the antithesis of the mock trial in Lviv. He understood Ms. Klein's dilemma. He also knew that he, like Nico, would not have backed down. Unlike Ukraine, here his Swiss peers were voting to keep him and not expel him. Whatever the outcome of the vote, he felt a kinship with strangers that he had never felt before.

Hans tallied the vote: forty-one for and none against. The group broke out in cheers. Those nearest to him hugged him. Maya kissed him on the lips. Ms. Klein, defeated, insisted that Alec sign a document in front of the entire group, releasing her and Swisscare from any liability resulting from his presence at the camp. She had prepared the document in German prior to the banquet in anticipation of such an eventuality. It was a small price to pay. He had signed similar documents before.

Alec signed the document without understanding a word of what it said. He did not look her in the eyes, because to an extent, he sympathized with her. He had turned her world upside down. She left Banja Luka the next morning and did not return.

The vote at the Palas Hotel was liberating. Nico was unanimously empowered to lead. Alec was unanimously accepted as a member of the group. He wondered what would happen if his generation suddenly took over the world. What if the police at the Democratic National Convention had conceded to the protestors? What if America brought her troops home? What if everyone, including him, suddenly embraced peace and love?

*　*　*

In celebration of their victory over the establishment, Nico gave the workers the day off. Most of the Swiss youth went into the city to enjoy their holiday. Alec stayed in camp to write a letter to his parents—he knew they would be panicked by now. He hadn't communicated with them since entering the Soviet Union, and he did not know if Father Collins had contacted them to let them know that he had left the tour for an unknown destination.

Dear Mama and Tato,

I am sorry that I have not written to you sooner. I know that you must be very worried. For these past few weeks I needed to disconnect from everything. I am safe and have joined a Swiss work camp in Banja Luka to help with reconstruction after the earthquake. We are building a school. They don't pay us anything but give us food and a place to sleep. My coworkers here are won-

derful—*young, independent, and unbelievably friendly.*

In a week I will be leaving here for Munich to join the Flight of Freedom tour. In Ukraine, I saw Aunt Ulana and Aunt Vera. Mama, your younger sister looks exactly like you! When we first met I thought I was talking to you—she is young, beautiful, and as you yourself say, she took after your father because she loves to talk. I'll tell you the story of how we met when I get back home.

I will always cherish the language and customs that you have taught me, but I need to find my own place in the world.

I know that you raised me to be Ukrainian, but Ukraine is not as you left her. The Soviet Union is hell. It's a terrifying, oppressive state. I was persecuted for my nationalistic views and officially expelled. I will always be Ukrainian because it's in my blood. I don't know, however, whether freedom for Ukraine should be my primary goal in life. I was born in America. I'm more American than Ukrainian.

For me, the Ukrainian diaspora community is my home. We are people without a country. I now understand that the pledge in our Ukrainian national anthem—"We will lay down our body and soul for independence"—are not just words; they are bound to sacrifice, suffering, and death. We need to think about what path we choose: do we choose struggle and imprisonment or freedom in the diaspora? You have chosen to live freely in America rather than imprisoned in Ukraine—as have I.

I am doing well here, better than on Father Collins's tour. I've met new people—I now have a new friend in every city in Switzerland! Next year, they might come to visit me in the States. We'll see. Don't worry about me. I have everything I need. I'll be coming home soon. I miss you.

Love, Alec.

Alec sealed the letter and addressed it to his home in Chicago. He still needed stamps. Nico had set up a small tent that served as the administrative headquarters. It held a wooden table and two metal chairs. He was there, was working on the camp budget.

"Nico, I need some stamps," Alec said. "I want to mail a letter to my parents in Chicago."

"Yes, of course." Nico pulled a leather briefcase from under the table and took out a sheet of Tito stamps. "One of these is enough to send a letter to Switzerland. Two should be enough for America. Do you miss your parents?"

"Yes, but I feel at home here. I'll see them soon enough. How much do I owe you?"

"Nothing. You are now an official member of our group and entitled to share our communal resources. Give me your letter. I'll take it to the post office on Monday and mail it with the rest."

"Thanks."

Nico took the letter and slipped it into a bundle of letters wrapped in twine. "There is something I might ask of you."

"Sure, anything."

"If I ever come to Chicago, take me to hear the blues."

***

Nico suggested that they go to the Roxolana Disco to celebrate their victory at the Palas. He even offered to pay for the beer with money that had been reserved for camp provisions. The disco was located in the ruins of an Ottoman castle on the other side of the river. The earthquake had done substantial damage to the walls, and large blocks of stone were strewn over the open courtyard that served as the dance floor. A crescent moon was rising over the ramparts.

The Doors' "Light My Fire" blared through enormous speakers that were suspended from a makeshift scaffold behind the DJ. The scaffold also held black lights, strobe lights, and rotating colored lights. The equalizer was set to emphasize the organ solo that reverberated through the ruins. There were two bars on opposite sides of the dance floor. Nico bought the first round of beers and set them on the round plastic table next to Alec, Maya, and Regina.

"To your health!" he shouted over the music and clinked the mouth of his bottle with each of them.

As the DJ was switching from the Doors to the Stones, Alec leaned over to Maya and spoke directly into her ear. "Roxolana was Ukrainian—she's the concubine who became a sultaness."

Maya nodded, but Alec doubted that she understood him. The equalizer was now set to amplify the base and drums, and their beers were reverberating on the table. Roxolana, like Helen of Troy and Cleopatra, was one of the most intriguing women in history. *She was the epitome of harmony between East and West,* Alec thought. At the age of fifteen, she was abducted from her home to serve in the harem of Suleiman II. Legend says that she bewitched him to fall in love with her. He was still writing her love letters when she was fifty. He broke Ottoman tradition and made her his sultaness, the most powerful woman in the empire. *Imagine,* he thought, *the daughter of an Orthodox priest becoming the queen of the Ottomans!* She embodied the triumph of love over politics and religion.

The Stones' "Sympathy for the Devil" blasted out over the speakers. Alec grabbed Maya by the hand. "Let's dance," he said and pulled her onto the dance floor.

The other dancers were locals, with the exception of several boys and girls that Alec recognized from the Yugoslav camp. Two of the girls had climbed on top of the stone blocks on the dance floor and were mimicking go-go dancers. As he was trying to get his dance moves in sync with the Stones, Alec saw that several of the dancers were intentionally bumping into other dancers to make them lose their balance. They would time their bumps to the "woo-woo" refrain in the song. One of the boys who had been bumped came crashing into them. He quickly got up without apologizing and went to look for the offender. There seemed to be an invisible line that bisected the dance floor that he was unwilling to cross. He could only bump opposing dancers who came close to the line. *Strange game*, thought Alec.

As the beat went on, it became more apparent that there were two separate groups of locals. They were physically indistinguishable but stuck to themselves like packs of wolves. They would dance up to the invisible line and try and ambush an opposing dancer. It didn't seem to matter that both girls and boys went flying to the floor. At first it seemed playful, but soon it turned ugly. The youths from the camp tried to keep their distance, but they were still the occasional unintended victims of the human projectiles. The DJ seemed oblivious to the dance floor drama and just kept pounding the beat.

One of the bumped girls fell face first into a stone block. Blood gushed from her nose and over her blouse. The boy who bumped her started jumping up and down in triumph. His friends joined in, and soon half the dance floor was jumping to the beat. The situation was getting scary. *More like baboons than wolves*, thought Alec. He pulled Maya off the dance floor and sat down in safety.

"It's getting rough in here!" he shouted to Nico. "Maybe we should leave."

"They're not after us," Nico replied. "We're foreigners."

"Who are they?"

"They're locals. Christians and Muslims."

CHAPTER 17

The Vrbas River flowed down into Banja Luka from the surrounding hills. It was a white-water river for much of its run, but by the time it reached the city, it had lost its turbulence and was simply cold and fast. The banks were mostly wild and undeveloped. It reminded Alec of the rivers in upstate New York where he and his friends had gone tubing as teenagers. The river was oblivious to the craziness around it.

Alec jumped into the river. Giving himself up to the current was exhilarating. The swift current carried him and his new Swiss friends from the bridge to a beach about a kilometer downriver. This was fun. It was free. Caught in the current, the past didn't really matter. The moment—the swirling blue water, the swiftly passing willows, and the laughter of his friends—was all that mattered. The river delivered them to a sandy stretch of beach where families had already staked out the best plots with towels. Alec and Maya sat down on the sand to dry off in the sun. Maya put her head on his shoulder, and he felt her long hair drape over his back.

"I love the fun," she said.

Alec loved it too. "Let's do it again," he said, and they hiked up the road to jump in again.

***

The highlight of the camp experience, and the reason why some had volunteered in the first place, was an excursion to Dubrovnik, once their job digging the foundation was almost completed. The trip would take them through Sarajevo and Mostar to Dubrovnik and then back again. Alec had been to Dubrovnik with Father Collins and Walrus two years before. They had stayed in one of the socialist youth recreation camps on the outskirts of the walled city and had partied with youth from Yugoslavia to Kazakhstan. Yugoslavia was looser than the Soviet Union, and Dubrovnik was one of the few luxurious escapes from the drudgery of life behind the Iron Curtain. One evening they had gotten into a heated discussion with Bulgarian engineering students about the merits of nationalism versus internationalism over a bottle of slivovitz. Walrus' toast was the one thing on which they could agree: "Let's drink to the end of 'isms'—I have them all up my ass!"

The Swiss had driven down to Banja Luka in an assortment of vehicles that included private cars and rented vans. Nico and Hans had driven down from Basel in his yellow Volkswagen Beetle. Alec had told Nico about his Karmann

Ghia, and Nico insisted that Alec drive his Beetle down to Dubrovnik. Nico would drive one of the vans.

"Alec, I will lead," said Nico, "and you follow in the rear. Maya can ride with you. If one of the other cars breaks down, you can help them get out of trouble. I will give you a map where I marked out our route. We need to get to Dubrovnik by nightfall."

The distance from Banja Luka to Dubrovnik was only 250 kilometers, but with stops in Sarajevo and Mostar, it would be a full day's drive. The road went through the very heart of Bosnia and Herzegovina. The caravan set out at daybreak. Nico wanted to cover the 140 kilometers to Sarajevo by noon. The winding drive took them through high, forested hills and deep river valleys. It was a beautiful but wild landscape. Alec worked the stick on the Beetle like a pro, downshifting on the declines to not overwork the brakes. Passing the occasional truck was tricky because there were few stretches of straight open road. Maya worked the channels on the radio, trying to find a rock station. The hills blocked the reception, and they heard mostly static.

"We'll try again when we get closer to the coast," said Alec. "What kind of music do you like?"

"I like many different musics," Maya replied. "In school, I play cello. To dance, I like rock."

"What bands?"

"Beatles. Doors," she replied. "What music do you like?"

Alec thought for a moment. He too had an eclectic taste in music. He and Serge favored acoustic over electric in their band. They wrote their own songs. Serge would compose the music, and Alec would write the lyrics. Serge liked the Beatles, while Alec favored the Stones. They both liked Crosby, Stills, Nash, and Young. Stills's "Love the One You're With" flashed through his head. Alec also liked the oldies, like "Unchained Melody," "Runaway," and "Dreams." They reminded him of skating at the Rainbow Ice Rink with girls from his eighth-grade class. The girls wore angora sweaters and tissue in their bras. Life seemed simpler then.

***

Driving down from the mountains, Alec could see the terra cotta roofs of Sarajevo spilling down from the hillsides into the Miljacka River valley. It was difficult to imagine that shots on the bank of this shallow river had set off the maelstrom that engulfed Europe in the First World War. Sarajevo was the hotbed of Bosnian Serb nationalism. The Serbs had rebelled against the same Austro-Hungarian Empire that had ruled Galicia. Was this cause worth thirty-seven million dead, he wondered, most of whom had never even seen this remote place or known what they had died for?

The Swiss campers had agreed to drive down Appel Quay and then rendezvous at the Bascarsija bazaar for lunch before heading south and west to Mostar.

"I have a map that marks the locations," Nico said. "First, we stop by the Cumurja Bridge, where Cabrinovic threw the bomb. Then we stop by Schiller's Delicatessen where Princip shot Franz Ferdinand and his wife, Sofia."

As they neared the Cumurja Bridge, Nico stopped his van in the middle of Appel Quay and hopped out. He made a motion of throwing a bomb and then pretended to jump into the river. The cars in back of the cavalcade began to beep, and they had to move on. When they reached the Lateiner Bridge, he turned left toward Franz Joseph Street and again jumped out of the car. He motioned to Alec to get out of the car. "Alec, come! You must see! This is the spot!"

A pair of footprints were embedded in the concrete.

"This is where Princip stood when he fired the two shots. The first pierced the duke's jugular vein and another ricocheted into his Sofia's stomach."

Alec stepped into the footprints.

"He was about your age when he fired those shots," Nico said.

A policeman came up to them briskly to make sure that the tourists were not defacing the spot. "*Ty je ctajao xepoj,*" he said waving them on.

"What did he say?" Nico asked.

"I think he said, 'Here stood a hero,'" Alec replied.

"Do you think he was a hero?"

"He was a hero to some and a villain to others," Alec said. "I wonder if he ever reflected on the consequences of his action."

"He was just the spark. Europe was ready to burn. Come, let's go to the bazaar."

Bascarsija was in Stari Grad, the historical and cultural heart of Sarajevo. They parked their motley assortment of vehicles and scattered in small groups, looking for souvenirs and food. They had only one hour to eat and shop if they wanted to see Mostar and still make it to Dubrovnik by nightfall. A restaurant would take up the full hour, so Alec and Maya decided to buy *cevapcici* and pita from a street vendor who had set up his grill near the entrance to the bazaar. The smell of grilled lamb was too tempting to pass up. Alec bought two beers from a tourist shop to quaff down the grilled sausages, onion, and pita. It was the perfect fast-food lunch.

Maya teamed up with Bridgette and Regina for the shopping. They darted in and out of shops filled with jewelry, copper, trinkets, and local handiwork.

"Alec, look here," Maya beckoned to him. The girls were looking at copper medallions with the signs of the zodiac. "What is your sign?" she asked him.

"I'm Scorpio."

She quickly rustled through the collection and found the Scorpio medallion. "I buy for you," she said.

"Thanks," he said and hung it over his neck. It was a welcome gift. It made him feel like a flower child. "What's your sign?"

"Taurus." Maya laughed, and her friends giggled. Then they ran off to look at earrings while Alec wandered back to the car.

Nico was already rounding up the troops. "It's about two hours to Mostar and then another three hours to Dubrovnik. If we get separated, we'll meet by the Old Bridge at 1600 hours. Alec, you are the last car. Make sure we don't forget anyone."

The drive south to Mostar took them along a river valley surrounded by mountains. It was the most scenic of the routes they had driven so far, and it was relaxing to just take in the view. They arrived in Mostar on schedule. The city was named after the Old Bridge, or *Stari Most*, that was built over the Neretva River by the Turks. It was quite an architectural feat to span the steep riverbanks with a single stone arch. Mostar was the most Ottoman of the cities they had seen. It was exotic. While there had been mosques in Banja Luka and Sarajevo, here the minarets were an essential part of the cityscape.

Alec and Maya peered down from the bridge into the swirling Neretva River. "It's not like the Vrbas," Alec said. "It looks too dangerous to swim in."

"Boys jump from the bridge into the river," Maya said and motioned a jump with her hand.

"To kill themselves?"

"No, to show they are brave."

Alec had had enough of bravery. He had nothing to prove. "Another day," he replied.

***

The road from Mostar took them toward the Adriatic. After an hour they descended from the mountains to the blue-green waters of the Dalmatian coast. Maya found a radio station that played more music than static. Alec heard Mick and Keith croon, "Because I used to love her, but it's all over now." The vegetation changed from pines to palms. The traffic along the two-lane coastal road now included tour buses heading south to Dubrovnik from Split. The road would hug the coast and then veer inland for several kilometers before coming out again. It was late afternoon, but it was hot.

"I could use a cool dip," Alec said. Just off the road, he spotted an abandoned quarry with a deep blue pond. Except for a narrow stretch, it was shielded from the road by rock piles. Alec pulled off the road next to the pond. "I'm going to jump in," he said.

"Me, too," Maya replied.

Their swimsuits were packed in the trunk. "Rather than unpack, how about if we just skinny-dip?"

"What is skinny-dip?" Maya asked with a half-knowing grin.

"We'll jump in naked. You first. I won't look."

But Alec did look. Maya turned her back to him and pulled off her blouse. She undid the clasps on her bra and let it fall to the ground. The tension from the clasps had left red impressions on her back. She then pulled down her shorts and panties with a few wiggles and twists. Rather than jump in, she turned around and said, "Now you."

In her nakedness, Maya looked like Aphrodite coming out of the sea. Alec felt himself getting hard. He pulled off his shirt and pulled down his pants. Maya grabbed him by the hand, and they jumped into the pond. The water was too deep to stand, so they held each other up like seahorses, treading water with their legs. Alec had gone skinny-dipping once before, with Stefi. It had been a moonlit night at summer camp. Their bodies were white in the moonlight, and the night had cloaked them in an illusion of modesty. Here by the quarry, it was completely different. They were naked in the sun. Their bodies were bronze and muscular from the month of digging trenches in the heat of summer. Alec looked up at the rock pile and saw that Regina and Bridgette had also stopped their car and had been watching them the whole time.

He waved to them from the water. "Come on in," he invited.

They laughed, stripped off their clothes, and jumped into the pond with Alec and Maya.

***

When they arrived at their campsite on the outskirts

of Dubrovnik, it was already dusk. The campsite was on a small hilltop with a trail that led down to the beach. They had rented the site for two nights and were the only occupants. The sun had set over the Adriatic, and the only lights came from the headlights of their cars. They had dallied too long in Mostar and missed their goal of setting up camp while it was still daylight. Maya had taken her bag and run off with her friends to find a place to sleep. Nico asked Alec to make sure that there was toilet paper in the latrines. By the time Alec returned to the car, it was twilight. He walked around the parked cars, trying to remember the direction that Maya and her friends had taken, but it was impossible to find them in the dark. He had to find a place where he could sleep alone. Nico's VW Beetle would be way too cramped.

Alec checked one of the vans and found that it was open and empty. He crawled into the backseat and stretched out as best he could. Within a few minutes, someone opened the front door of the van. As the door light went on, Alec could see it was Hans. Despite the heat, he was wearing long pants and a white shirt. Hans looked at Alec but didn't say a word.

"Plenty of room in here," Alec said, but Hans still did not speak. Alec closed his eyes and tried to sleep. From the front of the van, he could hear a deep, sonorous breathing. It wasn't like snoring; it was a more disturbing sound, like deep breathing on the other end of a telephone from an unwanted caller. Alec looked into the rearview mirror and saw that Hans was looking at him. It was too creepy. Alec mumbled something about forgetting something and escaped from the van. He found the VW Beetle, got into the passenger's seat, locked the doors, and tried to sleep.

CHAPTER 18

The hot morning sun evaporated the dew off the windshield of the yellow Beetle. Alec rolled down the window to let in some fresh air. He tried to figure out which one of his joints didn't hurt. He had tried multiple positions in his sleep but none of them were comfortable. It reminded him of the many times he had slept in his Karmann Ghia at summer camps, at Suzy-Q, and on the Jersey shore. He was free. He was happy. It was a brand new day.

The only other person up at dawn was Nico. Alec respected the type of leader he was, someone who took his responsibilities seriously and would make sure everyone was safe and accounted for before going to sleep himself. He also was the first one up, thinking about what they would do for breakfast.

"Alec, you're up," Nico greeted him. "Let's try to find a place where we can buy food."

"We'll need to ask," Alec replied. "I think I saw some campers about a kilometer down the hill, in the direction of Dubrovnik. They might know where we can find something."

"Good. It's a beautiful morning. Let's walk."

Nico and Alec set off along the dirt road they had driven up the evening before. It looked completely different in the daylight. The Adriatic shimmered white in the morning sun. The dry scrub was interspersed with patches of pomegranate trees and exotic palms that had been transplanted here by sailors over the centuries. About halfway down the hill, they ran into a local farmer with a goat.

"Hello," Nico said. "Do you speak English? *Sprechen sie Deutch? Parlez-vous français?*"

The goat herder shook his head, avoiding eye contact. Nico looked at Alec, indicating he should give it a try.

"*Gavarite po Ruske? Chu vy hovoryte po Ukrainske?*" Still no response.

Both Nico and Alec resorted to body language. Nico pretended to be drinking from an imaginary bottle, and Alec, eating from an imaginary plate. Finally, a flash of understanding lit up in the goat herder's eyes, and he pointed down the road. He gave them detailed directions in Croat, which neither of them could understand.

"It's funny," said Nico, "how we in Europe are so close to each other yet so different. Is it like that with you in America?"

"Yes and no," Alec replied. "We are a country of immigrants, but most seek to forget where they came from."

"You are different, yes?"

"I'm an American born to Ukrainian political immigrants. They did not come to America by choice. The war drove them from their homes—and the Communists."

"You are political, like them?"

"I thought I was. Now I think there is more to life than politics."

"We Swiss have always believed that," Nico replied. "I am happy that you found us. Whatever it is you're looking for, you just might find it here."

* * *

Dubrovnik was the pearl of the Adriatic. The white stone fortress glistened amid the clear blue sea. For centuries it had been the major maritime power on the Dalmatian coast and had even rivaled the Venetians. Today, it was the center of tourism in Eastern Europe. You could hear all the languages of both Western and Eastern Europe spoken within its walls. The only universal language one needed was money.

The Swiss tourists gleefully spread out to explore the medieval city. Alec had been here before, so he convinced Maya and her friends that it was worth the several dinars to see the city from walkways on top of the city walls. From the high vantage points, one could truly appreciate the beauty of the city and the sea. The castle looked impregnable. The cannons on its high ramparts would have easily sunk any approaching warships. From land, it was protected by steep hills that would have been difficult to scale by an approaching army. It was not surprising that the walled city had remained intact for all these centuries.

A small restaurant was tucked into a lower rampart on the wall, facing the sea. White-and-red Cinzano umbrellas shielded the diners from the noonday sun. To reach it, Alec and Maya had to descend steep stone stairs protected with a rusted handrail. A couple was vacating a table, and Alec and Maya quickly grabbed the table, not waiting for a hostess to seat them. When the waiter finally came to their table, Alec asked to see a menu.

"I am the menu," the waiter replied in English.

"What would you recommend?" Alec asked.

"Fish. Caught today. Grilled."

"And to drink?"

"Croatian wine."

Alec turned to Maya. "We asked, and he recommended. I say we go with grilled fish and the local wine."

Alec was content to sit silently. He and Maya had a connection, but it was difficult for them to converse freely. He didn't understand German, and her English was limited. She knew some basic words, but it was difficult for her to express anything complicated. For Alec, her body language was enough for now.

The waiter brought the local red wine in a carafe with two empty water glasses. Alec filled them halfway with wine and raised a toast. "To youth—may it last forever."

Maya clinked glasses and replied, "To you, too."

Alec wanted to ask her if she thought that he had the soul of a sailor, like an Argonaut in search of the Golden Fleece. From their perch on the wall, he could see sailboats and yachts sailing along the coastline. He loved adventure. He loved meeting new people and seeing new places. Sailors had no commitments, other than to the sea—a girl in every port, but none at home. He wondered where home was for him now. He was a different person from the idealistic youth who had left Chicago just two months before. He was thousands of miles from home, both in his heart and in his head.

The sea bream that the waiter brought them was fresh off the grill. The heads and tails were still attached and grill marks seared the body. Together with bread and olive oil, it was a simple and delicious lunch. The wine, too, was remarkably good. From their vantage point in the ramparts, they could see islands stretching up and down the coast about a kilometer offshore.

Maya pointed toward the direction of their camp that was on the other side of the peninsula. "We swim to island," she said. "After lunch."

"Sure," he replied. The wine had given him a pleasant buzz. He was not a strong swimmer, but the idea seemed thrilling. *Safer than jumping off the Stari Most in Mostar*, Alec thought. He would not back down from this latest challenge.

***

Alec dug into his knapsack to find his swimsuit. As he was fumbling through his clothes, he felt a hand touch his shoulder. It was Hans.

"Why did you leave last night?" Hans asked. He seemed hurt.

"I went to find Maya and her friends," Alec replied, "but it was too dark."

"To sleep with her?"

"To sleep next to her. We came up together in Nico's car. I thought she would be waiting for me." He omitted telling Hans that his sonorous breathing had made Alec very uncomfortable.

Maya ran up, ready to swim in a banana-colored bikini. "Alec, let's go swim!"

"Hans, we're going to swim to the island right off the beach. Would you like to join us? Several of us are going."

Hans hesitated for a moment, but then he agreed. He carefully removed his shirt and long pants, folded them, and placed them in the trunk of Nico's car. He was already wearing his black Speedos.

The island was about a kilometer off the beach. It rose about fifty meters above the Adriatic and was covered in pine, with stretches of open meadow. The shoreline looked rocky, but it was too far away to tell if there were any open stretches of sand. The swimmers included Maya, Hans, Regina, Bridgette, and Alec. Alec dove into the water. It was cool and invigorating, and after a few strokes, the chill was gone.

Alec's mother had taken him for swimming lessons at the local YMCA, once a week, when he was seven. All he remembered was that the water had always been cold and smelled of chlorine, that he would vomit after several laps, and that the older boys would snap their towels at him. He quit after a few lessons and learned to swim on his own. His biggest feat until today had been to wade and swim across the Wisconsin River at the age of ten. He didn't have the technique of a trained swimmer, but if he varied his strokes, he learned that he could swim a good distance.

Hans and Maya were strong swimmers and quickly put distance between them and the others. A strong current was pulling from north to south. Alec looked up from the water and saw that if he didn't make a correction, he would miss their designated landing point by a few hundred meters. He swam at an angle against the current, while Bridgette and Regina drifted south, oblivious to where they might land. *Just don't miss the island*, he thought, *or you'll be swept out to the open sea*.

Alec wanted to prove to Maya that he could do it. About half-way to the island, he began to tire. Hans and Maya were now only a few hundred meters away from the island, while Alec still had to cover the full five hundred. He was alone and equidistant from both shores. If he turned around, he would surely make it back to shore. If he continued to swim to the island, he would still need to swim back, and he wondered if he had the strength. Turning back, however, was not an option. After several strong strokes, he could finally see the bottom through the crystal blue-green water. It was now about ten meters deep. He cleared the fear from his mind by telling himself that the water was getting progressively shallower. He experimented with several strokes, and the breaststroke felt least exerting. It allowed him to keep his head out of the water and keep his eyes on the approaching shoreline. When he finally reached the shore, Hans reached out his hand and pulled him up the rocks.

"Alec, you made it!" Maya exclaimed. Hans, too, looked pleased.

"Yes, it was harder than it looked," Alec said. "I need to rest here for a while." He lay face down on a broad, flat rock that was comfortably warm from the midday sun.

"Bridgette and Regina landed somewhere behind those far rocks," Hans said. "I will find them and bring them here." Hans scampered up the rocks to the tree line and disappeared among the pines.

Maya came over to Alec and began to rub his shoulders and back. The tiredness eased from his body as he felt her hands knead his muscles. At first his muscles tensed, but then he closed his eyes, relaxed, and gave himself up to her. He could feel her breasts caress the back of his neck as she worked the muscles in his lower back. He was caught between the hardness of the rock and the softness of her body. It was a wonderful place to be.

"Now turn over," she said.

Alec turned, knowing that she would see his erection. It might have been the reaction she was hoping for. She began massaging his legs and slowly moved up his body. She lingered for a long moment over his tented trunks and then moved up to his abdomen and then to his chest. Her eyes were focused on the parts she was working on. Her long wet hair draped the sides of his body. She was now straddling him and slowly rocking back and forth. She closed her eyes. Alec wanted to embrace her, but that would break their charade. Her rhythm quickened, then slowed, and then quickened again. She tensed and dug her fingers into the back of his shoulders. Then she relaxed and opened her eyes. She leaned over and kissed him on the lips.

"Silly boy," she said.

Hans and the girls came bursting out of the pines. Alec quickly rolled onto his stomach.

"I found them!" Hans proudly exclaimed. "They were almost at the end of the island!"

Regina and Bridgette were giggling. "Hans saved us," Regina said and gave Bridgette a hug of mock relief. "What happened to your back, Alec?" Bridgette asked, giggling again.

Alec touched his shoulder blades and could feel that they were scratched. "I scratched my back on the rocks when Hans was pulling me up."

"Hans or Maya?" Bridgette asked.

Maya shot Bridgette a look that could have turned her to stone, but when she saw that Bridgette would behave, Maya grabbed Bridgette and Regina by the hands and climbed up the rocks. "We go to do what girls do," she said, and the three of them disappeared into the pines.

Hans saw the scratches on Alec's back and smiled. "I understand," he said. Alec was not quite sure what he understood, but he was happy that Hans was friendly again.

***

The swim back from the island was easier than the swim there. They were accustomed to the current and started their swim farther down the island to allow for the drift. Maya swam back with Alec, while Hans played the lifeguard for Regina and Bridgette. When Maya reached the shore, she stood up, swung back her head, and squeezed the salt water out of her long hair. She knew Alec was watching. He again imagined Aphrodite coming out of the sea.

When he tried to hold her hand, she coyly pulled it back. She acted as if nothing had happened between them. Alec wasn't sure what to make of this unexpected gesture. Perhaps her friends had teased her, and she was embarrassed. Perhaps she had a boyfriend and was ashamed. He had never asked her. He walked back to camp with her without saying a word.

The sunset over the Adriatic was magnificent. A few clouds on the horizon imbued the sky with evolving hues of yellow, orange, and red. Night came quickly. It was the night of a dark moon. Nico and Hans had started a campfire, and Les had pulled out his guitar. The Swiss campers sang songs in German that Alec had never heard. They would laugh in unison at certain refrains. After several such songs, Les handed the guitar to Alec.

"Alec, sing us a song," he said.

"American or Ukrainian?" Alec asked.

"One of each!" The campers started clapping, encouraging him to play.

"OK, first a Ukrainian song. It's called 'Halya.'" Alec knew the song well. It was a favorite at Ukrainian campfires. It had a haunting melody and a lively beat, but it was a terrible song about a girl who was abducted and raped by Cossacks and then tied to a tree and burned. The song had a moral: that parents shouldn't let their daughters wander with Cossacks in the night. Luckily, no one understood the words.

"Now sing an American song," Les insisted.

"OK, but you have to sing along with me. It's called 'Barbara Ann.' It's by the Beach Boys. All you have to do is sing 'Barbara Ann' with me on the refrain and just keep singing it while I sing the rest of the words." The group caught on easily and were delighted that Alec had taught them an American song. Alec looked around the fire for Maya, but he didn't see her.

As the fire died down, most of the group slowly broke apart and wandered off to sleep, but Alec and Les remained by the embers, taking turns playing the guitar. The songs became more soulful and melancholy when Alec began strumming the chords to Neil Young's "Down by the River."

"What is the song about?" Les asked Alec.

Alec smiled ruefully as he handed the guitar back to Les. "It's about a man who shoots his girlfriend," he answered quietly, "and forfeits his soul."

CHAPTER 19

After their return from Dubrovnik, the Swisscare volunteers went back to digging the foundation for the new school. Most were already thinking ahead to returning home and seeing their family and friends. Maya was cordial with Alec but acted as if he had somehow offended her.

Alec had the inspired idea of having everyone in camp sign his bag as a remembrance. He asked them to write something personal in whatever language they wanted. Alec also made a point of taking everyone's picture when they signed his bag. His favorite inscription was from Les, who wrote, "*Live is hard.*"

When Alec gave his bag to Maya, she thought for a moment and then wrote, "*I miss you.*"

"I'll miss you too," he told her. "Give me your address and phone number, and I will come visit you. I promise." He gave her a piece of paper, and she wrote down her numbers in Zurich.

"Be with me tonight," she said.

After dinner, as Alec packed his few belongings, he read each of the inscriptions on his bag. There was not enough room on the outside of the bag, and some of them had written on the inside and even over the United Nations insignia. The bag with its forty inscriptions was a symbol of friendship that he would cherish for life. He left his belongings in the tent and went to find Maya.

It was another night of the dark moon. They had planned to meet in a secluded glen just outside the camp. Maya had already laid out a blanket and was waiting for him.

"Why did you not sleep with me in Dubrovnik?" she asked.

Alec was taken aback. "I thought you were angry at me."

"You should have followed me. I waited for you." Maya was beautiful, lying on the Bosnian earth with her dark hair flowing beneath and around her, like black tendrils that were waiting to envelop him. He stroked her face, and she opened her mouth as he kissed her. He moved his hands around her hips and up her thighs. She was wet and waiting. He knew she wanted him to enter her. She was not thrusting. He had to be the one to take her.

Alec felt a confusion he had never felt before. He had wanted to immerse himself in the here and now, and now she was here, opening herself to him. In the heat of the night, he could easily lose himself in her. She did not know or care about his past sins. The only sin that mattered was the one now. He was caught between the earth and the sky. He thought of Stefi, who had faded into memory. He thought of the gold charm he had bought her just two months before and of their promise to kiss in front of the Eiffel Tower.

Maya was not seducing him; she was waiting for him to take her, but it had to be his choice. His body wanted her, but his mind could not take the plunge.

"I can't make love to you," he said. "There's a girl I love. I am meeting her in Munich."

When Maya sighed, it seemed to come from deep in her heart, from a place where love and pain intersect. She had let him into her secret garden, and he had hurt her. He had befriended her and flirted with her. He had led her to believe they had a special connection. Now, on their last night together, he had pulled away.

"Then just stay with me tonight," she said. She put her head on his shoulder and kissed him. There was tenderness and vulnerability in her kiss that expressed all they had not been able to communicate to each other in those past few weeks.

Alec gazed up at the starlight while Maya slept. He realized that he had just gone through another test, but he wasn't sure if he had passed or failed.

***

Alec decided to take a train to Munich, which would get him there by morning; he wanted to be there when Stefi's bus arrived. Nico had offered him a lift, but Nico and Hans were taking the route through Trieste and Como, and dropping him off would have been out of their way. The Beetle was also filled with gear that they were bringing back to Basel.

The break-up of the camp was disorderly, as many were eager to get on the road at daybreak. Alec's train to Zagreb wasn't until five in the afternoon, so he spent most of the morning and early afternoon helping Nico break camp. They needed to take down the tents, fold them, and place them in one of the vans without losing any stakes or poles. They had to account for the all of the picks and shovels. The pots and pans needed to be washed and scrubbed. Alec and Hans went through the camp, picking up litter and assorted items that the other campers had forgotten—single shoes, towels, and canteens. Nico would eventually drop these things off at the Swisscare office in case anyone wanted to claim them.

Maya had left after breakfast with Regina and Bridgette, but not before giving Alec a hug and kiss. He took one last picture together with her, sitting on the hood of the Beetle. They promised to stay in touch, if only as friends.

Alec took a picture of the finished foundation to show his friends what he'd been doing during the month of July. When Nico and Hans drove off, only Alec and Dieter remained.

Dieter was a serious young man from Bern who did not speak a word of English. His round, wire-rimmed glasses made him look studious, though Alec knew from being with him these past few weeks that he was both a hard worker and a partier. Dieter would travel with Alec as far as Ljublana, where he would switch to another train. They were camp mates and fellow workers, but they could barely communicate. Alec had learned a few words of German that were enough to get along, but Dieter couldn't utter a word of English.

"*Kommen*, Dieter," Alec said. "*Railstrasse.*" They grabbed their knapsacks and walked the few kilometers to the railway station. Alec checked the schedule, and the northbound train to Zagreb and Ljubljana was running on time. They still had two hours to kill. Dieter made a motion as if drinking coffee, and Alec nodded. They left the station and found a nice café overlooking the Vrbas and the old city, just a few blocks away from the station.

Dieter insisted on ordering. *"Dvi café, bitte."* The waiter brought them two Turkish coffees. Dieter made a ceremony out of adding the sugar until it was the perfect consistency. They looked at each other from across the table and sipped their coffee. Alec wished he'd been able to tell Dieter how much he had enjoyed their shared experience, how he respected Dieter as a coworker, and how wonderful it was to have met in this exotic place, but there was simply no way to do it. Sipping coffee together in a nice café on the Vrbas River would have to be enough.

The train to Munich left on time, and Alec bid Banja Luka good-bye. The rhythmic clanking of the wheels on the rails was surprisingly tranquil. As he reflected on the last several weeks, he realized it had been a transformative month. He had shared his life with friends who accepted him without knowing him, as well as with a beautiful girl who had given herself to him. Now it was all in the past. He was returning to the reality of his own existence. He looked out the window and thought of their swim in the Vrbas, the bridge in Mostar, skinny-dipping on the way to Dubrovnik, and especially their swim to the island. Had he taken Maya that last night, he would have been lost in that dream forever.

Alec looked at the inscriptions on his bag and smiled. "Live is hard." *Yes it is*, he thought, *and then you die*. There had to be more to life than that.

***

Alec arrived in Munich at eight o'clock the next morning. He pulled out the letter his mother had given him and called his distant uncle from a pay phone.

"Hello, Uncle Lev?" he asked in Ukrainian.

"Listening. Who is this?" a voice responded, also in Ukrainian.

"My name is Alec, from Chicago. My mother gave me your phone number. She explained to me that your grandmother and hers were sisters, and that you know of our family in Chicago. I am meeting the Ukrainian Youth group, which is arriving in Munich today. We are to meet at the Ukrainian Cultural Center."

"Yes, yes, Alec, of course. You have just arrived? Come to my home, and I will take you to the meeting place. Do you have my address?"

Alec replied that he did and that he would take a trolley to Uncle Lev's house. The directions to his house were simple enough, and Alec was there within twenty minutes.

Uncle Lev lived on the third story of a solid stone building that had survived the bombing during the war. Alec knocked on the heavy front door. It had three locks and reminded Alec of the doors in Ukraine.

A bookish man in his late sixties opened the door. He checked the vestibule to make sure that Alec was alone and then said, "Welcome. You must be Alec."

Alec gave him a perfunctory hug and stepped into an apartment that looked like it hadn't been updated in decades. There were decorative grates on the outside windows that would prevent anyone from climbing in. Books and papers were crammed into oak shelves and overflowed on the floor. Black-and-white photographs were scattered on a table in the middle of the room.

"You must forgive the mess," Uncle Lev said. "My wife passed away, and my son has emigrated to Canada."

"My mother asked me to give you this letter."

Uncle Lev took out his reading glasses, opened the envelope, and perused the letter. He then carefully refolded it, put it back in the envelope, and returned it to Alec. "How is she?" he asked. "I haven't seen her since she was a little girl."

"She's fine, thanks." Alec noticed a photograph of his mother and her sisters when they were still children in Ukraine. "Is this her in the picture?"

"Yes, that was taken in Horlivka," Lev said. "I pulled these out to show you. Your grandfather," he pointed to a young man in a cassock, "was a priest there. I remember he was very strict but a very intelligent man. Your grandmother was quite a lady. She had elegant manners—very Austro-Hungarian. We would visit on holidays. Here is a picture of me from the same place, but as you can see, I am a little older than your mother." In the photo, Uncle Lev had the look of a boy who had just been spanked behind the shed for pulling the girls' braids. Uncle Lev pointed out several other people in his photos, some of whom Alec had heard about and others whom he hadn't. Lev informed Alec which people in the photos had been killed and who had fled when the Soviet tanks rolled into Galicia. "But enough about history. Your mother says in her letter that you'll be joining Ukrainian Youth for a European tour. What places will you be visiting?"

"Germany, Italy, and France. The organizers wanted

to make sure we visit the sites important to the Ukrainian diaspora."

"Why Munich?"

"Isn't this where Stepan Bandera was assassinated?" Alec asked.

Uncle Lev looked out at the street through the iron grates. He glanced at the locks on the door. "And Rome?"

"To see Patriarch Slipyj."

"Yes, yes, of course. And I presume Paris because of Petlura's assassination?"

"I guess."

"Why did you not come to Europe with the rest of your tour?"

"I've been here since June. I joined an earlier tour with my former high school that included a visit to the Soviet Union."

"Did you visit Ukraine?"

"I was in Kiev and Lviv."

Uncle Lev began putting the photos back into a shoebox. "What were your impressions? Is Ukraine as you pictured her?"

"It was difficult. I was arrested."

"What? How? For what?"

"I met with dissidents. They were under surveillance. They gave me certain information. I was tried and deported for political activism."

Uncle Lev's face took on a look of horror. He rudely grabbed back the envelope. His name, address, and telephone number were spelled out on the cover. He stashed the envelope in his pocket. "Who else saw this letter?" he demanded.

"The Soviets found it when they searched me at the

border. Actually, they took a strange interest in the letter. They have gone through all my things multiple times."

"You can't stay here," Lev said abruptly. "I will take you to the Ukrainian Cultural Center, and you can wait for your group there. They'll be arriving in a few hours."

Uncle Lev had changed from a long-lost relative who was reminiscing over family photos to a rude stranger who clearly wanted to sever all connections with Alec.

Alec did not protest. *Strange man*, he thought. *My mother should have warned me.* At least he was safely in Munich, and Stefi was arriving in a few hours.

***

Alec was standing in front of the Ukrainian Cultural Center near Marienplatz when he ran into Stretch, a member of his volleyball team who, like Alec, was joining the Flight of Freedom tour in Munich. He'd spent the summer hitchhiking from the Costa del Sol to the Cote de Azur.

"Hey, Stretch, you hitchhike here from Nice?"

"No, I took the train. How about you?"

"Train from Banja Luka."

"So you've been bumming around Eastern Europe while I've been slumming along the Riviera," Stretch replied, laughing. "How was it?"

"What a long, strange trip it's been," Alec replied.

"Yeah, you learn a lot about yourself when you're on the road. I don't know if I'll be able to sit through a disciplined bus tour. If they start to hassle me, I might just take off on my own again."

"I know how you feel," Alec replied. "But I really need

to see Stefi. I don't think her parents would take kindly to me if I abducted her from the tour."

"She's not eighteen, is she? You'd probably land in jail."

"Crazy as it seems, I just broke out—hey, look, here come the buses!"

The tour buses pulled up in front of the Cultural Center, spewing diesel fumes. The buses had picked up the tour group at the airport in Luxembourg and driven them straight to Munich. The same buses would take them on a tour of the city before heading out to a Ukrainian Youth camp on the outskirts of Munich in the evening. The camp would serve as their base for touring Bavaria. The city tour was optional, and some could choose to rest or walk around Munich on their own.

Alec counted three buses. One hundred thirty-eight Ukrainian Youth members had registered for the trip. They had come from all over the United States and Canada. Most only knew the kids from their own city, so they were still clustered in cliques, identified by the brightly-colored kerchiefs of their uniforms. As the buses were unloading, Alec ran from one bus to the other, trying to catch a glimpse of Stefi or of anyone from Chicago. On the third bus, he saw Stefi looking out the window, trying to spot him. When she saw him, she started knocking on the window and smiled so broadly it seemed to light up the bus. He blew her a kiss and ran around to the bus door to greet her.

Stefi ran down the stairs of the bus and literally jumped into Alec's arms. She kissed him on the face and lips, oblivious to the gapers around her. "I've missed you so much!" she said, starting to cry. "You stopped writing after Banja Luka. I didn't know what happened to you. Why did you stop writing? Why didn't you call? Do you have someone else?"

"It's a long story," Alec replied. "I love you. I missed you. Don't worry about all that now. The important thing is that we're together again."

Stefi had been the first one off the bus, followed by Alec's friends from Chicago—Serge, Razz, Sandy, and Chou. He was happy to see his friends again.

Razz was a dead ringer for Keith Richards. Alec had spent many of his boyhood summers at Razz's cottage on the bank of the Wisconsin River. The ancient tea-colored river that carved out the Dells teemed with fish and snapping turtles. He remembered how he, Walrus, and Razz would go fishing at dawn, when the mist was still on the water. They would sit together on the sandy banks and eye their lines; the current was rhythmic, while a nibble was erratic. They never knew what they might pull out of the water. The usual string included red horse, stripers, pike, and walleye, but on the lucky days, they would pull out a sturgeon. When the fish weren't biting, they skipped sand stones across the surface, discussed model airplanes, and watched the water bugs skim eddies by the shore. The river had forged a special bond between them. Razz would poke Alec in the chest and say, "You and me are blood. I would kill for you."

Sandy and Alec were volleyball teammates. Sandy had been recruited to play professional baseball straight out of high school, but his parents had advised him to finish college instead. He was strong, fast, and explosive. When the game was on the line, he wanted the ball. His Achilles' heel was that he was superstitious. He would only play well if he wore the lucky panties that a girl from Montreal had given him. He claimed that she was a distant cousin, but Alec knew there was more to those panties than kinship.

Alec had met Chou in seventh grade when his family immigrated to Chicago from Brazil. He was a dark, handsome boy with a wry sense of humor. His real name was Daniel, but Stefi's French niece had once referred to him as *"Mon petit chou,"* and the moniker had stuck. After their European tour, Chou planned to go to Vermont to attend acting school.

"We have a couple of hours before the buses leave for camp," Alec said to the group. "Let's go bum around Munich."

"The counselors said that after we eat, they'll take us on a bus tour," Stefi replied.

"It's up to you," Alec said, "but it's much more fun to walk around on our own."

"I'll walk around with you," Sandy volunteered.

"Me, too," Stefi chimed in. The others were content to rest, eat, and let the buses drive them around.

"We'll start in Marienplatz and then see the Rathause," Alec said, "and then hang around some beer gardens. If we have time, we'll jump in the Isar River for a swim. We'll be back before the buses return."

The three of them hopped on a trolley and headed off to Marienplatz. Stefi would not let go of Alec's hand. She seemed more frightened of losing him than of getting lost. In Marienplatz they bought some hot pretzels and a bunch of grapes.

"Watch this," Sandy said. He ran across to the other side of the street. "Throw me a grape." Alec hurled a grape high into the air and across the street. Sandy judged the flight of the grape like a trained seal and expertly let in plop in his mouth. "Again!" Alec threw and again the grape landed in Sandy's mouth.

"Amazing eye/mouth coordination," Alec laughed.

"It's no different from catching a fly ball in the out-field," Sandy replied.

"Let's have some real fun. How about a dip in the Isar?" Alec asked.

"I'm in if you are," Sandy replied.

"Just don't get the water in your mouth. I don't know where it's been."

They made their way to the bank of the slow-flowing river. Alec stripped down to his underwear and handed his clothes to Stefi. Sandy did the same.

"Don't think that I'm going in there with you," Stefi protested.

"No, it's OK," Alec replied. "Just hold on to our clothes and follow us down the banks."

Alec and Sandy jumped into the water and started to float through the center of town in their underwear.

"You're going to get arrested!" Stefi yelled to them from the bank.

"They'll have to catch us first," Alec yelled back.

The sport continued for a few hundred meters until they found a concrete bank to climb out.

"Pretty cool, no?" Alec asked Sandy. "When the current takes you, it's as if the world passes you by." Stefi handed them their clothes.

"Loved the rush," Sandy replied. "Now let's go get some beer."

"I saw a bunch of kids from our group at an outdoor café near Marienplatz," Stefi said. "Let's go join them."

***

The café turned out to be a wine garden. About fifteen white wooden tables were neatly arranged in a corner of an open square in front of the establishment. The kids from the East Coast had taken up most of the seats. From their raucous laughter, Alec could tell that they'd been there for a while. While Alec didn't know them, Stefi and Alec's friends had met them on the flight. A handsome couple that looked South American waved them over.

"Stefi, Sandy—come join us. You have to try the *junger Wein.*"

"Come meet George and Marijka," Stefi said. "They're a lot of fun. Marijka's dad owns a plantation in Venezuela, and her boyfriend, George, works there as an overseer."

George had an easy, self-assured style. He looked the part of a plantation overseer. He had Latin eyes and a well-trimmed moustache. Alec could picture him on a horse. His girlfriend was a raven-haired beauty. Both spoke English with a Spanish accent.

Stefi made the introductions. "This is my boyfriend, Alec. He's been bumming around Europe all summer. You know Sandy."

"You came on this trip all the way from Venezuela?" Alec asked.

"No, no. We live in New Jersey during the Venezuelan winter and only go down there for the tobacco-growing season," Marijka replied.

"You must try this *junger Wein,*" George said. "It's not like anything you've ever tasted before. It's fizzy and goes straight to your head."

"Just don't let the counselors catch you," Marijka warned. "Alcohol, smoking, sex ... they're on a long list of things we're not allowed to do."

A buxom waitress brought out several more glasses of

wine. She winked at George, and Marijka slapped him on the thigh. "Stop ogling every girl you see," she said. "Everything you need is right here."

"So you were bumming around Europe before we got here?" George asked. "Cool."

"I was on a European trip with my former high school for the first month. Then I hitchhiked to Yugoslavia and worked with the Swiss Peace Corps. Now I'm here with all of you for the next three weeks."

"It's going to be great fun," George assured him. "Look at all these pretty girls we're with. Watch out for this one," he said, pointing at Stefi, "or somebody like me is going to grab her." Marijka gave him another slap on the thigh.

"You'll protect me, won't you?" Stefi coyly asked Alec.

"Sure I will," Alec replied, but he wasn't really sure about Stefi now. He had changed, and she hadn't. He wasn't sure if their relationship could stay the same.

186

CHAPTER 20

The buses left for the Ukrainian Youth camp in a pouring rain. Part of the forest belonged to the Ukrainian Youth and the other part was reserved for nudists, who felt that nude bathing in the cold waters of the stream that ran down from the Bavarian Alps was good for the body and soul. The rumors of this unusual use of the property had quickly spread throughout the buses, and the teenagers were peering out the windows hoping to see some of the bathers.

Oddly enough, as the bus crossed the stream to enter the property, several nudists were bathing in the stream, even though it was pouring rain. It was difficult to see if they were male or female, but the boys concluded they were mostly female.

"Water nymphs," Alec informed them. "They lure you

into the water and then they drown you."

"Cut the crap," Serge said. "They're just naked women. The one on the left looked pretty hot. I'm pretty sure she was looking back at me."

When the buses arrived at their campsite a few kilometers away, the military surplus tents were already standing. The German Ukrainian scouts had done their best to make their international friends feel welcome. Only the weather wasn't cooperating. The group leader, Mr. Nalysnyk, ordered them to unpack the buses and put their luggage into the tents. Most had the type of hard, square luggage that one takes on leisure trips. Alec was one of the few who traveled with his belongings on his back.

After they had claimed their cots and nestled in, Serge pulled out his guitar. One of the boys from New Jersey had also brought a guitar, but Serge told him to hand his guitar to Alec. "Try this," Serge said. He showed Alec the base riff for the Stones' "Gimme Shelter." It was the right song for a night like this. The weather had worsened. A thunderstorm shook the sides of the tent.

Several girls came into the tent to listen to the music. They were wet from the rain but eager to party on their first night out. Most were still dressed in their uniforms, but one of the girls from New York had changed into a blouse that was sheer from the rain and clung to her ample cleavage. She had long blonde hair and had taken the time to put on some red lipstick. Chou knew her from a previous trip to Suzy-Q, the Ukrainian resort in the Catskills.

"Serge, Alec, I want you to meet my friend Katya," said Chou.

"I met Katya on the plane," Serge replied and kept

playing. Alec got up out of politeness to give her a friendly kiss on the cheek. Instead, she met him full on the lips and opened her mouth, inviting a French kiss.

"Nice to meet you too," Alec said and sat back down to continue playing. He was beginning to get the hang of the song. "Oh, a storm is threatening, my very life today ..."

Stefi walked into the tent, drenched from the rain. "I was waiting for you to come and get me," she said, sitting down on the cot next to Alec.

"We got caught up playing this new Stones song," Alec replied. He put a blanket around her and rubbed her shoulders. The drone of the rain on the canvas slowed to an intermittent patter.

"Let's take a walk," Alec suggested and Stefi nodded. They stepped out into the dark. The tents were interspersed in an old-growth forest that looked like it belonged in a Grimm's fairy tale. They walked a few hundred yards through the tall trees into a small clearing. The rain had subsided, but they could hear thunder and see distant flashes of lighting. The air smelled electric. Stefi still had Alec's blanket over her shoulders.

"I missed you so much," Stefi said. "I thought you forgot about me."

"I could never forget about you. I couldn't write. I've just lived through the hardest time of my life. I was arrested in the Soviet Union. I'm lucky to have gotten out."

"Why? What for? It was Johnny who put you up to whatever it is you did, wasn't it?"

"I can't say what I did, or why, or with whom. It's still too dangerous."

"Why is it dangerous?"

"I was followed when I left the Soviet Union. They

DANIEL HRYHORCZUK | 189

know about you and me. They read your letters. The less you know about what happened to me, the safer you'll be. Someday, years from now, I'll tell you the story."

"Why did you go to Banja Luka?"

"I needed to get away. I met a group of Swiss volunteers who were digging a foundation for a school. I've been living and working with them for the past month."

"You wrote that you were in a Yugoslav camp."

"I was, but then I ran into the Swiss. It was much easier to communicate."

"Why did you stop writing?"

"I just needed some time to myself to figure things out."

It was starting to rain again. Stefi put the blanket over their heads and kissed him. "I'm glad you're safe. You don't have to tell me any more until you want to." Alec gave her a long, soulful kiss. She took his hand and put it on her breast. The top buttons of her uniform were opened, and he felt a lacy bra covering her breast. She must have bought it especially for the trip. In the midst of the threatening storm, Alec wasn't ready for anything more than affection.

Stefi removed the blanket from their heads. She looked at him with consternation. "You seem distant. It's like you're a million miles away. Is there someone else?"

"No," he lied. "There's no one else. I've changed a lot over these past few weeks. I'm not the same boy who left. I'm still the boy who loves you, but I've discovered much more about the world and about myself. It's been overwhelming. I want you to love me for who I am today and not because you had a crush on a Northwestern kid with a Karmann Ghia. I'm thinking of maybe staying in Europe for a while and maybe even take a year off school."

Stefi pulled away. "Are you sure there's not more that you're not telling me?"

"No," he lied again.

"Lots of boys asked me out while you were gone."

"What did you tell them?"

"I told them I have a boyfriend. What should I tell them now?"

Alec didn't know how to reply. "Yes, you have a boyfriend. He's just trying to find himself."

She closed the buttons on her blouse but then took his hand. She was still wearing his school ring. "Johnny came over to see me just before we left."

"Johnny? Why? What could he possibly want from you?"

"He asked me to give you a message."

"What message?" Alec asked.

"He said 'Don't tell anyone what happened in Ukraine.'"

"Not anyone?"

"No, not anyone. He said especially not to tell your friends. Why do you think he said that?"

Alec let go of her hand. "It means we're all in this alone."

A flash of light illuminated the forest, followed by a deafening crack, and then a tree fell hard to the forest floor, missing them by just a few feet. The trunk was seared where it had been split.

Stefi clutched Alec for protection. "We need to get back to our tents. It's not safe here."

***

The Flight of Freedom tour was scheduled to stay at the camp near Munich for three more days and then head south to Innsbruck. When Alec woke up in the morning it was still raining. The camp was bound to be dreary and boring in such weather, and he craved adventure. *I need to get away to think*, he told himself, but he also wanted to apologize to Maya. After his heart-to-heart talk with Stefi, he realized that he had hurt and betrayed them both. He wanted to tell both girls how wrong he had been.

He suggested to his friends that they hitchhike with him to Switzerland for a few days and then rejoin the group in Innsbruck. Serge, Razz, and Stretch agreed to the adventure. It was only 250 kilometers to Zurich. "We should make it by nightfall," he told his friends. He took his knapsack and advised his friends to take their sleeping bags, just in case they had to sleep on the side of the road.

"What about Mr. Nalysnyk?" Stretch asked.

"We'll leave him a note," Alec replied. "We'll ask for his pardon when we get back."

They stood on the side of the highway in front of the camp with their thumbs out, hoping to catch a ride. Finally, after nearly two hours, a young French couple in a Peugeot picked them up and dropped them off in the center of Munich. It proved even more difficult to get a ride out of the center of the city. They decided to walk toward the highway to Memmingham.

"You sure this is a good idea?" Serge asked.

"Well, I guess hitchhiking alone is easier," Alec replied. "It's tough because there are four of us. Anyway, it's getting dark. Why don't we stay here for the night and head out in the morning?"

"Where are we going to sleep?" asked Razz.

"We'll find a public park and camp out there," Alec replied.

"Yeah, I've done that before," Stretch chimed in. "All the hippies do it. The police will probably leave us alone."

After walking several blocks, they found a small park in a quiet section of the city. It had a few trees, manicured bushes, and a freshly mowed lawn. Alec found a small grocery store in the vicinity and brought back four cold bottles of beer. They took long gulps of beer and lay down, staring up at the sky. Serge hadn't brought a sleeping bag, so he propped himself up against a tree and covered himself with Alec's blanket.

"I didn't think it'd be so tough to catch a ride," said Razz.

"People are probably afraid to stop for four of us," Stretch said, echoing Alec's earlier comment.

"You take a chance when you stick out your thumb, too," said Alec. "The guy picking you up could be some wacko. Serge and I once played a gig at a wedding in Cleveland. After the wedding, well past midnight, we decided to hitchhike to the youth camp about fifty miles away. We got picked up by some rednecks who wanted to crash a prom party—they thought they could get in by bringing their own band. When the prom queen turned them away, they drove us into the country, pulled out a gun, and tried to rob us. We scattered into the woods. It was too dark to chase us, so they just drove off. We ended up walking the last ten miles to the camp."

"I can top that hitchhiking story," Stretch said. "I was hitchhiking through France when some old dude in a convertible picked me up, and next thing I know, he's got his hand up my thigh, going for my balls."

"What'd you do?" asked Razz.

"I pulled out my knife and stabbed him in the hand.

He slammed on the brakes, and I jumped out of the car."

***

The next morning, they tried a different method. Alec bought a map at a gas station and would walk up to cars with single drivers, asking for directions to Zurich. When a driver was kind enough to point out the way, Alec would ask if he was heading in that direction and if he had room for four more. It was a workable strategy—they managed to find enough cars to take them at least part of the way, all along their route. They arrived in Zurich at one in the afternoon—tired, hungry, unwashed, and unshaven.

Alec had told his friends about the Swiss volunteers and the fun times that he had spent with them in Banja Luka. Now, he was determined to find Maya. Alec assured his friends that Maya would have friends for them. When they arrived in Zurich, Alec bought a city map and asked the shopkeeper for directions. The street he was searching for was only six tram stops away. When they got off the tram, they discovered that the house number was still far off, and they walked another two kilometers before finally arriving at Maya's door.

The house was not as Alec had imagined it. He had pictured a cozy chalet with a view of the Alps. Instead, it was a narrow brick home in a quiet residential neighborhood. Alec climbed the stairs and rang the doorbell. No one answered. He rang again—still, no answer. It had never occurred to him that no one would be at home. His friends were waiting on the sidewalk impatiently.

"I need to make a phone call," he said. "Wait for me here." He ran down the street until he found a public phone and dialed her number. Again, no one answered. He was at a loss as to what to do. He had dragged his friends to another country on an adventure that wasn't going according to plan. He slowly walked back down the street to his friends, who were eager to meet some European girls.

"She's not home, but I'll try again in an hour," he said. On the cover of his map he saw a picture of tourists feeding swans on the shores of Lake Zurich. "Let's go by the lake, grab something to eat, and figure out what to do next," he suggested.

The lakefront was as beautiful as the photo on the map. Swans and ducks paraded in front of the tourists, who threw them bread and snapped photos. Alec took a picture of his three friends with the swans in the background. They sent Razz to buy some food, and he came back with frankfurters that were a poor substitute for Chicago hot dogs.

"I don't want to spend another night in a park," Razz complained. "You promised us some chicks, but all we get to see are these fucking swans."

Alec sighed. Once when he was seven, he had told Walrus and Razz that a cow had fallen into a foxhole that he had dug when they were playing army. He had indeed dug a hole down to his waist, and there were cows in the pasture, but he'd captured the cow only in his imagination. Walrus and Razz, however, had insisted he show them the cow. When they didn't see one, Alec insisted, "The farmer must have helped it out." But they knew it wasn't true. This time, he'd promised his friends that Maya and her girlfriends would welcome them in Zurich. That promise was proving to be little more than another childish fib.

"Well, are you going to call your *girlfriend*?" pressed Serge.

"No, I don't think so," Alec replied.

"What the hell!" said Razz. "You make us hitchhike all the way to Switzerland and there are no girls? You probably made up the whole thing. It's like that time when we were seven, and you said there was a cow—"

"Be cool, man. Leave him alone," said Stretch. "Look, she's not home. We can't wait. We had our little adventure. Let's head to Innsbruck."

"No way am I hitchhiking," said Razz.

"We can take a train," Alec replied.

"I got ripped off at the airport," Razz replied. "I don't have money for a train."

"Serge, how about you? Do you have any money?" asked Alec.

"Not much. I left most of it with my stuff in the bus," he replied.

"Stretch?"

"Same deal," he said.

They walked over to the train station to check the schedule and the price of tickets to Innsbruck. The idea of sleeping on a train seemed luxurious. Luckily, there was a train leaving in less than an hour. The problem was that after pooling their resources, they had only enough money for two second-class tickets. Alec insisted that he would hitchhike back, since he had brought them on this wild goose chase. Serge offered to accompany him.

"Thanks, Serge," Alec said, happy that he wouldn't be traveling alone. Then he turned to Razz, asking, "Can you do me a favor? Would you give Stefi a note from me? I've been such a jerk to her." Alec pulled a piece of paper and a pen out of his knapsack. He knelt down and placed the paper on the marble floor of the train station. A muddy stain bled through the paper.

"Don't tell me you're going to apologize," said Serge.

"What do you mean?"

"You're kneeling on the floor of a railroad station, writing a note to some high school girl. No high school chick is worth groveling for."

"I hurt her. I should at least own up to it." He continued writing his note.

Dear Stefi,

Sorry for leaving without telling you. I wanted to come back with Razz, but my money is just about out. Serge and I are going to hitchhike to Innsbruck. I'll see you soon.

Love, Alec

CHAPTER 21

The road from Zurich to Innsbruck wound past blue lakes and through alpine meadows and mountain passes. Catching the first ride out of Zurich was easy. An American couple on holiday was happy to give them a lift to the next point of interest in their Michelin guidebook. They drove southeast toward Schulbelbach and then along the southern shore of Lake Zurich to Sargans. Their second ride took them north through Lichtenstein. The driver, a businessman in a black Audi, was heading through Schann to Schaanwald. On their map, it looked like a shortcut, because they could avoid going farther north than they needed. He dropped them off at a remote intersection in a birch forest and turned off to the south. From there, it was slow going. Few vehicles came by, and no one seemed to be heading east. Serge plopped down on the side of the road; Alec paced back and forth.

A truck heading west dropped off another young hitchhiker before it, too, turned south. The hitchhiker was tall and blond and looked Dutch, but it was difficult to tell. Alec pointed his thumb east to show him that they were heading in opposite directions. The Dutchman clambered over a steep rise on his side of the road, sat down in the tall grass, and un-packed his lunch. Alec and Serge were starving, but all they could do was watch as he bit into an apple and threw the core into the road.

"I wonder if he's got a few more apples," said Serge. "Let's go over and ask him."

"I'm sure he didn't pack a lunch for three," Alec re-plied. "Just let him be."

The Dutchman fumbled through his knapsack for several minutes and then yelled out across the road, "Have you a metal cutter?"

"A what?" Serge yelled back.

"A cutter ... for metal."

"You mean a can opener?" Serge replied. "Yeah, I've got one of those in my army knife!"

The Dutchman beckoned them to come over. He pulled out a can of sardines to show them what all the fuss was about. "We eat together," he propositioned.

Serge and Alec ran across the road and up the rise to take a closer look at the can. Serge pulled out his Swiss army knife and with due deliberation found the right utensil. He carefully pried up the tin with an up-and-down motion and exposed the oily contents, to everyone's delight. The Dutch-man pulled out a small box of crackers and handed each of them three. He divided the last cracker into three equal pieces. Alec imagined Wild West outlaws dividing their loot. The Dutchman used Serge's knife to delicately pull out the sardines and place them on the divided crackers. They devoured their portions in less than a minute. Afterward, they politely parted company to await the next ride.

They got lucky with their next ride. An older gentleman in a white Opal was heading ninety kilometers in the direction of Innsbruck. He said he was driving back from Zurich to his village, high in the Tyrolean Alps. He spoke limited English, but Alec and Serge understood that he would take them through the scenic route. The road climbed higher and higher into the Alps until they were well above the tree line, in a high plateau covered with snow and surrounded by majestic peaks. Their driver named the highest peaks as they drove by, but the names meant little to them. It was clear that their driver was proud of his country and wanted to show it off to these two young Americans. The drive to his village took well over two hours, and they arrived in the late afternoon. They hopped out of the car in the center of a storybook Tyrolean village. It looked like it had been frozen in time in the last century.

"I'm surprised we don't hear yodeling," Alec laughed.

"Well, at least it's civilization. They have to have some food somewhere. I'm starving."

The sardine canapés had been tasty, but now they needed to find some real food. They were almost out of shillings. The smell of bacon dumplings lured them to an inn with a silver Roadster parked by the entrance. The hewn-wood dining room opened onto a flower balcony with a vista of the Alps. A handsome couple sat at one of the two tables. The man sported driving gloves. The lady wore pearls.

"Let's enjoy the view," Alec said. He plopped his knapsack on a seat at the empty table. A fraulein in a dirndl rushed out to protest, but the man with the gloves waved her away.

"American," Alec offered apologetically.

The menu had much to offer but little that they could afford. Alec and Serge ordered two glasses of water and a plate of dumplings to split between them.

The man at the next table took off his gloves and gently touched the lady's hand. His gaze wouldn't leave her eyes. She smiled and fingered her pearls. They were speaking in German, and the two Americans had no clue as to what they were saying.

"She looks like Grace Kelly," Serge said. "Look at her pearls … and check out that dude's watch. It's solid gold. Some day we're going to live the good life."

"You forgot the Roadster," Alec added.

"He who dies with the most toys wins."

"Is that what you mean by a good life?"

"What else is there?"

Alec smiled. "Love, friendship, knowledge?" He turned his head to get a better look at the couple. "You know what's cool about them?"

"What?"

"They're over thirty, and they're still in love."

The fraulein brought out two serving dishes of pan-seared trout and a bottle of white wine.

Serge dug into his dumpling. "Whatever. All I know is that they're eating like royalty, while all we can afford are these damned dumplings."

The man at the other table turned around. The lady pulled back her hand. "My wife and I couldn't help but overhear you," he said in English. "You said you are Americans?"

Serge turned red. "You speak English?"

"Yes," the woman offered curtly, "and German and French and Italian."

"We're very sorry," Alec said. "Please don't take offense. We're students hitchhiking through Europe."

"My name is Carl, and this is my wife, Alina. We have a chalet near St. Anton. We would offer you a ride, but our car only seats two."

"Thanks, but we're heading east toward Innsbruck," Alec said.

Lights began coming on in the valley below. "We need to be on our way," Carl said offering his hand to Alina. He pointed to their unfinished plates. We cannot possibly finish all of this food. Please help yourselves."

The couple got up from the table without waiting for their bill.

"Oh, what the hell," Alec said. "I'm starving." He scooped up the leftover trout, bread, and fruit, wrapped them in a napkin, and tucked them in his knapsack. Serge took the unfinished bottle of wine. They left what few shillings they had on the coin dish and hurried out into the street.

After fifty meters, Serge handed the wine to Alec.

"Have a swig of Gruner Veltliner. Here's to trickle-down economics."

Alec took a sip of the white wine. "We need to get back to the main road soon. It'll be dark in another hour."

Before they could retrieve the rest of the food, they were startled by a command of "Stoppen! Hands up!" They turned around and saw a policeman pointing a shaking pistol at their chests. "Hands up!" he ordered again. He pointed the pistol at Serge, then at Alec, and then back at Serge, as if not knowing whom to shoot first.

Alec and Serge raised their hands. Alec was still holding the bottle of wine.

"Turn around! Hands up! March!" The policeman
acted as if he had never actually pointed his pistol at anyone.
Several locals stopped what they were doing and stared at the
spectacle. The arrest of foreign scofflaws in broad daylight
was undoubtedly a rare occurrence, and they would probably
be talking about it for years. The policeman kept repeating
"March!" making sure that those within earshot would know
that he was earning his keep. He was also demonstrating his
command of English. He marched them into a tiny police station with a single cell and ordered them to sit down. He still
had his gun drawn. Alec again thought of westerns, when the
local sheriff arrests the outlaws in front of the saloon.

"Passports!" he demanded. Alec and Serge handed
him their passports. The policeman holstered his gun and du-
tifully logged their names, citizenship, and passport numbers.
He read them the statutes they had violated from an Austrian
codex. They didn't understand a word, but it was apparent that
they had been arrested for stealing. The fraulein came into the
police station and identified them as the Americans who had
stolen from her patrons. This was duly noted in the police report. He photographed the wine, fish, napkin, bread, and fruit
as evidence of the crime. The fraulein signed the complaint,
retrieved her cloth napkin, and walked out in a huff. The policeman placed their passports in his desk drawer and locked it.

"Look, we are starving students. We have no money,"
said Alec. To demonstrate that they were telling the truth, he
pulled out his wallet and opened it, showing the policeman
that it was empty. He then pulled his pockets inside out, prov-

ing that he had no coins. He motioned to Serge to do the same.

"I'm not giving him my wallet," Serge hissed.

"Don't be a fool. He'll add resisting arrest to the charges."

Serge reluctantly handed his wallet to the policeman and then pulled out his pockets. The policeman carefully went through each wallet to see if there were any hidden bills. He found a Trojan tucked in behind Serge's license.

Alec looked at Serge, who looked flustered. If they were locked up and detained, who knew when there would be a judicial hearing? And if they were found guilty, which was likely, they would have no way to pay the fine. They would have to contact their parents and have money wired to a bank in Austria. They would miss their group in Innsbruck, which would likely panic the group leader, since the last anyone knew, they were hitchhiking through the Alps.

Alec found their situation increasingly Kafkaesque. He had survived interrogation and near imprisonment by the KGB. He had been tried and sentenced by a Soviet kangaroo court for political activism that could have sent him to the Gulag. To be arrested for stealing leftovers in a remote village in the Tyrolean Alps by a Mayberry policeman was downright ridiculous.

Alec looked directly at the policeman. "Look, we're innocent. It's a simple misunderstanding. You are faced with a choice. You can arrest us, or you can let us go with a warning. If you arrest us, we will need to call our American embassy and let them know that you have imprisoned two starving students. You will need to deal with them and with your own officials, which will result in a great deal of paperwork. It may develop into an international incident. The leftovers were not eaten. They have been returned. Is the crime worth the punishment? Do you want to be in the newspapers as the policeman who arrested two starving students for stealing leftovers?"

The policeman deliberated for a few moments. He saw the logic in Alec's argument. He wrote some additional lines in the police report then said, "Leave now. Never come back again."

Alec and Serge retrieved their passports and their wallets and stepped out of the police station. Several villagers had gathered across the street to witness the drama. The policeman yelled something about "Amerikaner" and waved them on. Alec and Serge walked past their stares to the edge of the village to thumb their next ride. A milk delivery truck came lumbering down the road, and they jumped into the middle of the narrow road, forcing the truck to stop. Serge ran over to the side of the driver, who clearly looked frightened. "Please," Serge begged, "just take us to the main road."

"*Funf kilometers—nicht weiter*," the driver said. They jumped into the front of the truck and sat down on the metal floor for the bumpy ride back to the main road.

"You were pretty cool back there," Serge said. "I thought we were in deep doo-doo."

"I've been through worse," Alec replied.

***

The milk truck dropped them off at the intersection with the main highway. The sun had disappeared over the mountains, and it was unlikely that someone would stop for two hitchhikers on a desolate mountain road in the dark. They needed to make plans for the night. They had only one blanket and one sleeping bag.

"Let's camp on the side of road," Alec suggested, "and wait until morning to catch the next ride. I'll see if I can find some wood to make a fire. Let's hope building a campfire isn't a crime here as well." But Alec came back empty-handed. "Everything's wet or green. There's no dry wood. I've got a blanket and a sleeping bag in my knapsack."

Night was setting in quickly. The moon lit up the snow-covered peaks, and a cold wind blew down off the mountain. Alec and Serge covered themselves with the blanket and huddled together to stay warm. It was the time and place for friends to have a heart-to-heart talk.

"This reminds me of our hike in the Rockies last summer with Johnny and the other guys from the Brotherhood," Alec said.

"Yeah, but at least we had our own sleeping bags."

"I felt like I really got to know those guys."

"They're too idealistic for me," Serge replied. "They think they can liberate Ukraine on their own by taking an oath of Brotherhood. It's not up to us; it's up to the people who live there. I know; I've been there. We all need to row our own boat."

The temperature had dropped, and now Alec began to shiver.

"So what happened in Ukraine?" Serge asked, drawing the blanket more tightly around them.

"What do you mean?"

Serge rolled his eyes. "Don't BS me. Luka called his parents. He said you got busted for pornography."

"It wasn't like that."

"So what was it?"

"I really can't talk about. We got deported, and I ditched the tour. I went to Banja Luka to help with the reconstruction. I met up with the Swiss Peace Corps and hung out with them."

"So?" Serge prompted. "Come on—what happened?"

"Look, I really can't talk about it," Alec insisted. After a moment, he added, "I don't want to put anyone else in danger."

"What about the people who put you in danger?" Serge demanded. "They don't give a damn about you. They probably threw you to the wolves."

"You look for the worst in people," Alec sighed.

"I look for the worst and let the best take me by surprise."

"Oh? What's the worst in me?" asked Alec.

"Do you really want to know?"

"Of course."

"All right, then. You're a sucker. You want to believe everybody. It allows people to take advantage of you. And you think you're better than the rest of us."

"I don't think I'm better than everyone else," Alec protested.

"Well, that's how you act, whether you think so or not. Even now, you think I can't handle the truth. Who can you trust if you can't trust your best friend?"

They barely squeezed into the single sleeping bag. A howl echoed through the moonlit mountains.

"What's that?" asked Serge nervously.

"Sounds like wolves," Alec replied.

CHAPTER 22

Alec and Serge rejoined their group in Innsbruck as two returning war heroes. Rumors of their exploits had quickly spread through the group, embellished by Stretch and Razz. Serge recounted their exploits with the policeman in the Tyrolean Alps, and their status as the coolest guys in the group was firmly established. Mr. Nalysnyk was relieved to have them back and made them promise not to leave the group again.

Stefi was sitting on the bus with Sandy. When Alec approached, Sandy moved to another seat.

"Did you get my note?" Alec asked her.

"Razz gave it to me. He said you wrote it on the floor of some train station."

"It's not like it seems. I really missed you."

"You don't see me for months, and then you take off as soon as I arrive?"

"I'm sorry. I don't know what I'm looking for. Everything seems so meaningless. I'm searching for answers."

"Someday you'll realize that everything you're looking for is right here," she said.

"It's a big world. We're just a small part of it."

"Who's to say that our part isn't the most important of all?" she replied.

"Maybe you're right."

"You promised to protect me," she sniffed, turning to look out the bus window.

He put his hand on her shoulder and kissed her tousled hair. He smelled the familiar scent of hyacinths. For the first time, he noticed that she was wearing her charm bracelet with the gold Eiffel Tower.

"I want to chase the moonlight with my Cinnamon Girl," he said.

"You can't have it all," she replied coolly. "You need to choose."

***

The highlight of the alpine leg of their itinerary was the Passion Play in Oberammergau. It took place only once a decade. The people in the town had promised God back in 1633 that if he spared them from the Black Death they would continue to reenact the Passion Play every decade in perpetuity. The tradition had continued for centuries. Now, the entire town participated in one way or another—as actors, directors, stagehands, or observers. The play lasted for several hours and reenacted the crucifixion of Christ.

The plan was to attend the play, look around town, and meet at the buses at the designated time to take them to Vienna.

On the way to the play, Serge found one of the few bars that was still open. "The play's going to be boring. Let's hang out here instead," he suggested. "We can come in for the Resurrection." Alec and Stefi were happy to comply. So were Razz, Stretch, Chou, and Katya. The bar was empty. The usual patrons were most likely at the play.

"Beer, all the way around," Serge said. "First round is on me." He had recovered the cash that he had left on the bus with the rest of his belongings. The bartender was a weary man who looked like he had seen enough of the world.

"I wonder why he's not at the play?" asked Chou.

"He's probably been in it at least five times," Serge replied. "Same play, over and over. Must get boring after a while. Christ gets crucified, dies, and resurrects after three days. I got it. What I can't figure out is, if Christ is God, why does he have to die?"

"He died for our sins," Katya offered. She was toying with a gold cross that hung from her neck on a delicate chain.

"Why couldn't he just forgive us and be done with it?" Serge countered.

"I think it relates to the cycle of the seasons," Alec surmised. "We talked about it in my World Lit class. In nature, things have to die before they are reborn. It's a common archetype in many cultures."

"Do you guys believe in life after death?" asked Katya.

"I believe in this," Serge said, as he grabbed his balls, and everyone laughed. "I believe in the here and now. Most everything else is bullshit."

"Do you believe in good and evil?" Alec challenged him.

"There's no absolute right or wrong. You just have to make the most of the time you have," he replied.

"Maybe you're right," said Alec, "but I hope there's more to life than that. Otherwise why are we here? I know there's a difference between good and evil. I've lived through it. The choices we make define who we are."

"What happens if you don't want to choose?" asked Katya. "Do you just go to hell?"

"I don't know if there's a heaven or hell, the way we were taught in catechism," Alec replied, "but I do believe there's a spiritual side to us. I guess you can call it a soul. I think to realize it, though, you have to find yourself first."

Razz waved down the bartender. "We'll have another round."

"So how do you find yourself?" Katya asked. "By bumming around Europe?"

Alec was surprised that he had captured her attention. At first, he thought she was just egging him on, but her eyes said otherwise. "I thought I'd find myself by visiting different places, meeting new people, and having new experiences. I've been around the world. I realized on this trip that to find yourself, you have to look inward."

"What do you see when you look inward?" she asked.

"You see yourself for who you really are. It's like the vision you get when you think you're about to die. In Stockholm, I went into this crazy-hot sauna and lost track of time. My body temperature skyrocketed. My whole life flashed in front of me. I had the feeling that I was living my life over again.

Everything seemed to make sense. I was free of the present. Then my friend Bill snapped me out of it. If he hadn't found me, I could have died."

"What happens if you never find yourself," asked Katya.

"Probably nothing," Alec replied. "You waste your opportunity. You become a lost soul—something that could have been but wasn't."

"What do you do once you find your soul?" she pressed. Serge was rolling his eyes.

"You need to redeem it," Alec said and reached for his beer.

"How?"

He thought of Maksym, Taras, and Mariana. "You need to figure out who you are, what you've done, and why you did it. Then you need to figure out what you're going to do. You need to seek forgiveness from those you've wronged."

"My plan is to live it up and repent just before I check out," said Serge. "It gets me to heaven, and I can leave my sins on earth."

"To be forgiven you need to forgive yourself first," Alec said. "You can only repent if you see yourself for who you really are."

Katya leaned forward. Her cross plunged into her cleavage. "So we can erase our sins?"

Alec followed the chain as it disappeared into her bosom. The beer was getting to his head. He wondered if she too was searching for redemption. "I don't think you can change what you've done," Alec replied. "But you can still change yourself."

"That sounds a lot like that transcendental crap that

Father Riley tried to teach us in senior religion class," Razz interjected.

"Each of us is incredibly special," Alec continued, undeterred. "Think about it. We're the product of an endless series of improbabilities. We can believe that our being here is random and meaningless, or we can believe that we're here for a reason."

"What's the reason?" Serge asked. "To serve God?"

"Maybe. We get a rare chance to live, and we should try to make it meaningful. Whether God exists or not, we do. Figuring out who we are seems like a good place to start."

"What if you're wrong?" Serge challenged him. "What if you have no soul? What if all you have is the here and now?"

Alec looked across the empty beer bottles at his best friend. "Then you can at least choose to live your life gracefully."

"Hey, Stretch!" Razz interjected. "Do you remember that song we used to sing to Father Riley when he was feeding us that bullshit? You know ... 'Give me that old time religion. It was good enough for Moses, and it's good enough for me.'"

Alec laughed and joined in the song. Serge and Stretch quickly caught on to the refrain as they continued through the prophets. "It was good enough for Jesus, and it's good enough for me."

The bartender looked at them with a scowl.

Alec downed the last of his beer and put his arm around Stefi. "How about you, Stefi? What do you believe in?"

"I believe in us," she said. She put her hand on his thigh and squeezed. She knew how to bridge the gap between the spiritual and material worlds.

"That's good enough for me," Alec replied.

The conversation switched from metaphysics to politics to sports. They left their empty beer bottles on the table to keep score. After forty-two beers, they got up and left to catch the Resurrection.

***

When the buses pulled into Vienna that evening, Stefi was asleep on Alec's shoulder. He reflected on the discussion he'd had with his friends in the bar in Oberammergau. It might just have been sophomore philosophy, but it felt good to transcend the superficial chatter. He felt like a character in Dostoevsky's *Notes from the Underground*, who would refuse to leave a bar at daybreak because he and his friends had not yet resolved the question of the existence of God. He convinced himself that getting to the truth of things was important. *It's why we are here*, he thought. Sharing what you've learned with people you care about was also important.

The group checked into a youth hostel that accommodated over two hundred guests. The beds were laid out in military rows in four large rooms, two rooms for the boys and two for the girls. Their group occupied all but about fifty of the beds; the rest of the hostel was filled with students from Europe and the Americas. The hostel operator warned them that theft was common, and that for a small fee they could keep their valuables in the lockers. There were only seventy-five lockers, each with a single key, so Alec shared his locker with Stretch.

Alec and Stefi had planned their first full day in Vienna on the bus ride from Oberammergau. They needed to reconnect with each other. At breakfast, she'd playfully stuck her finger in his ear. "Today, you're mine," she said. "Today, I'm not sharing you with anyone. You promised to take me on the Ferris wheel."

The Ferris wheel at Prater was their ultimate destination, but Alec wanted to save it for the evening. First, they toured the heart of Vienna. They drank Viennese coffee at a small café near Stephansplatze. They climbed the 343 steps to the tower at St. Stephen's Cathedral, from where they could see the Ferris wheel in the distance. For lunch, they bought some bread, cheese, and beer and picnicked in the Green Prater before entering the amusement park. Their conversation was light—neither wanted to delve into the whys and why-nots of the last several weeks.

As the sun was beginning to set, they bought their tickets for the Ferris wheel and climbed into the swinging wagon that would take them high above the park. Through their windows they could see the lights of the city. Alec snuck his hand down the back of Stefi's skirt and past the elastic in her panties. From her body language he knew it was exactly what she wanted.

"I have a confession to make," she said. Alec flinched and started to take his hand out of her panties. "No, nothing like that," she said and pulled his hand back down. "I bewitched you." She laughed.

"Bewitched me? How?"

"At summer camp in Wisconsin, on the eve of the feast of Ivana Kupala, I made a flower wreath for you. I lit a candle, placed it in the wreath, and let it float down the river, knowing it would somehow reach you. I said a prayer that if you ever swam in a river while you were away, you would fall under my spell. You would be mine forever."

"I swam in the Dnipro," he said. "I swam in the Vrbas."

"See? I knew it would work!" she beamed.

"And what kind of spell was it?"

"A love spell. That I would be the only girl that you would ever truly love."

Alec looked out the window over the waxing moon that was rising over Vienna. He knew in his heart that her spell had worked.

***

When Alec and Stefi returned to the hostel near midnight, Mr. Nalysnyk was waiting for them in the lobby.

"We lost track of the time—" Alec began.

"There's been a theft," Mr. Nalysnyk interrupted. "Your locker was broken into."

"My locker? And how many others?"

"Only yours. They stole the passports and the cameras."

Alec immediately realized what had happened. They were after *his* passport and his camera. They wanted to know what happened to him when they lost track of him in Constanta. They needed to account for the missing month. He thought he had escaped. He thought they were done with him. Why was his fate so important to them? Other than pure paranoia, it made no sense. How did they know which locker was his? Now, Stretch was yet another innocent victim of his misadventures.

Alec suddenly realized who had taken the photo in the Rockies. The revelation hit him like a bullet to the back of the head. Then he dismissed the possibility just as quickly. The betrayal was too great to contemplate. "It's a city of thieves," he said to Mr. Nalysnyk.

Mr. Nalysnyk looked at him with suspicion. "Are you

sure there's nothing more to it?"

"No," Alec replied. "They got my camera. It's a Zeiss. It's worth a lot of money. Luckily I had my wallet on me."

"I've called the embassy," Mr. Nalysnyk said. "You have an appointment there at nine in the morning. It will take at least two days to get temporary passports. We're leaving the day after tomorrow. You'll need to catch up to us in Italy by train."

"Where's the first overnight stop?"

"Parma," Mr. Nalysnyk replied. "I'll give you the co-ordinates."

Alec looked over at Stefi. "Did you bring my letters with you to Europe?"

"Yes."

"Ask one of your girlfriends to hold on to them for you until we get back home."

"OK, but—"

"Trust me. Just do it. I'll explain later."

***

Alec awoke in the dark. For a terrifying moment, he thought he was back in the camp in Lviv. He looked under the bed to see if a cord was running into the mattress. The reassuring snores of his friends reoriented him. The light from the streetlights glowed through the windows and cast moving shadows on the ceiling. They circled his bed like ghosts. He recollected fragments of horrific dreams about betrayal, confinement, and dismemberment. He felt the chill of the Rockies. He smelled sweet tobacco and acetaldehyde. He heard paper tearing. Dead eyes stared at him through spectacles. He recalled how the mirrors in the Tivoli fun house had cut his body into pieces. His mind flashed to the men's room in Tivoli. "Silly boy," the blonde girl had said. He wondered if he was silly or simply a fool.

***

CHAPTER 23

While most of their stays had been in youth hostels and scouting camps, Parma was different. It was an actual hotel with an outdoor swimming pool and a patio. When Alec and Stretch arrived at the hotel two days after the rest of the group, it was already dark—Serge had saved a place for Alec in his room—and most of the Chicago group were hanging around the patio by the pool. Stefi ran up to him and kissed him to show Katya and the other girls that Alec was off limits. Serge threw him a key. "You got the bed by the window," he said. "Throw your stuff in there and then come out here and join the party. Stretch, you come too."

"What are you guys drinking?" asked Alec. "Water?"

"Exactly," said Serge. He passed a glass to Alec.

Alec took a gulp and coughed. "It's straight rum!"

"You got it," Serge said, and everyone laughed. "You're way behind us. You need to take some penalty shots." Alec picked up the glass and downed the remaining third, while everyone yelled, "Chug, chug, chug." It burned the back of his throat and almost came up twice. Serge refilled the glass to the top and began to pass it around again. Except for a New Jersey girl nicknamed Hot Pants, the girls took mainly ceremonious sips. The boys, on the other hand, were eager to outdo one another. Any boy who didn't take a manly swig was labeled a needle dick.

"Where's Sandy?" Alec asked.

"You didn't hear?" Serge replied. "He had to go to the hospital to get some stitches."

"Why, what happened?"

"Ask your girlfriend," Serge replied. "She's the one who was flirting with him."

Stefi turned red. "We were just fooling around," she said. "Remember you told me about his lucky panties? Well, he brought them to play volleyball at Suzy-Q. I found them in his bag and ran to show them to the rest of the group. He started chasing me, and I closed a glass door behind me. He didn't see the door and crashed through it."

"Is he OK?" Alec asked.

"I think so," she replied. "He cut his forehead, but I think he's going to be OK."

"I can't leave you alone for a day without your causing some trouble," Alec said, half jokingly. His image of Stefi was sliding from innocent to flirtatious. His woolen mitten was starting to get crowded. "Time to drink!" he said. "Pour me some more of that stuff."

Another East Coast girl named Melanie poured him a

healthy shot of rum, and Alec downed it in one swig.

It didn't take long to lose control. Serge, not wanting to be outdone, filled the glass to the brim and drank it all down in one long swig. His inebriation accelerated like a rocket. He insisted that every girl at the table give him a kiss, which they did. Melanie and Katya took turns sitting on his lap, but Melanie politely changed seats when his groping became too public. "Let's dance," said Katya.

Serge and Katya proceeded to slow dance without music. Serge's steps were becoming increasingly faster and less stable. Out of the blue, he began to do cartwheels around the pool.

"Amazing," laughed Razz. "I didn't know he could do that."

"He probably didn't know it either, until now," said Chou.

Alec admired Serge's ability to seize the moment. The show stopped when Mr. Nalysnyk suddenly appeared and ordered everyone back to the rooms. He took Serge aside, but in the middle of their conversation, Serge began to sway. Mr. Nalysnyk walked up to the table and tasted what was in the water glass. He looked at Alec, who was doing his best imitation of sobriety. "I don't care if you're over eighteen. Drinking is forbidden. Get him back to the room," he said. "We'll talk about this in the morning."

Alec had hoped to spend an intimate night with Stefi, but the evening again ended in frustration. It seemed to him that the world was conspiring to keep them apart.

***

The celebration of mass with the Ukrainian patriarch at St. Sophia's in Rome was the religious apex of the Flight of Freedom Tour. For Ukrainian Catholics, meeting His Beatitude Cardinal Josyf Slipyj was more important than an audience with the Holy Father himself. The patriarch had been the archbishop of Lviv and successor to Sheptytsky before being arrested by the NKVD—the People's Commissariat for Internal Affairs—during the war and sentenced to hard labor in the Siberian Gulag. Pope Pius XII had secretly named him a cardinal. He was freed from the Gulag after President Kennedy and Pope John XXIII pressured Khrushchev for his release in time to participate in the Second Vatican Council. Ukrainian Catholics revered him as their patriarch, even though Pope Paul VI refused to grant him that title. Slipyj embodied the very soul of the Ukrainian Catholic Church.

Alec wanted to meet Slipyj. The patriarch had endured the Gulag and it had not broken him. He was good when those around him had lost faith in goodness. Alec needed to know where he found his strength. Was it simply faith?

Alec believed in God, but he found it hard to believe in the cruel God of the Old Testament, who was constantly testing man and finding him wanting. Alec had been a dutiful Catholic. He had been baptized and confirmed, confessed his sins, and had taken Holy Communion over a thousand times. Every morning at St. Nicholas Grammar School began with the celebration of mass in the cathedral. The religious mosaics were engrained in his brain. As a child, he had prayed to his guardian angel before going to sleep. As a boy, he had prayed to the Blessed Virgin Mary when he was in need. As a teenager he had drunk holy water at Lourdes. Yet there was much about the church that disturbed him.

When he was seven, his father had given him a dollar to buy penny candies at the school store during lunch. A dime would have sufficed, so he decided to do a good deed, spend the entire dollar, and give the candy away to all of the children in his second-grade class. Sister Teresa sold him the bag of candy with a scowl. After recess was over, he was expecting her to praise him for his benevolence. Instead, she pulled him out from behind his desk by his ear, made him kneel by the blackboard with his arms extended, and placed a heavy book in each hand.

"You glutton!" she screamed.

He was shocked and confused. He began to cry. Instead of being rewarded for his good deed, he was publically declared a sinner and crucified in front of his peers. Why had God not informed the good sister that he was anything but a glutton? After an agonizing several minutes, a girl was brave enough to raise her hand and say, "Sister, he bought the candy for all of us." Sister Teresa did not concede her error. She had made her point that sinners have to suffer.

Crimes against humanity were committed in the name of God. The Inquisition had tortured, mutilated, and killed innocents for heresy in order to save their souls. Men of the cloth had burned young women at the stake whose only sin may have been madness or a desire to commune with nature. The church had tried and imprisoned Galileo for seeking the truth through science.

Still, Alec believed that Christ had died for our sins to redeem our souls. He believed in the words of Jesus and in a kingdom of God that was not of this earth. He just wasn't sure that man had interpreted God's words correctly. He needed to find out for himself. There was comfort in knowing that if you lived your life according to the teachings of the church that you would find eternal salvation. If you stayed within the flock the shepherd would deliver you from evil. He wondered if the sheep that strayed from the flock—not through sin but through curiosity of the world around it—would also be saved. He hoped so.

The youth assembled in the courtyard of St. Sophia's Church, awaiting the entrance of the patriarch. There were too many of them to fit inside the church, so mass would be celebrated outside. It was sunny, and they were hot, dressed in their full uniforms. The uniforms were decorated with badges. Alec's uniform was sparser than most. He wore the insignia of the Brotherhood on his right arm. He had two badges over his heart from the children's camps where he had served as commandant. He could have added many more, but those were the few that held real meaning for him.

The patriarch made his entrance at the end of a procession of altar boys and priests. He was a tall man with a long white beard. On his head he wore a stiff headpiece—a *kamilavka*—with a cross and white veil. His eyes were alive, unlike the eyes of his inquisitor in Chernivtsi.

The patriarch began to sing the High Mass. His voice was strong and unwavering. Alec also knew most of the Mass of St. John the Chrysostom by heart. He had listened to it a thousand times before. What he enjoyed most about the mass was the choral music of the Eastern rite.

The patriarch's sermon was not pious; it was political.

"My dearly beloved. Today I will talk about the need for great deeds. Those who have come before you have begun the work of building Ukraine, but it is up to you to you to finish it. If there is hope, if there is a future, then the future is up to you. I pray that you young people will take the burden on your shoulders. There is a great deal that needs to be done. Perhaps in a few years, when I have stepped out of the arena, you will enter to take my place. The work of gaining our freedom must continue. Only God knows what the future holds. We must each work to reclaim our rights to profess our faith and practice our religion. These are the God-given rights of every man …"

Alec's thoughts were beginning to drift in the heat of the day. He had been expecting to receive insight into the spiritual rather than the material world. He had done his great deed. *But it's not just what you say,* he figured, *it's how you choose to live your life.* The man himself was inspiration enough. At the end of mass, the youth filed up to the patriarch to kiss his ring. When Alec kissed the jeweled ring, he was hoping to experience a flow of grace. He hoped that some of the goodness in the man would enlighten the darker reaches of his soul. But he did not experience the spiritual enlightenment he was hoping for. Perhaps he was not worthy enough, even though he had confessed his sins to the Orthodox priest in Banja Luka. Or perhaps he too had become a lost soul, with little hope of escaping the current.

***

At dinner that evening, Mr. Nalysnyk announced that they would be having guests. A glee club from St. Patrick's High School in Detroit was on a European tour and would be performing for them after dinner in the church hall. The Ukrainian Youth, in exchange, would sing some Ukrainian songs and perform some Ukrainian dances. The glee club was made up of about thirty students. The lead singer was a black boy with a wide smile and a booming voice. Their first number was "Oh Happy Day," a joyous gospel song that was clearly one of their favorites. They followed it with "America the Beautiful."

This is the best of America, Alec thought. *Not a melting pot, but a place where people from all over the world are welcome and can maintain and share their cultures.* Everyone other than the Native Americans had come from elsewhere, but they had left behind their troubles and brought their hopes and dreams with them.

Now it was the Ukrainians' turn to perform. Ukrainian music was beautiful of itself, but the dancing was particularly rousing. They decided to perform the Arkan and finish with the Hopak. The Arkan was the traditional Hutsul dance, which was danced in a circle, often around a fire. The Hopak was the dance of the Cossacks—it was wild, acrobatic, and free. The key male step was the *prycidka*, in which the men would dance from a crouched, almost sitting position, kicking out their legs in rhythm to the music. There were countless variations, some imitating swordplay, others drunken rolls, and the most dramatic, high leaps into the air. In addition to the standard choreography, the dancers gathered in a circle and tried to outdo one another with their moves. The result was a dance that began civilly enough but then crescendoed into a wild free-for-all until the dancers were all exhausted. Alec stopped taking Ukrainian dance lessons at the age of twelve, when the instructor had forced the boys to wear tights. Now, he regretted quitting, because he would have loved to join his friends in dancing the Hopak. Stefi had danced in one of the troupes and thrilled the crowd with her spritely steps and engaging smile. It was moments like this that made him proud to be Ukrainian.

After the performance, the singers and dancers intermingled in the church hall. There was great positive energy in the room. Hearts were still racing, pheromones were flying, and new friendships were igniting from the spark that was their shared love of music and dance. This wasn't the sterile, homogenizing effect of a Top 10 pop culture, Alec realized. It was the liberating effect of diversity. *We can all be very different, and we can all still be Americans. That is the promise of America. There is hope for us in America*, Alec thought. His parents' generation had isolated themselves in the comfort of ethnic ghettoes. They had built churches and schools and financial institutions, all with Ukrainian names and Ukrainian members. It was a remarkable generation—fleeing the horrors of World War II as teenagers, living communally in displaced persons camps, emigrating to the Free World, and building vibrant communities in the diaspora. Their kids were trapped between two worlds; they were Ukrainian and everyone else was "American."

Alec had been born in Champaign, Illinois—in "the heart of the heart of the country," as he liked to say. Yet had he been born in a Displaced Persons camp in Regensburg, like his cousin Zack, his life in America would not have been much different.

"I was born in Clinton, Illinois," the black singer replied when Alec told him of his roots. "My name's Trevonne. We're practically neighbors."

"I really enjoyed your gospel number."

"I've got to learn some of those crazy Ukrainian dance moves," Trevonne replied. "What other kind of music do you like?"

"I'm pretty eclectic. Stones, folk rock, blues ..."

"How does a white-ass Ukrainian dig the blues?" Trevonne asked, laughing.

"Easy. I'm from Chicago."

Trevonne let out a long hearty laugh. "You're my man," he said.

"God bless America," Alec replied, and he meant it.

***

Alec stood in the forum at Pompeii and stared out at the silhouette of Mount Vesuvius. The sun-washed ruins belied the horror of what had happened here almost two millennia before. Their tour buses had brought them from the Eternal City to the City of the Dead. It was an obligatory stop for most educational tours of Europe. The city was preserved almost as it was; there was still carbonized bread in the bakery ovens and fruit in glass jars in the merchants' shops. Only the inhabitants were missing. Even their bodies were gone. All that remained were the "hollow men": plaster casts made from the cavities in the volcanic ash where they had been buried alive.

Alec had read the eyewitness account of Pliny the Younger in Latin class at Loyola. He remembered translating the terrifying lines: *"You could hear the shrieks of women, the wailing of infants, and the shouting of men. ... Many besought the aid of the gods, but still more imagined there were not gods left and that the universe was plunged into eternal darkness."*

"Alec, you have to see the brothels," Stefi called out to him from across the forum, "and the public toilets. They're really cool!"

Most of the kids were scampering around the ruins without guidebooks, oblivious to the historical significance of what they were seeing. Alec preferred to understand what he was looking at. He had bought a guidebook of the ruins for a few thousand liras at the entrance to the excavations and was working his way through the highlights. Now, he sidetracked his planned route to join Stefi and see the brothels.

"Do you remember in Oberammergau when Katya asked if we believed in life after death?" he asked.

"Yeah, what about it?"

"We never answered the question."

"So?"

"So all those people who died here … do you think they live on?"

"What are you talking about?"

"Do you think they found eternal life, or did their existence end here?"

"I think they live on," she replied.

"Do you think they were redeemed?"

"The good went to heaven, the bad went to hell, and the others went to purgatory."

"Do you really believe that?"

"I want to believe that," she replied. "I was raised a Catholic, just like you. I believe that Christ died for our sins, so that we could defeat death and live forever."

"And you believe in heaven and hell?"

"I believe we live on. I don't know if it's hell or Hades, but heaven sounds like the place to be," she replied.

"If there was no life after death, how would you imagine it to be?" he asked.

"Like nothing."

"What do you mean?"

"Do you remember what it was like during the Second World War?" she asked him.

"Of course not; I wasn't born yet."

"So if there is no life after death, then you won't know it either—it's pretty much the same, isn't it?"

"So what really matters is that we're living here and

now?" he asked. "But it's not enough. What if we weren't caught in the current? What if we could go back and forth, like a water bug in a stream?"

"I don't think you could change things," she said. "There's a lot I would have done differently if I could, but I can't go back. You said yourself that you can only change things going forward."

"Life is too short," Alec replied. "We're here, and then we're gone. For some, like those who died here, death grabs them before they can figure things out. Some were just children; others were in the womb. There has to be something more."

"You want to live forever," she said.

"We all do. It's our biggest fear—that there is nothing beyond death, that *this* is all there is. That's why boys want to be immortalized as heroes—so they can live on, at least in the imagination of others."

"So you want a constellation named after you?"

"No." He put his hand on the nape of her neck and kissed her smiling lips. "Like you said, I want our love to live on forever, even it's only in the minds of others—like Romeo and Juliet, Anthony and Cleopatra, Alec and Stefi …"

"Alec and Stefi?" she interjected. "Why does your name always come first?"

"OK, Stefi and Alec," he conceded. As they passed the brothel, Razz peeked out and called out, "Hey guys, you have to see this." He pointed to an erotic fresco of a prostitute and client, lying on a bed, with him entering her from behind. "Pretty damn hot," Razz concluded.

"That's the other way to defeat death," Alec said to Stefi. "The rapture of orgasm. For that brief moment, we seem immortal."

"And art," she replied. "Whoever painted that fresco, we're still admiring their work today."

"Hey Razz, Stefi and I have figured out how to live forever. You can be a hero, an artist, or a great lover."

"What's there to figure out?" Razz said. "I've got to go find myself a girl."

CHAPTER 24

Paris was the last stop on the Flight of Freedom tour. Stefi was in seventh heaven. She peered out of the window of the bus and poked Alec every time she saw something romantic, which was about twice every minute. Her older sister had come to Paris after college and had fallen in love with a boy from Buyukada who was tending his aunt's hotel. Stefi could not imagine anything more romantic.

Stefi leaned over toward Alec and put her tongue in his ear. "You and I were meant to come here," she whispered. She reached into her purse and pulled out her charm bracelet. "Can you put it on for me?"

Alec took the bracelet from her and looked at the gold charms. They were the usual charms of a teenage girl—a four-leaf clover, a teddy bear, a diploma, and the Eiffel Tower that he had given her.

"This one is my favorite," he said as he fastened it onto her wrist.

"Mine too." She fondled the Eiffel Tower. "Do you love me?" she asked suddenly.

Alec was startled by the obviousness of her question. "Yes, I love you."

"Am I the only love in your life?" she asked tentatively.

"You're the only one I love."

She put her head on his shoulder. "I've felt you drifting away from me," she said. "I thought I would lose you."

"I've been confused," he said. "I just needed to find myself first."

"I worry that I'm not good enough for you, that you'll find someone prettier, more accomplished. I may act flirtatious and sure of myself, but deep inside, I'm not sure of myself at all. I worry that I'm not good enough."

"Stop ..."

"No, let me finish. I never had the things you had. I never traveled to Europe. My parents aren't doctors or engineers. The only time I got close to realizing my dreams was in eighth grade, when Sister Anna said I would be an angel in the St. Mary May Day procession."

"You must have been a beautiful angel."

"No, my mother came home late from work and got me to the procession just before it started. Sister Anna had already given my robe and wings to another girl. I cried for a week. Nothing good or exciting happened to me until you came along. A Northwestern boy in a Karmann Ghia, picking me up from high school—I was the envy of my friends! You're my rock. You're my everything. Don't ever leave me."

Alec put his arm around her, looked into her frightened eyes, and kissed her. "Don't worry," he said. "We're soul mates. No matter what happens to us in the future, you will always be a part of me."

"I'm never letting you go," she said and moved her hand up his thigh. Suddenly, she bolted up. "Oh look, look! I can see the Eiffel Tower!"

Alec looked out the window, where the Eiffel Tower rose in the distance. "Beautiful," he said, "and very romantic."

"My sister told me what we have to see. We'll start at the Left Bank, then go to Notre Dame, the Louvre, Tuileries Garden, Champs de Elysees, and finish at the Eiffel Tower." Stefi was beaming. The last time Alec had seen her so happy was on the rocks by Northwestern when he had given her the golden charm.

***

Stefi and Alec left the hostel right after breakfast and took the metro to St. Michele. They had only two and a half days in Paris, and there was so much to see. Stefi wore a white blouse over her blue jeans. The blouse was tied at the waist with an embroidered cloth belt. They wandered down the narrow streets of the Left Bank past cafès, bistros, bookstores, and shops. The streets were already bustling with tourists. Alec was drawn to a rack of postcards in front of a souvenir shop. The postcards were in black-and-white and depicted scenes from Paris in a bygone era. In one, a group of eight young men in suits were gawking at a young, well-dressed Parisian woman. In another, a man with a waxed moustache and bowler hat sat at a café table with an enormous mug of beer.

"Stefi, take a look at these." On the rack with the colored postcards were two other postcards that caught his eye. The first was an aquarelle of a young boy with a Beatles haircut and a guitar, hitching a ride. The second was an aquarelle of a blonde girl with a bindle, walking along the Seine. "These remind me of us," he said. He pulled out two francs and bought them.

"That might be you," she said. "You would hitchhike all over Europe if you could."

"Wouldn't you?"

"No. This is fun, but I miss home. I want you home with me."

"Do you smell that?" he asked. The aroma of chocolate, cinnamon, and burnt orange came from a creperie stand across the street. Alec walked over and ordered two Grand Marnier crepes, which were folded into triangles and served hot in napkins.

"Are you still thinking of staying in Europe?" Stefi asked.

"No."

"What made you change your mind?"

"Two things," he replied. "First—and most important—you did. Second, I thought I needed to get away to find myself, but now I think the answers I'm looking for are closer to home."

"What do you mean?"

"I was questioning my direction in life. I was rebelling against my background and my upbringing."

"And you're not now?"

"It's complicated," he said. "Being Ukrainian is who I am. I didn't choose it, but it's still who I am. I'm also American.

I need to find out where I fit in. The best place to figure it out is back home in America. Here in Europe, I'm just a drifter with no roots, a displaced person like my parents."

"Well I'm glad, for our sake, that you came to your senses."

"Your hot body brought me to my senses."

"You got that right." She took his hand and led him across the Petit Pont bridge toward Île de la Cité, the natural island on the Seine that housed the Notre Dame cathedral. She stopped at the arch in the bridge and pointed to an old building a stone's throw from the cathedral. "Do you see that window up on the top floor? That's where my sister lived when she first came to Paris. She showed me the building in a photo."

"It must have been pretty neat," Alec said. "Living in the heart of Paris in an apartment overlooking the Seine."

"She loved it. She's like you—she was trying to find herself. She found her soul mate, and they went off to California together. From the way she talks about Paris, I'm pretty sure they'll be back."

Notre Dame reigned over the Île de la Cité in all her splendor. Masons and pilgrims had dedicated their lives to her over the centuries. Alec found the fantastic gargoyles on Notre Dame's edifice to be the most interesting architectural features.

"Each one looks different from down here," he said. "The stoneworkers let their imaginations go wild."

"Sister Chrysanthemum told us the story in our Art and Architecture class of how they started," Stefi said. "A fire-breathing dragon named Gargouille was terrorizing the people of Rouen. The people fed him convicts to keep him from burning down the town."

"In the movies, those dragons always prefer maidens,"

Alec interjected.

Stefi laughed. "I think they might have thrown in a maiden or two on holidays. Anyway, this saint named Romain offered to kill the dragon if the people got baptized and build a church."

"Was he like a St. George or something?"

"No, not at all. He subdued the dragon with a crucifix and then led him back into town on a leash made from his robe."

"If he used his robe, then what was he wearing?"

"Stop it! Let me finish the story. So the townspeople killed the dragon and burned him, except that the head and neck didn't burn because they were too tempered from his own fiery breath. They then hung those remains on a wall, and it became the first gargoyle."

"Pretty cool."

"I thought you'd like that story. Come on—we have to go in and see the rose windows."

They entered through the Portail de Sainte-Anne into the womb of the cathedral. They bowed and crossed themselves in the style of the Eastern rite.

"It's beautiful," Stefi said. He held her hand as they marveled together at the glory of God and the art of man.

***

The Louvre was overwhelming. Works of art that captured moments in time and place—lovers and landscapes, virgin births and crucifixions, triumphs and tragedies—were all assembled and concentrated in one place. When an individual work caught someone's eye, it was only for the briefest of moments, as hundreds more cried out for attention.

"We need to have a plan," Alec recommended. "Let's pick just a few things we really want to see. We would need several lifetimes to appreciate them all."

"I want to see the *Mona Lisa*," Stefi replied. "How about you?"

"I want to see *Winged Victory*."

The statue of the *Winged Victory of Samothrace* stood in a vestibule at the top of a flight of stairs. Even incomplete, she was magnificent. The statue portrayed the goddess Nike on the prow of a ship, celebrating a victory at sea. Her wings were outstretched as her robe rippled against her body in the wind. What Alec found most intriguing was the balance and tenseness of the muscles in her legs as she weathered the sea and the wind.

"She has your legs," Alec pointed out to Stefi.

"Who is she?"

"Nike, the goddess of victory."

"Why is victory female?"

"I don't know," Alec replied. "War is male. I guess men fight, but it's the women who choose the victor in the end."

"So I get to decide if you're my victor or not?"

"That must be the way it works."

"I'm going to have to think about this one," Stefi replied. "You haven't told me what great deeds you've done to earn me."

"Love isn't enough?"

"Oh, I don't know. Girls want their princes and heroes. Are you my prince?"

"I'll be your prince. I thought I could be your hero, but sometimes the dragon wins."

"What do you mean?"

"Someday I'll explain it to you," he said.

"If you had a son, what would you name him?" she asked.

"I like the name Nike ... Victory. I guess the male equivalent would be Nick. I would name my son Nicholas."

"So would I," she replied and rushed off toward the *Mona Lisa* before he could respond.

Alec found her on the fringe of a crowd of admirers, all trying to get a glimpse of the most famous painting in the world. Stefi deftly worked her way through the crowd and disappeared for a full minute, as the rest pushed and elbowed to budge her from her vantage point. Then she popped out with a smile.

"You're not going to see her?" she asked.

"No, it's way too crowded. I've seen her before. So what do you think?"

"Much smaller than I imagined, but she really does look right at you. It's like she knows something that she's not telling."

"I find that to be true of most girls."

"We like to keep you guessing."

There really is a mystery to the Mona Lisa, *he thought, and Stefi is right—it's that she knows something that you don't and is tempting you to find out what it is.*

"How's my smile?" Stefi asked.

"There's a mystery about you too," Alec replied, "but it's not just in your smile. Your smile lights up a room. It's the rest of you that I can't figure out."

"I just have to keep you guessing," she laughed. "Time to go—I want to see the Garden."

***

The Tuileries Garden had been a playground for ordinary Parisians since the nineteenth century. Stefi's sister had spent her summer afternoons in the Garden when she had lived in Paris. She delighted Stefi with stories of puppet shows, acrobats, boats, and donkey rides. The formal basins and plantings contrasted with the informality of children running, lovers kissing, and tourists taking photos. Stefi saw Razz and Sandy ogling some French girls and ran over to meet them.

"Hi, guys! I thought you'd be holed up in some bar on the Left Bank," she said.

"We brought the wine with us," Sandy replied. He pulled out a half-empty bottle of white wine and offered it to Stefi and Alec.

Stefi took a sip and immediately made a face. "This stuff is terrible. What is it?"

"It's chicken wine," Razz replied. "We walked into a grocery store and asked for some white wine. The guy didn't understand us, so I pretended I was pouring a glass and Sandy was flapping his hands like a chicken. The guy said, '*Oui, vin de poulet*,' and this is what he gave us. You just have to guzzle it quickly without tasting it."

Alec heeded his advice and took a gulp, trying to avoid his taste buds. "I think it's cooking wine," he said. "It's not meant for drinking."

"The person who has the last sip is the chicken," Sandy yelled out, and the three of them took off running in different directions. Alec figured there was no way he was going to catch Sandy, so he took off after Razz. As he ran after him, he almost knocked over a stroller. The mother gave him a dirty look, but he turned around long enough to say "*Pardon*" before resuming his sprint. Razz was now a quarter of the way around the basin, and there would be no way to cut him off. He needed a new target, so he went after Stefi.

Stefi and Sandy were hiding behind the statue of Nymphe. Alec mingled with a group of nuns in starched white habits that were circling the basin. They did not seem to mind a fox in their midst. He snuck up to the Nymphe statue from behind and grabbed Stefi around her waist. "Now you're the chicken!"

"How did you sneak up on us?" she laughed.

"I got a little help from some friends."

She lunged toward him faster than he anticipated, and he barely dodged her tag. The promenade was packed with tourists, and he had nowhere to maneuver without knocking over more strollers. He jumped knee-deep into the Tuileries fountain. Stefi was not deterred. She kicked off her shoes and jumped in after him until they both tumbled in the water.

"You think the fountain would stop me?" she asked. Her white linen blouse was soaked, revealing the swells of her breasts. She was panting from exertion. She straddled him and pushed his head under the water. They were like kids playing in the water. She had her face to the sun, and whenever she would let his head out of the water, he saw her vivid green eyes, sun-drenched hair, and smile that lit up the Tuileries Garden. She was a rainbow in the fountain. She could make all his troubles disappear.

"Thought you could get away from me so easily?" she asked. "I'm not going to let you get away again."

"You two are attracting a crowd," Razz said as he pointed to the nuns who were ogling them from the edge of the basin. "I see some bushes over there. You might want to bring it to a climax," he joked.

"Not so soon," Stefi said. "I need to make him pay first. He has a lot of making up to do." She got up slowly, making sure to press her knee against his groin to see if she had gotten the reaction she expected. She had. "I'm hot and wet," she said. "Let's get an ice cream cone. I saw an ice cream vendor on the other side of the basin."

"Not for me," Sandy said. "Razz and I are sticking with wine."

Alec took off his shirt and wrung out the water; then he and Stefi walked over to the ice cream vendor. "What flavor would you like?" he asked.

"Pistachio, if he has it."

Alec nodded and said to the vendor, "One cone of pistachio."

"*Oui. Un pistache. Quatre francs.*" The vendor scooped out a generous cone and presented it to Stefi. "*Pour mademoiselle,*" he said with a wink as he leered at her wet figure.

Stefi took the cone and tasted the ice cream with the tip of her tongue. She looked at Alec with her green eyes and began circling the cone with her tongue, as the warm sun sent green trickles down the side of the cone. She then put the entire top of the cone into her mouth and brought it out again. "Bet you didn't think I could do that," she said.

"Pretty impressive. What other surprises do you have for me?" he asked.

"Do you want to taste it?"

"It looks delicious."

Stefi put the ice cream cone back in her mouth and then pulled it out and gave Alec a long, French kiss. Her tongue tasted of pistachio.

"You're delicious," he said.

"You haven't tasted anything yet," she purred.

"You drive me over the rainbow."

***

The last day of the tour began with mass at the Cathedral of St. Volodomyr the Great on Rue de Saints Peres. Uniforms were obligatory. In his sermon, the pastor explained why this cathedral was sacred to Ukrainians. Simon Petlura, the Ukrainian national hero, had been pronounced dead on this very spot. He was shot on May 25, 1925, just a few blocks away, by Sholom Schwartzbard, a Ukrainian-born Jew. The site on which the cathedral was built was once a hospital.

Alec had learned about Petlura in Ukrainian Saturday school. He had been head of the newly independent state between 1917 and 1920, until it was taken over by the Bolsheviks. Since Petlura had died on this very spot, he was curious to learn more. When mass was over, he opened the side gate of the wooden iconostas and ventured into the sacristy where the pastor was removing his vestments.

"Glory to Jesus Christ," Alec said.

The pastor was surprised that someone was bold enough to cross the iconostas without being invited. "How can I help you, my son?"

"I had a question about your sermon."

"Yes?"

"You had said that Petlura was not an anti-Semite. He had forbidden pogroms, yet he was killed by a Ukrainian Jew."

"Despite his orders, thousands of Jews were killed

during the conflict. Schwartzbard claimed he was avenging the deaths of his brothers and sisters."

"Could Schwartzbard have been working for the Soviets? I mean, they admitted to killing Bandera. Wasn't it in their interest to assassinate the leader of the Ukrainian independence movement?"

"At his trial, the prosecution tried to prove that Schwartzbard was a Soviet agent, but he was acquitted. Petlura's wife was awarded one franc in damages."

"Do you think he was a Soviet agent?"

"I think the Soviets are capable of anything," the pastor replied. "His two sisters, Orthodox nuns who had remained in Ukraine, were arrested and shot by the NKVD. It was long ago—an important part of our history but long ago."

After mass they were driven to Montparnasse Cemetery to lay flowers on Petlura's grave. Alec recalled the Patriarch's sermon in Rome on the need for great deeds. Petlura, Schwartzbard, and the Bolsheviks were indeed all guilty of great deeds.

***

Alec was glad that he and Stefi had walked through Paris by themselves the day before. Seeing Paris through a tour bus window was not the same as frolicking in the fountain in the Tuileries Garden. The one highlight they were still missing was the Eiffel Tower.

"There it is!" Stefi pointed through the window. "We're getting closer."

The buses parked by Trocadero, and the kids piled out to see the sites. Mr. Nalysnyk instructed them to be back before sunset. Their flight was departing from Luxembourg the next morning, and their buses would need to leave Paris at midnight.

"My sister told me that the best view is from Palais de Chaillot." She ran ahead to convince herself that it was. Alec and Razz walked quickly but soon had to jog just to keep up with her. She wanted to be the first one there.

"This is the spot! It's perfect," Stefi said. "Razz, take a picture of us with my camera but make sure that you catch the Eiffel Tower. I want to keep this picture forever. Take your time." She handed him her Kodak Brownie, took Alec by the hand, and walked toward the monument until she was sure that they wouldn't be overheard.

"I've been waiting for this moment all summer. I want it to be perfect."

"So you've been planning this all along?" Alec said with a smile. "I always thought of you as spontaneous."

"Do you remember the moment when you gave this to me?" She raised her hand to reveal the gold charm on her wrist.

"Yes. It seems like a lifetime ago."

"Well, now we're here with the real thing. I can't imagine anything more romantic. I thought I might lose you, but you came back to me."

"You could have given up on me."

She put her arms around his neck and thrust her hips up against his. "Do you remember how I danced with you?" she asked. She started to sway her hips to the rhythm of a song that he had almost forgotten.

Alec felt the same intense attraction that had bewitched him during their first dance. He gazed into her sea-green eyes. Their hips were opposite poles of a magnet. He couldn't and didn't want to resist the pull. She was no longer the innocent schoolgirl that he had imagined her to be. She was the woman who had captured his heart and soul. She felt the erection in his pants and drew herself even closer.

"Do you love me?" she asked.

"Yes." Alec didn't need to think about his reply. "I've loved you since the day I met you. I love you now and forever."

"Hey, guys, it's just a photo," Razz shouted out. "I'm not making a movie."

Alec cradled the small of her back with both hands and said, "Lean back. Let yourself go." Stefi leaned back until the Eiffel Tower rose between them in all its magnificence. Alec leaned forward and kissed her open lips.

"You're whole again," she whispered.

"Got it," Razz shouted. "This one's for the cover of *Life* magazine!"

* * *

Stefi slept on Alec's shoulder for most of the plane ride from Paris to Kennedy Airport. They covered themselves with an airplane blanket. He loved holding her in his arms and whispering naughty things in her ear when she was asleep. He kept his other hand above her knee.

At Kennedy, she and most of the Chicago kids would be changing planes to fly back home. Alec would be staying in New York State for a few more days. Together with Serge, Razz, Stretch, and Sandy, Alec planned to spend Labor Day at Suzy-Q, the Ukrainian resort in the Catskills. Many of their new friends from New York and New Jersey would be there as well. Alec had tried to convince Stefi to go, but her parents wouldn't allow it. Chou wasn't going but he had arranged a ride for Alec with his friend Raya from Long Island.

Alec woke Stefi as the plane was descending into the lights of New York City. She opened her eyes and nuzzled up against his neck.

He covered her with the airline blanket, slipped his hand under her blouse, and gently cupped her breast. Her breathing accelerated. She gave him a hickey on his neck to mark him.

"That's in case anyone gets any ideas," she said.

"You don't need to worry about me."

"Remember what you told me at the Eiffel Tower. Promise me you won't do anything crazy at Suzy-Q. I've heard stories about what goes on there on Labor Day."

"I'll be playing volleyball with Sandy most of the time. He's staying in one of the rooms with his cousin and her friends from Toronto. I'll probably end up sleeping in the woods."

"Promise me you'll be careful. Don't chase any girls. I trust you, but I don't trust them."

Alec didn't tell Stefi that he was meeting Boyan at Suzy-Q for his debriefing. He was eager to have it over and done with. Suzy-Q was the perfect place. It would be natural for them to bump into each other during the Labor Day festivities. They wouldn't be noticed in the crowd.

"There's one more thing I need to ask you," she said.

"What's that?"

"Am I still your Cinnamon Girl?"

As he went to kiss her, she opened her mouth, inviting his tongue.

"Yes, you are," he said and plunged into the moment.

CHAPTER 25

Raya was a blonde, blue-eyed flower child. Last year, Chou had gone with her to the Woodstock festival. They had met at Suzy-Q and hitchhiked the forty miles to Yasgur's farm together. Chou had described her as a free spirit. He said she had dropped out of Columbia University after her brother died; she wanted to find herself. Alec was looking forward to meeting a kindred spirit.

Raya was waiting for him outside of customs. He spotted her instantly. Chou had told him, "Look for 'Judy Blue Eyes' with golden hair." There was only one girl in the crowd that matched that description.

"Hi, I'm Alec. You must be Raya."

"How'd you know?"

"You're just as Chou described you," he replied.

"You guys must have had a blast in Europe."

"It was pretty wild, but I'm glad to be home. I'm looking forward to Labor Day at Suzy-Q."

She led him to her VW Beetle in the parking lot. It had a peace sticker on the bumper. Steven Stills' "Love the One You're With" was playing on the radio. "We'll sleep at my father's place tonight," she said. "He's really straight, so don't let him get to you. He's a judge, and that's just the way he is."

They pulled up to a beach house on Long Island Sound that looked like it could easily sleep ten. A tall, elegant-looking man with gray, slicked-back hair opened the door—Raya's father. He was wearing a starched white shirt under his smoking jacket.

"Good afternoon, sir," Alec said, putting out his hand. "My name is Alec. I'm a friend of Chou's."

"Chou is the boy I met at Woodstock," Raya interjected.

"Where's Chou?" her father asked, looking behind them.

"He couldn't make it. He had to leave for school in Vermont," Alec replied. "They started classes before Labor Day. He'd already missed a week by going with us to Europe."

"Please come in," Raya's father said. A marble table with an empty vase graced the spacious foyer. "Are you in school, Alec?"

"I'm a junior at Northwestern. I'm doing pre-med."

"Doctors, lawyers, engineers—all respectable professions," her father said, looking at Raya.

"My mom's a doctor, and my father's an engineer," Alec said. "I guess they want me to follow in their footsteps."

Alec recalled how Stefi's father had eyed him with the same suspicion when they were first introduced, though at that time, Alec had been wearing beads and lace-up sandals that he had bought from a cobbler in Crete.

"You can sleep in the living room on the sofa," Raya's father said as he turned to leave the room. He seemed satisfied that his daughter had not brought home another stray.

"Give me your dirty clothes," Raya said. "I'll throw them in the wash. I'm washing my stuff anyway." She tipped her head toward the door where her father had exited. "Sorry about the sofa," she said. "He wants to leave the other bedrooms undisturbed. I think he's hoping they're going to come back."

"Who?"

"My mother and brother."

"Chou told me that your brother had passed away. He didn't say anything about your mother."

"She's still alive, but we live apart."

"Sorry, it's none of my business … I wish Chou could have joined us," Alec said to change the subject.

Raya nodded. "We had a groovy time in Woodstock. We were in front of the stage when Crosby, Stills, Nash, and Young played 'Judy Blue Eyes,' and you should have seen Joe Cocker play air guitar!"

"Sounds like fun."

"It was magic. We were all part of the scene."

Alec reclined on the couch and closed his eyes, trying to imagine what it must have been like. The jet lag was catching up to him. He dreamt of youth and free love and rock and roll.

Raya woke him up at dawn and pressed her finger to his lips. She was wearing a Ukrainian blouse with an embroidered belt over a pair of cut-off shorts that were barely visible below the hem of her blouse. "Sh-h-h," she whispered. "I don't want to wake my dad. I folded your clothes and put them in your knapsack."

Alec tiptoed to the bathroom. He washed his face and brushed his teeth. He still had the hard-on he had woken up with. The windowsill was cluttered with cosmetics. When he flushed the toilet, he heard someone stirring on the second floor.

Raya was waiting for him by the door to the garage. "Let's go. I want to get an early start. I want to claim my place by the river."

"Do the campsites fill up so quickly?"

"Most of the kids get there in the afternoon. It'll be packed by nightfall."

They threw their stuff under the hood and hopped into the car. "Would you believe that the Man got elected sheriff of Kerhonkson?" she said. "It's not enough that he hassles us on Suzy-Q every year. Now he and his rent-a-cops can chase us all over the county!"

"He won't find our campsite, will he?"

"I doubt it," she replied. "It's pretty remote. It's not on Suzy-Q property. You have to know it's there. The only way in and out is through a cornfield."

Alec saw Raya's father in the doorway as they were pulling away. She waved to him and yelled out, "I'll be back on Monday!"

Suzy-Q was about a hundred miles north of New York City. The easiest way to get there was to go up the interstate and exit at New Paltz, drive west on Route 299, and then up Route 44 towards Kerhonkson.

"Chou called from Vermont last night to see if you made it to my place," Raya said. "You were asleep, so I didn't wake you. He also said that you've had quite a wild summer."

"He told you about the Soviet Union?" He was surprised because he had mentioned very little to his friends about his arrest.

"No, he told me about Yugoslavia, and your trip to Zurich, and your having your passport stolen. But what's this about the Soviet Union?"

Even though Johnny had warned him, Alec needed to tell someone what happened. He hadn't shared the details of his story with Stefi or Serge or any of his friends on the trip. It might be easier to unload on Raya, since she was a stranger. She also seemed to look at the world differently than most people did.

"I was on a trip to the Soviet Union with my former high school and got caught meeting with dissidents. I was tried and deported."

"Was it your idea to meet with dissidents?"

"No, not really. My friends talked me into it. They knew I was going to Ukraine, and they asked me to bring back some information."

Raya upshifted and stepped on the gas. "So you wanted to be a hero?"

The question surprised him with its directness. "Yeah, I guess so," he replied.

"Why?"

He braced his hands on the dashboard as the speedometer hit ninety. "I wanted to make up for being a coward. My best friend drowned when I was ten. I was afraid to save him."

"Ten? You would have drowned with him."

"I dared him to go in."

"You were a child."

"Still, I should have gone in after him."

"So you're looking for redemption?"

"Yes ... no ... I wasn't a hero then. I thought I could be a hero now."

"Are you a hero?"

"No."

"Good. I can understand sacrificing yourself for those you love, but society exploits heroes. My brother, Mark, wanted to be a hero, so he enlisted in the army. He came back from Vietnam in a body bag. My parents blamed themselves, and now they're divorced. The whole hero thing is way overrated."

"Chou told me your brother had died, but he didn't say how. I'm sorry. I'm opposed to the war ... we all are."

"But you're OK fighting in the Cold War? I don't see a difference. Is it your war or your parents' war? It's only your war if you believe in what you're fighting for, not if the bastards draft you. Older people force their values on us. I'm not saying you have to challenge everything they say, but if you choose to do something dangerous and risk getting imprisoned or killed, you had better believe in what you're doing."

"They told me it was my duty."

"Would you do it again?"

"I don't know ... maybe ... I would really need to think about it."

"Good," she said as she decelerated back to the speed limit. "Think about it. Figure out what you believe in and then go ahead and be a hero. Live your own life. Don't live someone else's."

"Well, at least heroes live on, if only in our memories."

"Bullshit. The irony is that heroes want to live forever, yet they give up their lives for it ... and the lives of others."

Alec leaned back against the headrest. He closed

his eyes and recalled the footprints embedded in concrete. "When I was in Sarajevo, I saw the spot where Archduke Ferdinand was assassinated. Princip was my age when he fired those shots. Four years later, thirty-seven million people were dead. Then their children unleashed the horror all over again." He opened his eyes and looked at Raya. "Do you think that we inherit the sins of our fathers?"

"No," she replied. "I think we commit our own sins."

Alec sighed. "So there's still hope for us?"

"I'm an optimist," she replied. "I really think our generation is different than the ones before us. We're going to lead this world into a new age."

"The Age of Aquarius?"

"Yeah," she smiled and put on her turn signal.

They got off the interstate at New Paltz and took Route 299 West. New Paltz was a college town. Freaks with tie-dyed T-shirts were jaywalking from one head shop to another. "This is where I want to go to school," Raya said, "but my father says he won't pay for it. He thinks I'm going to run off again. He'd rather have me go back to Columbia, where he can keep an eye on me."

"And you're buying into his values?"

Raya laughed. "You got me there! I haven't made up my mind yet."

As the road climbed up into the Catskills, Raya abruptly announced, "We have to pull off the road." She pulled the car off into the grass next to an apple orchard. "These are the best apples in the world," she said. "You have to taste one. I always stop here on my way to Suzy-Q on Labor Day weekend."

They got out of the car and climbed through a hole in a barbed wire fence to get into the orchard. The branches were heavy with ripe, red apples. She picked one, took a bite, and handed it to Alec. He too took a bite. He wasn't sure if it was the apple, Raya, or the spontaneity of the moment, but it was the best apple he had ever tasted. They each took an apple for later.

"So what's better?" she asked. "Eating apples in the Catskills or chasing dragons?"

"The apples. Especially sharing one with you."

***

In the 1930s, Suzy-Q had been a retreat for the well-to-do from New York City who suffered from melancholy and other disorders that could be cured by mountain air and good company. The Ukrainian National Association had bought it at a good price in the 1950s and converted it into a resort for Ukrainian Americans. The association went to great lengths to remodel it in the Hutsul style, so it would remind their guests of the homes they had left behind in the Carpathian Mountains. The Catskills were very similar to the Ukrainian Carpathians in height, flora, and fauna. It was easy to imagine that a magic mountain had been trans-located from Yaremche to Kerhonkson for their enjoyment. The manager, whom the kids nicknamed "the Man," ran it like an emperor. He was about five feet tall, replete with a badge and a Napoleon complex. Suzy-Q was tucked in amid the famous resorts of the Borscht Belt, such as Mohonk and Nevele, but all of the ethnic and social cliques kept pretty much to themselves. Like Galicia, the Catskills were big enough for everyone.

The road up the mountain was dotted with Ukrainian establishments that thrived from the overflow visitors to Suzy-Q. Suzy-Q had only ninety rooms, and the crowd on Labor

Day numbered in the thousands. One of the most famous establishments was a restaurant/bar called the Log Cabin that specialized in cold beer and Ukrainian food at reasonable prices. Raya suggested that they stop in for lunch before staking out a place to camp by the river. They walked in to find Razz and Hot Pants playing pool.

"Hey, Alec! Over here," Razz called out.

"Hi, guys," Alec said. "This is my friend Raya. She's a friend of Chou's. She gave me a ride to Suzy-Q. Raya, this is Razz and Hot Pants."

"Two more kovbasa sandwiches," Razz called out to the bartender, "and two Rolling Rocks."

"Have you guys staked out a place yet?" Alec asked.

"Hot Pants is staying with six friends at a room in Suzy-Q," Razz replied. "I'll probably need to crash with you guys down by the river. By the way, the Montreal boys were here about an hour ago. They said your buddy Joker is the Kerhonkson jail."

"Why? What happened?"

"As they were driving into Suzy-Q, he hit some old lady."

"Is she OK?

"She's not hurt, but the Man had the ambulance come and take her away anyway. He dragged Joker over to Kerhonkson jail, and the boys came in here for a couple of beers, trying to raise some money for bail. Hot Pants gave them a few bucks, but I'm pretty much broke."

"Why do they call him Joker?" Raya asked.

"He believes that life is one big joke, like some Divine Comedy. He's one hell of a volleyball player, though," Alec replied. "I'll pitch in some bail money when I see them."

"I know a lot of people around here," Raya said. "I'm sure we can raise enough money to get him out."

The kovbasa sandwiches were delicious. They were pan-fried Polish sausages, cut length-wise, and served on fresh rye bread, with a dill pickle, tomato, onions, and horseradish.

"Another beer?" the bartender asked when he brought out their lunch.

"You go ahead," said Raya. "I'm good with just one." The thought of Joker hitting some old lady with his car just as the weekend was starting was sobering.

"I'm fine, too," Alec replied. "I want to drop off our stuff by the river and head over to Suzy-Q."

***

The road from the Log Cabin to Suzy-Q led straight up the mountain. To enter the resort, they needed to purchase a day ticket from a teenage staff member, who had the misfortune of working at the entrance rather than at the pool or bar for the weekend.

"We'll buy our tickets later," Raya suggested. "Let's drop off our stuff first." The road continued down the mountain, between cornfields, and over a bridge that crossed Rondout Creek. Small streams trickled down from the mountain to feed the creek. As a young boy, Alec had tried to find the place from where the streams flowed. He had hiked upstream, up a waterfall, and past lichen-covered boulders, but the quest for the source had proved elusive. With the August rains, the trickles turned to torrents and became impassable. The creek swelled into a meandering river that flowed into the Hudson and then into the sea.

Just past the bridge, Raya turned off the road and followed a series of car tracks through a cornfield that led to a wooded clearing on the bank of the river. There were already several cars parked in the clearing with license plates from Illinois, Ohio, and Quebec. The kids from New York and New Jersey usually stayed at the summer homes of friends and had no need to camp by the river. Pup tents and sleeping bags were strewn about the makeshift campsite. Raya pulled her bag out of the car and claimed her spot near a willow that branched onto the river.

"We'll camp here," she said. Alec was pleasantly surprised that she seemed to be taking him under her wing for the weekend. He had been to Suzy-Q several times before with his parents, but never like this—communing with his peers. Alec laid his knapsack against the willow and covered it with a poncho, even though he had little of value, other than his replacement passport, his plane ticket, and his wallet with about forty dollars.

"Our stuff will be safe here," Raya said. "Just take your wallet. We'll go to Joe's later, and you'll need to have your ID. Let's walk back up to Suzy-Q. There won't be any place to park, and we can probably sneak past the gate."

The twenty-minute uphill walk to Suzy-Q went quickly as they looked forward to seeing their many friends. They told the boy at the gate that they had paid earlier, and he let them pass without a hassle. The place was packed with vacationing families, middle-aged singles, and teenagers who had come to party. There was a tennis crowd, a volleyball crowd, and a bar crowd. Most of the families were jammed in and around the large pool and patio that overlooked the valley below. Raya saw some friends from New York and ran over, telling Alec, "I'll catch you later." Alec went by the volleyball court to see if he could get in on a game of triples.

He saw Sandy and Stretch patiently sitting on the sidelines. When Sandy saw him, he elbowed Stretch and pointed at Alec. "You're our third. We were about ready to give up on you. We're on in four." Alec nodded and then walked toward the bar to see who else had come up for the weekend. As he was walking up the steps, he saw Boyan sitting on a bench near the Taras Shevchenko bust, looking directly at him. Boyan made a slight motion with his cigarette, which Alec understood as a signal to join him.

Alec climbed the few steps and sat down on the bench across from Boyan.

"Cigarette?" Boyan offered.

"Sure." Alec took the lit cigarette, even though he didn't smoke.

"Do you want to talk now?" Boyan asked.

"What do you know about what happened?"

"Enough. But I need to know everything."

"I got caught. I was arrested, tried, and deported."

"Start from the beginning. Where did you enter the Soviet Union?"

"I came in from Finland by minibus."

"Were you searched?" Boyan spoke without a hint of emotion. His face remained expressionless, except for the enjoyment he drew from his cigarette.

"I was singled out from the group and stripped down to my underwear."

"Why do you think they singled you out?"

"I'm not sure, but I think they knew what my purpose was."

"They prescreen everyone, especially anyone from

the diaspora."

"But there were other Ukrainian Americans on my trip. They got through without any problems."

"Interesting. Did they take anything from you?"

"Only a letter, but they gave it back."

Boyan raised one of his droopy lids at the mention of the letter. "What letter?"

"My mother had written a letter of introduction for me to give to some distant uncle in Munich."

"What is your uncle's name?" When Alec mentioned the name, Boyan took a long drag of his cigarette, lit a new one, and put the old one out. "Cigarette?" he asked Alec.

Alec's cigarette had burned down to the filter. "Sure."

Boyan handed the lit cigarette to Alec and lit another one for himself. "Continue," he said.

"In Kiev, I looked up Johnny's friend, Taras."

"Tell me about Taras."

"Johnny met him in Kiev last summer. He's about thirty … single; I'm not sure what he does. He's a close friend of the Sixtiers. Taras led me to Mariana and then to visit Maksym at the hospital."

"What did Maksym tell you?"

"Can I have another cigarette?" Sharing the cigarettes at least made it seem like they were confidants. As Boyan lit him another cigarette, Alec began to unload the information that he had tried so hard to protect from his interrogators. As he rattled off names and arrests and even trivial things that Maksym had told him, he felt a huge wave of release. He'd been sent to gather information, bring it back, and relay it. Now he was relaying it. He had delivered his package, and he was glad to be rid of it. He didn't know if Boyan was recording him, and he didn't care. He was just glad to be done with it.

"Your trial in Lviv made the news. You were on Soviet television."

"I was interrogated in our camp in Lviv. I had written some cryptic notes, and they were confiscated."

"I see."

Alec was expecting some rebuke, but there was none.

"Did they make you sign a confession?" Boyan asked.

"Yes, in Chernivtsi, at the border. I was detained again for several hours."

"Do you know who interrogated you?"

"He didn't say his real name. He called himself Damian."

"Curious. Does that name have any meaning to you?"

"It's the name of my best friend from childhood. He drowned when I was ten."

Boyan took a long drag of his cigarette and let the name pass. "Can you describe your interrogator?"

"He was different than the others, much more sophisticated—well dressed, almost Western."

"About forty? Sandy hair? Wire-rimmed glasses?"

"Yes, that's him. Who is he? I've told you everything that I know. Tell me what you know," Alec demanded.

"You've confirmed what we suspected. The man who interrogated you was the head of the KGB in Ukraine. I was surprised that he took such an interest in your case. It should have been routine and relegated to underlings, but now I understand. The letter your mother gave you was addressed to … you said your uncle? How well do you know this man?"

"I never met him before."

"Your uncle is a high-ranking member of the

Organization of Ukrainian Nationalists. After the KGB assassinated Stepan Bandera, your uncle was third or fourth on their hit list. Did you tell him about what happened to you?"

"I did—and he became very agitated."

"The KGB did not understand who you were working for. The letter to your uncle suggested you were working for the Banderivtsi, and they were probably surprised that you were naïve enough to carry the letter through the border. When you ditched them in Kiev, they got nervous, until you showed up at the dispensary. They get paranoid when there's something they can't figure out. The head of the KGB in Ukraine came down to Chernivtsi to interrogate you personally."

"He had a photograph of me, Johnny, and CK."

"Where was it taken?"

"On a climb in the Rockies."

"Who took the photo?"

Alec snapped his cigarette. He checked behind his back and then whispered the name in Boyan's ear. "Johnny tried to warn me. Could they really have infiltrated the Brotherhood?"

"Let us worry about that. If one of your own has turned, we can turn him again."

"Isn't the photo proof enough?"

"There are many ways they could have obtained that photo."

"You would know better than I."

"You're lucky you got out. There was a debate between the Kiev and Lviv branches of the KGB as to what to do with you. The Kiev branch wanted to make an example of you, probably because you embarrassed them. The Lviv branch wanted to let you go. The director himself made the decision to let you go."

"How do you know this?"

"We talked to one of your interrogators from Lviv. He recently escorted a Soviet dance ensemble to New York City. We exchanged some information."

Alec wondered what Boyan had revealed in return. Information for which he had risked his life could just as easily have been exchanged on a street corner in New York City.

"They tailed me in Romania," Alec said. "I left my group and hitchhiked to Banja Luka."

"You created quite a stir. They caught up with you again when you joined your group in Munich. Then they lost track of you again until Vienna. They took your camera and your passport to see where you'd been."

"And what about Taras and Mariana and Maksym?"

"We don't know about Taras. We're working on that. Johnny should not have given you his name without telling me. The Soviet Union is a complicated place. There are layers upon layers of complexity. Taras may be working for them. We don't know at this point. Mariana and Maksym are under constant surveillance. The KGB accumulates evidence against them and prosecutes when it's expedient for them to do so."

"I feel that I betrayed them by being caught."

"They would give their lives for Ukraine. You almost gave yours. It was not our intention for you to get so near the center. Your mother's letter ... Johnny sending you to Taras— a series of unfortunate circumstances."

"The KGB said they might contact me again."

"Yes, of course," Boyan replied. "They probably tried to set you up with some 'friends'—attractive women, most likely."

"Yes, they did."

"Did you take their bait?"

"No."

"If they contact you, let me know. Otherwise, go on with your life."

***

"Where you been?" Sandy asked when Alec returned. "Stretch and I had almost given up on you. It's game point. We were going to play them doubles if you didn't show up."

"I ran into someone I knew and had to unload some shit," Alec replied.

Playing triples in Suzy-Q on Labor Day was like playing King of the Mountain. Once you won, you stayed on the court until someone knocked you off. The New York boys had been on since morning. It was their home court, and they weren't ready to yield. The court was dug into the side of the hill. Most of the spectators watched from the top of a retaining wall, where a path led from the main house to the bar and swimming pool.

Sandy, Stretch, and Alec played the rest of the afternoon against an assortment of challengers, without losing a single game. At six o'clock they conceded the court out of sheer exhaustion and the need for beer. The first round of beers at the Veselka Lounge was on the house. The second and third rounds were bought by the vanquished. Alec saw Serge at the end of the bar, talking to Bogey, who had just driven up from Chicago in his new Dodge Charger.

"Hey, Alec, who's that dude you were smoking with by the Shevchenko statue?" Serge asked.

"An uncle on my mother's side," Alec responded.

"What's his name?"

Alec tried to read his eyes. "Damian."

Serge looked at him quizzically.

Am I being paranoid? Alec thought. *Who am I to speculate? We are all guilty of something. Let Boyan—or better yet, let God—be the judge.*

"I thought you guys would die from heat stroke on the volleyball court," said Serge. "You've been out there for hours."

"Time is what you make of it," Alec replied. "Hey, Bogey, what do you think of Suzy-Q so far?"

"It's teenage heaven."

"More like a teenage wasteland," Serge countered.

"Yeah, but no better place to be on Labor Day," said Alec. "So what are your plans for tonight?"

"We're going to hang out here for a while and check out the dance," Serge replied. "Try to pick up some chicks. How about you?"

"We'll probably hang around 'til midnight and then head into New Paltz. My friend Raya says there's a bar there called Joe's that rocks all night long. I think the Montreal boys are heading there too."

"Sounds like fun. Bogey's got his brand new ride. If we're not too high to drive, we'll see you there. First, you have to join us for a shot of tequila." Serge ordered another round. "Here's how you do it," he instructed. "Lick your hand at the base of the thumb and pour a little salt on it; then lick the salt, down your shot, and bite into a lime."

"Hey, check it out," Alec said. "The Montreal boys are here, and they're finally showing their true colors."

Joker walked into the lounge with a wicked smirk,

as if he had just shot the sheriff. "The old lady's fine," he said. "She's not pressing charges, but the Man wrote me up for all kinds of bullshit. The boys bailed me out, but I have to show up in court on Tuesday morning. I told them I have to get back to work in Montreal, but they said if I skip the country, they're not letting me back in." Joker was soon joined by Eric, the setter for the Montreal team, and by Tiny, their middle blocker. All three were dressed in drag.

"What's with the dresses?" Bogey asked.

"The Man was putting our asses to the fire, so we thought we'd give him another scandal to worry about," Joker replied, and all three started laughing. "There's no law about coming here in drag, is there?"

The girls at the bar were playing along as well. "Hey, Hot Lips! How about a little girl-to-girl action?" asked one of the cuties at the bar. She was wearing a slinky black dress with spaghetti straps. Joker curtsied, took her by the hand, and led her out to the dance floor.

"I heard you guys are heading out to Joe's," Alec said.

"Yeah, probably around midnight," Eric replied. We first have to find Rascal and Snake. They walked here from the river. They're either on the dance floor or partying with the workers. How about you?"

"I'm heading out to Joe's with Raya. We'll catch you there."

* * *

The band at Suzy-Q had been OK—waltzes, tangos, polkas, and the occasional rock song. Joe's was pure rock and roll. Raya disappeared soon after paying the five-dollar cover.

Alec had gone to buy them some beers and saw her on the dance floor with the local college kids from New Paltz.

The DJ put on a tune that Alec had never heard before. It had a haunting guitar riff and a voice that seemed to come from beyond the grave. The bass shook the floor. Raya grabbed him by the arm and pulled him onto the dance floor.

"Alec, we have to dance to this," she shouted above the music and the noise.

"Who is this?" he shouted back.

"Creedence Clearwater. 'Born on the Bayou.' It rocks!" Raya undulated to the beat of the music. Alec imagined her dancing on the bayou in the moonlight. He had never met anyone so uninhibited. Raya put her arm around his neck and pulled his face towards her lips. The song had just finished and the DJ was fumbling for another record. "Let's get high and make love tonight," she said.

Alec's heart skipped a beat. "I have to tell you … I'm in love with someone," he said. "My girlfriend, Stefi. She's my soul mate. She's everything I've imagined in a girl."

"I see." Raya smiled. "I can tell by the mark on your neck. Can I give you some advice?"

"What's that?"

"Sounds to me like you're idealizing her. The next time you're with her, make love to her like there's no tomorrow. She won't be your goddess forever." She gave him a quick kiss on the lips and disappeared back into the dancing crowd.

Alec was drenched in sweat from the hot, crowded dance floor. He needed to get some air. At the exit he showed the back of his hand to the bouncer, and the stamp "Joe's" lit up under the black light. "Cover's good all night," the bouncer assured him. There were dozens of teenagers hanging out outside. The smell of grass hung in the air. The bass boomed through the walls. Alec noticed a girl that he knew from Chicago, making out with a boy from New York. She was not especially attractive, at least not to the boys in Chicago, yet here she had found her one-night romance. *That's what's so special about Suzy-Q on Labor Day*, he thought.

A station wagon with Quebec plates pulled into the parking lot. The Montreal boys piled out. They had changed back into their jeans, as cool as ever.

"Eh, Alec," said Joker. "You still rocking?"

"I'm having a blast. Chicks everywhere," he replied, though the only chick he really wanted to be with was a million miles away.

"Your buddies from Suzy-Q were in an accident up the road," Joker said. "Don't worry; they're all fine. Car's trashed, though."

"What happened?"

"They were too fast coming down the mountain and couldn't make the turn. They skidded out and rammed into the gas station at the intersection. The car got wedged between the gas pumps. The whole place could've blown up."

"Are the police there?"

"No, the gas station was closed. We got there first and gave them a ride back to the Log Cabin."

"They just abandoned the car?"

"They had to; otherwise, the police would have hauled them away. They'll get it towed out in the morning."

"You sure they're OK?"

"Oh yeah, they're not hurt. Your friend Serge looked a bit freaked out, though."

"Was he the one driving?" Alec asked.

"Yeah," said Joker. "He looked like he came face-to-face with God."

CHAPTER 26

Alec woke up on Saturday morning with the riff from "Born on the Bayou" still twanging in his head. The sun was high in the sky, and their camp by the river was almost empty. He took a pee and rolled up his sleeping bag. He didn't remember who had brought him back from Joe's or when. Still, it had been fun. He saw Razz coming back from the cornfield with a roll of toilet paper.

"You couldn't wait for a real toilet?" Alec asked him.

"What's the difference?" Razz replied. "I'm just helping the farmer fertilize his corn. Did you want me to crap in the creek instead? Raya would freak out if I defiled her place. By the way, what happened to you last night?"

"I went to Joe's with Raya. The Montreal boys were

there. You heard what happened to Bogey and Serge?"

"Yeah, they got up early this morning to tow Bogey's car. The cook from Suzy-Q knows the guy from the gas station, so they're trying to work things out without anyone going to jail."

"Those turns down the mountain are treacherous at night."

"Highway to hell," Razz replied. "Let's walk up to Su-zy-Q and grab some food. Maybe we'll get lucky and hitch a ride up from someone. I really don't want to walk up that hill."

Alec and Razz followed the trail through the cornfield to the asphalt road that led over the bridge and up the hill to Suzy-Q. The walk was flat for about a half mile before beginning its steep climb. They saw a station wagon with Quebec plates coming down the road and stuck out their thumbs.

"We're in luck," Alec said. "It's the Montreal boys. I wonder if they slept at all." The station wagon came to a screeching halt beside them and the back window rolled down. Out popped an arm, holding a jug of wine. Alec took a long sip and gave the jug to Razz. Razz took an even longer sip and gave the jug back to the outstretched arm. The jug went back into the car, the window rolled up, and the station wagon pulled away in the direction of Suzy-Q without anyone saying a word.

"I guess they didn't have any room," Razz said.

"Guess not," Alec replied.

***

The pool at Suzy-Q was laid out on a broad concrete deck that overlooked the valley below. The veranda from the Veselka Lounge overlooked the pool and had enough room for hundreds of onlookers. Alec grabbed a fried kovbasa sandwich from the snack bar and sat on a table on the veranda with Bogey. He was on his third Fanta.

"Too early for beer?" Alec asked.

"No, you go ahead. I'm going to lay off alcohol for a while."

"I heard what happened. Sorry about your car. Lucky everyone's OK."

"Yeah," Bogey replied. "The car was packed—me, Serge, and four girls from the East Coast. I don't remember their names."

"How'd you lose control?"

"It was freaky. We came off the turn too fast and spun out. It was all a blur. We slammed on the brakes but the gas station was right in front of us. We got wedged in between the pumps. An inch to the right or left and we would have been toast! It seemed to last forever. My whole life flashed in front of me."

"I know the feeling. Time just folds into itself."

"We tried to push my car out, but no way. I had to pry Serge's hands off the steering wheel. The girls were crying, but no one was hurt. Lucky for us, the Montreal boys showed up a few minutes later. We packed into their station wagon—I mean, like twelve people—and just left my car. They dropped us off at the Log Cabin. From there we walked back up to Suzy-Q. I mean, they could have at least driven us all the way up."

"They're like that. Did they offer you any wine?"

"What?"

"Just kidding," Alec said, but he knew it wasn't funny.

An announcement blared out over the loudspeakers: "The Suzy-Q annual swim meet will begin in fifteen minutes.

First event is the 100-meter freestyle."

"I'm going to go swim," Bogey said calmly. "I need to burn off some stress before I call my parents about the car."

"Now?" Alec asked. "You can't go into the pool until the competition is over."

"I'm going to compete in the freestyle," Bogey replied.

"Those jocks have been training for this all summer," Alec told him. "They'll be kicking you in the face in the water."

"I'm still going to swim." Bogey downed his orange soda and walked down the stairs to the referee table to register his intention. Alec saw him pull down his shorts to reveal what looked like Speedos. Then he calmly walked up to the outside lane, got into a competitive crouch, and waited for the starting gun. When the gun popped, he dove into the water with a power and elegance that Alec had not expected. Bogey cut through the water in perfect form and quickly pulled out ahead of most of the other swimmers. On the return lap, he was neck and neck with a kid from Cleveland who had been to the US Junior National Championships. The finish was too close to call from Alec's perch on the veranda, but the referee gave it to the Cleveland boy. Bogey placed second.

Bogey walked back up to the veranda, sat down next to Alec, and ordered another Fanta.

"I'm pretty sure I beat him," Bogey said.

"That was amazing! I didn't know you could swim!"

"I was the Illinois high school champion in freestyle."

"Wow! You never told me that."

Bogey laughed. "You never asked. There's a lot about your friends that you don't know. Most of the time, you've got your head up your ass."

***

The Saturday night dance was the highlight of the Labor Day weekend at Suzy-Q. Management spared no expense and brought in the best Ukrainian American band available. This year it was Tempo, from New York. The dress code was more formal than the night before, and many of the girls showed up in long dresses. Alec didn't have a dress shirt or jacket, so he simply wore his jeans with a short-sleeved white linen shirt.

The band was set up on the veranda on a plywood stage—with a canopy, in case it rained. For some reason, it always rained on Suzy-Q on Labor Day.

The Man and his rent-a-cops were everywhere. He had briefed his deputies to keep a special watch on the boys from Montreal and the boys from Chicago. Besides the veranda, the most crowded stretch was the path that led from the main building, past the volleyball court, to the Veselka Lounge. Alec realized he couldn't walk that stretch without bumping into at least ten people that he knew. Most were laughing, some were crying, and a few were still waiting for Godot. Alec ran into several of the kids from the Flight of Freedom tour who had come up from New York and New Jersey for the dance. Even though they had parted just a few days before, he was happy to see them.

Razz had already picked up a girl at the bar, and Alec saw them head into the woods. Sandy and Serge were partying with the Montreal boys in the parking lot. Alec danced with several of the girls from the tour. He saw George and Marijka sitting at a table overlooking the pool.

"OK if I join you?" Alec asked.

"Alec!" George replied. "You don't have to ask. Hot Pants was sitting here, but she went to the bar to get some drinks. I heard Stefi flew back to Chicago."

"Yeah, her parents wouldn't let her stay. There were no rooms available, and the only place to sleep is in the woods."

"Rumor is you came up with Raya," Marijka said. "She's pretty wild."

"She's also smart," Alec replied. "And fun."

"You guys set up camp down by the river?"

"Yeah," Alec replied. "It's pretty much me, Raya, the Chicago boys, the Montreal boys, and a bunch of girls—I'm not sure where they're from."

"Who cares?" George started laughing. "As long as they're hot. You realize that if you sleep there, you have to go skinny-dipping."

"Why is that?" Alec asked.

"It's a long-standing tradition. It's a like a communal ritual for the hippies who sleep there."

"Fine with me," Alec said. "As long as we don't get too high and drown."

"It's pretty shallow," George replied, "except after a rain. The current gets swift, but it rarely gets deeper than your waist."

"So you've been down there?"

"We tried it once," Marijka replied with a naughty grin.

"Then I'll definitely have to do it."

The dance on the veranda was brought to an untimely end by a sudden thunderstorm. The dancers scattered for shelter. Most squeezed into the Veselka Lounge. The musicians covered their instruments to avoid electrocution. The bar was packed with wet, horny teenagers and middle-aged men and women, hoping to find Ukrainian mates. John, the assistant manager, rounded up the house pickup band and set them up in the corner by the window to play some tunes. The cook played guitar, a bartender played base, and a regular from Kerhonkson banged the drums. John blew the blues harp, and when he lit into "Sweet Home Chicago," the crowd went wild. Alec saw Raya at the bar and worked his way through the crowd to join her.

Raya handed him a shot of tequila without missing a beat and started dancing in place to "Soul Man." She grabbed Alec by his hips and made him dance with her. It felt good to move to the music. *Raya has danced with lots of boys tonight,* he thought. *Chou was right—she is a free spirit.* She belonged to no one except the person she was with at the moment.

Every room at Suzy-Q was taken, so those who had camped by the river had nowhere to take shelter from the storm. The rain was unrelenting, and they knew that they would be soaked and sick by morning. Joker had the brilliant idea of stealing a carpet from the main building so they could use it as a canopy. He figured the Man owed it to him after all the hassle he had put him though. Joker and Alec nonchalantly rolled up the oriental carpet, threw it over their shoulders, and hiked down the road and through the cornfield to their camp by the river. By then, the rain had slowed to a drizzle and the clouds began to break. The only illumination in the camp was the intermittent reflection of the moon off the creek. Several of the Montreal boys were already back at camp, banging girls and getting high.

Alec and Joker passed Rascal as he was making love to a girl on a wet poncho. The girl, who Alec didn't recognize, did not seem to mind their intrusion. Rascal paused to see what his friends were carrying. "Cool idea. Where'd you guys score the carpet?"

"We got it from the main building," Alec replied. "We'll bring it back in the morning."

"You should be able to fit four or five of us under there," Rascal said. "Mind if Julie and I sleep with you if we can't find another place to crash?"

"No problem," Joker replied. "We just have to get stoned and pass out, and everyone is welcome."

"Snake scored some peyote," Rascal said. "He's a little freaked out. He's over there in the river. I'm sure he'll give you some."

Alec and Joker unrolled the carpet and went to find Snake before he drowned. The rain had subsided to an on-and-off drizzle.

Snake was naked and wandering knee-deep in the river. He was hallucinating. Alec and Joker waded in and brought him back to the bank. "This water is magic," Snake said. "It's been everywhere. All these molecules have a history, a path they've taken. This one came from the Nile just a few weeks ago. That one was at the Red Sea when it parted. This one claims to have been pissed out by Alexander the Great in India. Now they're all here—it's freaking psychedelic!"

"Do you have any more of that shit?" Joker asked him.

"Yeah, man," Snake replied. "In my pants pocket, wrapped in foil."

Joker found Snake's jeans on the bank and pulled out a handful of dried buttons and offered a couple to Alec.

"No thanks," Alec said. "I'm high enough on tequila. That stuff is just going to mess up my mind. I'm not into drugs."

"This stuff is just cactus, 100 percent natural."

"It's still a chemical."

"We're all just chemistry," Joker replied. "We're just a bunch of molecules, a little more complicated than earthworms, but still the same." He popped a few buttons in his mouth and started to chew. "Yucch—nasty stuff! It's like Snake was saying, we're just molecules connecting with other molecules."

"What about love?" Alec challenged him.

"All chemistry, man. It's all just hormones," he mumbled between the buttons. "We got no control over that shit. You think you love someone, but it's just her chemistry interacting with your chemistry."

"I think there's more to it than that," Alec replied. "There has to be. Otherwise, what's the point of it all?"

"The point is to get high," Joker replied. "It's like Timothy Leary said, 'You got to turn on, tune in, and drop out.' Look at Snake. He's flying."

"If we're all just chemistry, then there's no right or wrong," Alec continued. "There's no higher truth. Our bodies are physical, sure, but I really believe there's another side to us. You just have to find it."

"You can start by looking in your pants," Joker offered.

"That's the only head you ever think with," Alec replied.

"Well, did you find yours?" Snake asked. Alec was surprised that Snake, sitting on the bank, naked and conversing with the water, was still tuned in to their conversation.

"I'm still looking," Alec said, "but I think I'm getting closer."

"You need to find an oracle who can show you the

way," said Snake. He was speaking slowly. "This molecule here says it rolled down the Pythia's cheek at Delphi."

"Do they have to be virgins?" Joker interjected.

"No, they probably just have to be pure in spirit," Alec replied. "When I really think about it, three girls did show me the way—Stefi, Maya, and Raya—and I'm a real dick because I hurt the ones who helped me the most."

"You banged them all?" asked Snake.

"No, but I connected with them in other ways."

Both Joker and Snake started laughing. "There's only one way to connect with a chick," said Joker. "Take a look at Rascal over there. He'll show you where to find the entrance."

"You guys are high. There's more to women than just sex. I love Stefi physically, sure, but our love goes deeper than that." He knew he was baring his soul, but he didn't care. "I felt trapped and adrift—and she wouldn't give up on me. She lit up the darkness ... like the moon over the sea."

"She can moon me any time," said Joker.

"She's not like anyone else I've known. There's something special about her. It's more than just physical."

"You're just under her spell," Joker replied. "She probably slipped you a love potion."

Alec laughed. "Well, you're right about that. She did cast a spell to lure me back. I thought I could find myself by escaping my past ... and I almost lost her."

"And what about the mystery girl from Switzerland? Razz was complaining that you took him on some wild goose chase to Zurich to find her."

"Her name was Maya. She brought me back down to earth. She turned me on to the beauty and transience of the world. And I hurt her too. I pulled away from her when she needed me most."

"And Raya?" asked Joker. "Looks like you've got the hots for her."

"Raya's a flower child," Alec replied. "She looks at the world differently. She doesn't live by other people's values. She told me to decide for myself what's worth dying for. I finally get the whole hippie thing—it's our generation trying to change the world. We believe in peace and love rather than hate and war. She says we're entering a new age. You know, the Age of Aquarius."

"Don't go astral on us," Joker said. "This whole Age of Aquarius stuff is all bullshit."

"Maybe," Alec replied. "It might not be real in our physical world, but it's real enough in a symbolic sense."

Joker started crooning, "When the moon is in the seventh house …"

Alec realized there was little point in talking to two guys who were high on mescaline. Mostly, he'd been talking to himself.

"Someday I'll help you find yourselves," Alec said. He walked back to where they had spread out the carpet. Rascal and Julie had finished their lovemaking and had laid down their ponchos as the floor for their carpet shelter. Both were already snuggled under the carpet. Alec took off his wet clothes, down to his underwear, and crawled in next to Julie. He brushed against her buttocks and realized she was naked. She smelled of sex. He turned so they would be back to back. The rain picked up again. A few minutes later, someone else crawled in next to Alec and placed her arm around his neck.

"Do you have room for one more?" Raya whispered. Alec thought of the rainstorm at the camp in Munich and of playing "Gimme Shelter" on guitar with Serge.

"Sure," he said and put his arm around her waist to share her warmth.

***

Alec awoke to the sound of birds singing. The patter of rain on the carpet had stopped long ago. The morning sun was burning the dew off the grass. Alec stuck his head out from under the carpet. His bedfellows were gone. He noticed a strange, orange mass of fungi that seemed to be slowly inching its way across the grass toward him. It was feeding on decay and getting larger. He had never seen anything like it before. *It's the creeping crud*, he thought to himself. *Amazing.*

He crawled out from underneath the carpet to witness a glorious morning. Sunlight was streaming in through the breaks in the trees. He stood up and looked around the makeshift camp. Snake and Joker were passed out under a tree. Rascal and Julie were frolicking and splashing themselves a few hundred feet downriver. Raya was nowhere to be seen.

Alec walked down to the river's edge and peered in. He looked for his reflection in the running water. He saw only a blur. A water bug was effortlessly flitting against the current. It reminded him of his boyhood days on the Wisconsin River. *The universe must seem very different to it*, he thought, *with the sun reflecting off the water, sticks the size of trees streaming down the river, some strange being peering down from above*. Yet was it any less valid a view than his? There were many ways to look at things. He wondered if his life would leave a trace in the world or if it would be like the dance of a water bug in a running stream. There had to be more to life than just chemistry.

If he could only transcend the physical into the spiritual, there might be meaning to his existence.

"Why are you always so absorbed in yourself?" Raya asked. "You're like a fish in a bowl, staring at its own reflection in the glass." She had come up behind him and surprised him. She was wearing the T-shirt and panties that she had slept in. "You've got to get past this 'I'm the center of the universe' mind-set. We're all God's children. He meant us to enjoy the time we have with the people we have. I need to pull you out of your fishbowl and throw you back into the river."

Alec gazed into her blue eyes. She revealed a secret to him in her sacred wood: if you view the world through your eyes only, then all you perceive is yourself. If you can learn to see the world through the eyes of others, then there are as many paths to enlightenment as there are rivers running into the sea.

He looked at himself through the eyes of his inquisitor. He had tried to be a hero, but he saw that there were heroes on both sides of a war. His ordeal seemed less relevant now. From the Soviet perspective, he was the villain and his inquisitor was the hero. Were some perspectives right and others wrong, or was morality relative? He thought about his essay on *Paradise Lost*. He had not yet found the answer, but at least he had found himself. He realized he had the freedom to choose.

He put his hand in the river and the let the water stream through his fingers. He had aspired to find secret knowledge. What did he know now that he hadn't known before?

He recalled the verse from the Old Slavonic Bible that he had read at the atheist museum in Kiev: "*He who increases knowledge increases sorrow.*" He knew that love had brought him happiness, while knowledge had brought him sorrow. He still needed answers, but he needed love even more. Stefi was more precious to him now than all the knowledge in the world. Before they kissed by the Eiffel Tower, she had asked him if he loved her. Yes, he loved her, more than he loved himself. No matter what the future might hold, not even the devil could take that moment away from them.

The water streamed over his hand. The current had quickened from the late summer rain. He gave in to the moment. He knew now that to find himself, he needed to lose his self. He needed to stop gazing into the water, looking for his own reflection. He must learn to appreciate the communion of others. Perhaps that's why Lucifer had been cast out of heaven. He refused to acknowledge that he was not the center of his own existence. He laid countless souls to waste for his vanity.

"So what matters to you?" he asked Raya.

"We matter—you, me, now, and this wonderful place around us. What matters is knowing that we're alive."

Raya took off her T-shirt and panties and stepped into the stream. The morning sun reflected off her golden hair, back, and buttocks. She looked like a nymph immersed in her own element. She turned around to face him. "You need to stop gazing inward and come into the water," she beckoned to him.

Alec hesitated but then gave in. He stood up, took off his clothes, and followed her into the river—body and soul.

***

The American Airlines 727 descended toward Chicago, heading west over Lake Michigan. Sailboats dotted the blue expanse. The setting sun illuminated the skyline. The thirteen green domes of St. Nicholas Cathedral rose to his left. The Northwestern campus jutted into the lake to his right. Classes would begin in another three weeks. Stefi was still his Cinnamon Girl. He knew where he belonged. He was whole again.

ACKNOWLEDGMENTS

Caught in the Current is a novel about the loss of innocence, the voyage of discovery, and the redeeming power of love. Alec embarks on a "Magical Mystery Tour" through the world of my youth—offbeat Europe and ethnic America during the psychedelic sixties. Many of us who are first-generation Americans are caught in the countercurrents of conflicting cultures. Most get swept into the mainstream. We owe it to ourselves to ask who we are and where we're going before we're gone.

I want to thank my wife, Christine, and my sons, Nicholas and Alex, to whom this book is dedicated. Christine, my high school sweetheart, inspired the character of Stefi. Nicholas, an English major and doctoral student, brought many of the scenes to life. His best advice was to let the characters speak for themselves. Alex, a philosophy major, lawyer, and avid reader of the classics, kept me from getting lost in the fun house. My mother, Natalia, a remarkably erudite woman, helped frame the historical and cultural context of the novel.

I wish to thank my friend Andy Ripecky and my nephew Marko Mazurkevich, who is also an aspiring writer, for encouraging me to pursue my passion. I am especially indebted to my dear friend Jurij Strutynsky, an artist in his own right, for his help in editing. He embarked on this task with the observation that "it's an achievement to put pen to paper for so many pages," and ended with "it's a very good novel." I am grateful to my professional editor, Marna Poole, for her insightful recommendations and expert edits—she made the book better.

I also wish to thank Professor John Serio, the past editor of the *Wallace Stevens Journal* and winner of the 2012 Distinguished Editor Award from the Council of Editors of Learned Journals, for his willingness to review my novel. His encouraging review helped assure me that my first attempt at literary fiction was indeed literary.